ACES
WILD

A HEIST

FOR MY MOM, ALWAYS.

—A. D.

Published by Peachtree Teen
An imprint of PEACHTREE PUBLISHING COMPANY INC.
1700 Chattahoochee Avenue
Atlanta, Georgia 30318-2112
PeachtreeBooks.com

Text © 2022 by Amanda DeWitt
Cover image © 2022 by Victor Bregante

Edited by Ashley Hearn
Design and composition by Lily Steele
Cover design by Adela Pons

Printed and bound in July 2022 at Lake Book Manufacturing, Melrose Park, IL, USA.
10 9 8 7 6 5 4 3 2 1
First Edition
ISBN: 978-1-68263-466-0

Cataloging-in-Publication Data is available from the Library of Congress.

ACES
WILD

A HEIST

AMANDA DEWITT

A NOTE ON EXPECTATIONS

LET'S GET ONE THING STRAIGHT: THIS IS NOT A love story.

I know that's what you're expecting. That's what everyone expects, whether you know it or not. My sister Beth likes to say that everything is a love story if you wait long enough, but Beth believes a lot of things that belong inside a Hallmark card. I don't.

I should warn you that none of the names in this account are real. Close, sometimes, but everything has been shifted slightly to the left. I don't want to lie to you—not here at the beginning, at least. There will be several crimes committed before we're done. As you might imagine, there will be a lot of lying later on.

This is just a story. My story. My therapist says that when you can't say things out loud, you should write them down. It's cathartic. \kə-ˈthär-tik\, adjective, providing psychological relief through the open expression of strong emotions; causing catharsis. She also helped me on the SAT.

My name is Jack Shannon, and this is not a love story.
It's a confession.

BLACKJACK

THERE WERE THREE THINGS TO KNOW ABOUT Elkhollow Preparatory Academy before choosing to attend its hallowed halls.

One: It was very old. Red-brick and white gabled roofs, so Revolutionary War it made you want to pick up a musket and die on a hill. They didn't advertise the draft that came from the old windows in the pamphlet.

Two: It was very expensive. *Tuition that looked like a zip code* kind of expensive. If Elkhollow could have found a way to keep their lawn green through the Massachusetts winter by raising the tuition to six digits, they would have done so already. And plenty of senators, Wall Street suits, and old-money widows would've paid it.

Three: Like many very old and very expensive institutions, it carried a proud history of secret societies. A lot of them. At some point, they started to lose their meaning, if you asked me, but no one was really asking me anything. In fact, in the three years I'd attended Elkhollow Preparatory

Academy, no one had invited me to join a secret society at all.

So I did what any enterprising young Elkhollow student would do: I founded my own.

Well. Sort of. I liked to think of it as an underground service. Filling a niche. Because as much as every secret society, group, and club on the unwritten roster liked to chant and force one another to run naked through the forest, a part of them wanted more. They wanted to pretend to be their mothers and fathers: sophisticated, powerful, and rich enough to afford to send their spawn to Elkhollow Prep.

They wanted to spend large sums of money, and they wanted to feel clever doing it.

That was where I came in.

The Beginner's Blackjack Club was an official club, though not one that Elkhollow advertised very well. It had a (bored) faculty adviser, met in a (cramped) classroom off the library, and received a (paltry) stipend every year. As far as the school administration knew, it boasted a small, rotating cast of nervous freshmen fumbling with cards and not much else.

The truth was a little more exciting.

The truth was a room in the back of the library's basement, the lights just yellowed and dim enough to cast the kind of ambiance that made people think they were in a mob movie. Unlike a mob movie, there was no smoking, no drinking, and no fighting. They could do that somewhere else, I didn't care, but I wasn't going to risk taking heat for extraneous crimes. I didn't bother with chips either, no matter how many people asked. There was no betting anything but simple, anonymous cash. It was a good system. It worked.

Blackjack Club wasn't the problem.

Tuesday night found me leaning against the wall, arms folded across my chest as I watched one of the tables. It was the last week of the semester, that hazy period post exams but pre summer, so the crowd was pushing at the seams of the little room. The mood was buoyant, the *thwap* of shuffling cards punctuated by laughter and groans of despair. By next week, half of them would be gone, jetting off to vacations in Greece and internships at their grandfather's company.

And I would be there, like I was every summer, probably training incoming sophomores how to deal correctly so there would be someone left to take over the club when I graduated next year. No rest for the wicked.

Speaking of. I pushed myself off the wall and sauntered toward the closest table. There were five players considering their cards. A girl leaning forward on her elbows, a busted hand on the table in front of her. I scanned the cards without even thinking. A king, a five, and a nine. Two lacrosse players sat next to her, a graduating senior with a hand of three fives beside them, and a junior from my English class at the end. A king and an ace sat in front of him. Blackjack.

"Bryan," I said, coming up next to the dealer. "Why don't you tell me what went wrong here?"

Bryan twitched, sweat beading his forehead. He wasn't one of my better dealers, but I'd been hoping he might improve. So much for that.

"Um," he said eloquently. "The house lost."

Two cards sat in front of him, a ten and a seven. Enough to beat the senior girl's fifteen and the bigger lacrosse player's twelve but not the junior's hand. Each king was worth ten, the ace either a one or an eleven. The only way to beat a twenty-one was to match it.

I shook my head. "Sometimes the house loses. That's the game." What we were betting, what every casino bet, was that the house would win more than it lost. Considering Bryan collected cash from four out of five players at the table, it wasn't a bad bet. "But not when you cheat."

"Card counting isn't cheating," the junior with blackjack blurted out, which was a very good way to sound guilty. He clutched his cash like he was considering making a run for it. Also not a great strategy. One of the lacrosse players met my eyes and gave his chin a little jerk. I always made sure the team had a little better luck than average, with the understanding that their luck depended on mine. The junior wouldn't be getting far if he did make a bad decision.

I gave my head an infinitesimal shake. I didn't think it would come to that.

"It's not," I agreed. Not technically, though technicality wouldn't keep you from getting kicked out if you got caught. I swept the cards from the table and rejoined them with the deck, my hands falling into the familiar pattern of shuffling. The decks we used were comfortable and well-worn, like old friends. "There's a reason we play blackjack here. And not because it's simple."

Which it was anyway, luckily. At least for our purposes. A real dealer's shoe could have up to eight decks in it at a time when you got to the big leagues. I kept it simple. One deck, fifty-two cards, one number in each suit. Numbered cards were worth their numerical value while face cards were worth ten. An ace could be either an eleven or a one. You got two cards in a hand and could take a hit from the dealer until you got to twenty-one, or close enough that you were confident that your hand would be higher than the dealer's. Or you could go over twenty-one and bust.

I ran my thumb over the edge of the cards. "Because it can be beaten. Count all you want." If only. I had yet to meet a decent card counter in the halls of Elkhollow Prep, but I was still holding out hope that there might be a real challenge out there somewhere. Sometimes running the club felt more like playing solitaire. Or herding cats. "Actually, let's count them together."

The rest of the table shifted uncomfortably as I spread the cards across the table, letting them slide in a neat row. The girl on the end leaned forward a little farther, her chin resting on her hands.

"One." I slid the ace of diamonds out of line with one finger.

"Two." Ace of hearts.

"Three." Ace of spades.

"Four." Ace of clubs.

And . . .

"My grandfather used to have a saying," I said. "Anyone can get lucky. But sometimes—" I pulled a second ace of hearts from the deck and held it up between two fingers with a smirk. I couldn't help it. I liked to win. "You need five aces to win." I showed it to Bryan, who had gone pale and tight-lipped. The smirk grew teeth. "You're in the Magic Club, Bryan. I know you can do sleight of hand."

Someone was always watching. Better they learned that now, before they tried it at a real casino. *That* was how you got blacklisted. If you were lucky.

I struck Bryan's name from my list of dealers and let the junior leave with his money, but I made a note to keep an eye on him in the future. Contrary to what Bryan might have thought, I wasn't mad—the winnings from the rest of the table more than made up for whatever the junior took home, and this venture was never really about money. This was Elkhollow. We all had money.

It was about the game.

"Jack Shannon?" The girl from the table, the one who'd been so interested in my little show, stood behind me. She didn't look like someone who frequented the library basement, but I'd learned to stop trying to pigeonhole my clientele. There were even teachers down there from time to time, which was a little concerning. No way Elkhollow paid well enough to support a gambling habit. "Aileen Shannon's son, right?"

I eyed her warily. At Elkhollow, everyone sold themselves like trading cards—this senator's son, this pharmaceutical CEO's daughter. It was practically in every introduction. *Jack Shannon: son of Aileen Shannon, CEO of the Golden Age Hotel and Casino. Have you heard of it?* It had been easy to start the club, even as a freshman. It was what they expected out of me anyway.

"Yeah," I said. "Why?"

Did she want to replace Bryan as a dealer? I already had a waiting list, but I was willing to shuffle it around for someone who showed promise. Plenty of people wanted to deal for me—the thrill of the game but with the house edge—but not all had the confidence to pull it off. Or, like Magic Bryan, they had a little too much.

"I was just wondering if I could get a statement for the school paper." The girl's smile slid a little wider. "About your mother."

I started to refuse—the wannabe journalists at the school paper tried to crack open the story about a secret, underage, definitely illegal gambling ring in the library basement every couple of months, usually when someone new joined the staff. They never got far, thanks to the lacrosse team. So no, I wasn't interested in talking to the paper. I was interested in finding Lacrosse Benjy and dropping some hints that he might need to revisit their offices.

But I stopped, my mouth still hanging open. This wasn't the usual line of questioning. Mom? Their interest in her usually began and ended at her name and occupation. A casino mogul really wasn't that interesting at a place like Elkhollow. Even the (alleged) mob ties weren't really remarkable when there were members of the student body who came from mobsters themselves.

"What about her?"

The girl's eyebrows climbed upward. "You haven't heard?"

My hand flew to my pocket. I kept my phone off during blackjack nights, or else I'd be on it instead of watching the tables. Bad habits, bad business. Mom liked to say that.

The girl was faster. She unlocked her phone with a swipe and pulled up CNN. She flipped it around with a gleeful flourish so I could see the screen.

I knew I shouldn't look. I should have told her to leave. I should have closed early for the night, paid the dealers and packed up the cash in the lockbox to let the old basement rest for the night. At least then I might have gone to bed and left my life to fall apart in the morning.

But as you might imagine, that was the first of what would amount to many questionable decisions. I leaned forward and read the headline splashed over the familiar red-and-white website.

CASINO MOGUL AILEEN SHANNON BROUGHT IN ON MULTIPLE COUNTS OF FRAUD, TIES TO ORGANIZED CRIME. Underneath it was a picture of my mom, her blond hair perfectly swept into place and her white suit jacket unbuttoned so that I could see the gold-satin lining. She looked like she just stepped out of a board meeting, except for the pair of FBI agents leading her out of the Golden Age Hotel and Casino in handcuffs.

"Oh," I said as the first hairline crack raced down my heart. The first tremor, the first warning that my life was about to fall apart, and it very well might take me with it.

The girl leaned in. "Can I get that on the record?"

READ 'EM AND WEEP

VOICEMAIL: BETH SHANNON
MAY 26, 8:34 P.M.

"Jack, call me back as soon as you get this. I know it's getting late over there, but it's important. Okay? I mean it. Love you."

VOICEMAIL: BETH SHANNON
MAY 26, 8:47 P.M.

"Listen, something's happened. It's—everyone is alive. But it's really important that you call me back right away. I don't want you hearing it from someone else first. Call me. Please."

VOICEMAIL: KERRY SHANNON
MAY 26, 9:00 P.M.

"Oh my God, can you answer your phone? Beth is losing her mind. Please indulge her fake-mom instincts for, like, two seconds so she'll stop calling me."

VOICEMAIL: ROBERT CASTLE
MAY 26, 9:02 P.M.

"Hey, it's me. It's Dad. I heard about your mom. Just wanted to make sure you're—you know. I'll, uh, I'll try you later. Okay. Bye."

VOICEMAIL: BETH SHANNON
MAY 26, 9:28 P.M.

"Call me when you're ready. I love you, Jay."

♠

I stared down at my phone as we were taxiing on the runway. It was a six-hour flight from Boston Logan International Airport to McCarran International Airport in Las Vegas, Nevada. Plenty of time to nurse the emotional breakdown I could feel growing in my chest and enjoy the complimentary Wi-Fi.

I probably should have responded to Beth's flurry of texts about my arrival time and what gate I'd be at and if the people at the airport were nice to me, as if I were seven and not seventeen, but I didn't want to say something I'd regret later. Like how I started flying as an unaccompanied minor at age eight because our dad couldn't find the time to watch me for the weekend and thought that a two-hour flight to Grandma's house in Portland was the best alternative. I could handle a six-hour flight.

I muted my text messages and opened the Hullabaloo app instead.

12

The cheerful elephant mascot winked at me as it loaded, struggling through the airplane's sluggish Wi-Fi. It was late in Massachusetts, nearly midnight, but I knew my friends would still be awake in their respective corners of the country. Call it Internet addiction or call it fate, but they had a knack for being online when I needed them to be.

I exhaled as the chat filled with my missed messages, like I'd been holding my breath the whole time. I'd missed a lot in the last couple hours of awkward phone calls and shuffling through airport security to catch a last-minute red-eye flight.

[gabe]: it's a metaphor ok

[lucky]: dogsledding is a metaphor

[lucky]: for what???

[gabe]: FOR LOVE

[georgia]: You're the most romantic aromantic I've ever met

[gabe]: there are many kinds of love, my dear

[gabe]: the most important of which is between man and dog

[lucky]: ha. gross.

[gabe]: srgdjflmj stop

[remy]: do the dogs talk?

[gabe]: do you really think i'd be watching a dog-sledding anime if the dogs didn't talk?

I cracked a smile, for a moment caught up in the normalcy of it all. It didn't last long. My thumb hovered over the familiar gray text box, the reality of the situation looming over my shoulder, waiting to see what I would say. What was I *supposed* to say? My friends weren't just my casual Internet acquaintances anymore. After a year, we'd definitely transitioned into spill-your-guts-at-three-in-the-morning friends, but that didn't mean the actual gut spilling came easily. I needed to say *something*, but every time I tried, my fingers wouldn't cooperate. I could have pretended like nothing was wrong, but that felt too much like lying. At some point happy-normal Jack would deviate so far from the truth that it would technically become catfishing, and I wasn't interested in ending up on MTV.

Besides, they'd notice my change in time zones pretty quick. It would look at lot more suspicious if I didn't say something now. A half-truth, then. They knew I was from Las Vegas, at least. It was the *everything else* part that I'd never figured out how to tell them, and I certainly wasn't up to it now.

I took a picture of the runway lights out the window and put it on Instagram with a plane emoji in the caption and BOS → LAS. The coward's way out, but that's why social media was invented. To fulfill social obligations without having to actually speak to anyone.

I hit Post. The response was almost immediate. A red notification bubble appeared over the Hullabaloo app.

[remy]: *@jack* where are u going?
[georgia]: I thought he had club today?
[remy]: ya but it ends before MIDNIGHT

[remy]: I think. look at insta
[lucky]: LAS is vegas
[lucky]: take me with you bitch
[gabe]: skipping blackjack to go to VEGAS? what a bad boy
[gabe]: baby's going big league

A bit of relief unspooled in my chest. I was glad, now, that I'd never found a way to drop into casual conversation just *how* Vegas my family was. Despite what turning my high-school experience into an underground poker club might make it look like, I didn't like my background touching every part of my life. Sometimes it was nice to pretend to be normal.

Because it was definitely the last of normal I'd be seeing for a while, I was sure of that. I coughed and itched my nose, turning away from the woman sitting next to me. The runway lights blurred dangerously. Jesus Christ. I was not going to cry on a plane. Mom would never forgive me. I was a Shannon. We were supposed to be proud or whatever.

[jack]: hardly
[jack]: I'm from Vegas, remember?
[georgia]: Yeah I STILL don't know how you survive the snow
[gabe]: because some of us aren't babies, georgie
[remy]: and jack is one of them??
[lucky]: LMAO
[jack]: you guys are so funny I can't even stand it

[gabe]: I know!

[jack]: I was going to stay at elkhollow over the summer but my sister decided she wants to get us all together like last minute

[jack]: like some big family bonding thing I guess

I chewed on my bottom lip. Not totally a lie. Playing damage control after Mom's arrest was hardly the kind of family fun they write about on sitcoms, but it was definitely bonding. It would be the first time I'd been home since Mom's birthday in August. We did Christmas in Aspen last year.

[remy] is typing . . . popped up and disappeared again. My stomach churned in a way that had little to do with the plane leaving the earth. Remy knew I was lying, or at least they could tell that there was more to it than that. Remy could always tell.

I had to be normal. Throw them off the scent of my rapidly deteriorating composure. I typed the first thing I could think of.

[jack]: it's dumb but whatever at least the city is cool

[jack]: it's been a while since I've seen my mom

[georgia]: Awww

[gabe]: awwwwwwww

[remy]: b'aaaw

[lucky]: aAaAwWw

[jack]: shut up

[jack]: It's a six-hour flight help me pick a movie

HOME SWEET STRIP

QUESTION 1: WHICH OF THE FOLLOWING IS A shining example of the American dream?

A) In 1963, Samuel Shannon immigrated from Dublin, Ireland, to the United States with little else but the shirt on his back. He went west, looking for opportunity, and settled in Las Vegas, where, with a lot of hard work and bootstrap pulling, he went on to found the Golden Age Hotel and Casino, one of the Strip's many glittering jewels.

B) In 1963, Samuel McNabb fled Galway, Ireland, after killing his brother and stealing his inheritance. He went west, where he changed his name to Shannon to avoid being found and extradited back to Ireland, and he settled in Las Vegas. With a lot of careful investments in real estate and a comfortable relationship with the Carlevaro crime family, he went on to found the Golden Age Hotel and Casino, a sprawling testament to the gross decadence of the past, present, and future.

QUESTION 2: Which is the truth?

I stood at the floor-to-ceiling windows, looking out over the Las Vegas Strip from the Shannon penthouse. Despite leaving at midnight from Boston, I landed in Las Vegas at three in the morning local time, so tired that I tried to tip the driver Beth sent with a playing card. The ace of hearts, Magic Bryan's lucky fifth ace. Rather than sleeping, I'd been flipping it restlessly between my fingers ever since.

It was almost 6:00 a.m. Even in the hazy, early morning light, Vegas managed to glitter, the molten Nevada sun catching off miles of steel and glass. I rubbed at my eyes, itchy with exhaustion. I'd been awake for nearly twenty-four hours, but I knew sleep wasn't going to be an option for a while. Not on the plane and especially not here. Being home always threw me off.

Everything was white in the penthouse, from the plush carpet to the rigid furniture, giving it a cold, untouched look that I supposed wasn't untrue. I didn't know the last time someone actually lived there full-time. I'd been at Elkhollow since I started high school, and a different, similarly pretentious boarding school before that. Kerry too, before she graduated and got into some art school in California. Dad came into our lives irregularly, which was usually for the best, and Beth hadn't stepped through that door since the day she turned eighteen.

And Mom—

There was a shuffle and bang from the front hallway. My sisters moved like a herd of elephants, giving me plenty of warning before they appeared. Kerry dragged a suitcase behind her and an overstuffed backpack over one shoulder. She dumped them gracelessly at the edge of the white carpet. Despite only having an hour-and-a-half-long flight from San Francisco, she still managed to arrive after me.

Beth followed, looking harried. Her usual high ponytail was now a low ponytail, half the hair escaped and falling in her face. She clearly hadn't slept either. "Jack, you made it, thank God," she breathed out, pulling me into a hug like I went through a war zone and not just six hours in business class. Close, but less leg room. "I'm sorry I couldn't pick you up from the airport. Everything has just been so—"

"It's fine," I mumbled into her shoulder. My hands hung uselessly at my sides. Hugs were supposed to last fifteen seconds maximum. After that, I wasn't really sure what to do, and my oldest sister refused to let me go. "You've been busy." Beth had been talking with lawyers and playing damage control since the first available flight from Phoenix had landed, I was sure.

And that, at least, gave me a spark of confidence. It would all be sorted out soon. Mom had the best lawyers available, and there was a reason the Shannon family had managed to be so successful in the city of sin. We didn't go down that easily.

I cleared my throat. "You should probably get some sleep."

"Sleep? I've never heard of it." Beth laughed hollowly and finally detangled herself. She threw her massive purse onto one of the immaculate white couches. "Kerry, hug your brother."

19

My dear, middlest sister pulled a face. "I don't really want to do that."

I pulled a face right back. "I don't really want her to do that."

We weren't a family of huggers. Beth never got the memo.

Beth sighed. "God, you're such children." She disappeared into the kitchen. My oldest sister was only twenty-three, but she'd qualified as a responsible adult for about as long as I could remember. At least by Shannon family standards.

Kerry slouched against the wall, her hands sunk deep in her hoodie pockets. She looked every bit the rebellious middle child, from her lip ring to the disinterested expression. Kerry made it into an art form. She raised her eyebrows.

"Dad's coming," she said.

Oh God. "He's *here*?"

Kerry nodded. "Saw him across the atrium from the elevator," she said. "I think he already had a cocktail."

"The sun is barely up."

"For what it's worth, it might have been a Bloody Mary."

I snorted. "Sounds about right."

She pushed off the wall and came to join me by the windows, looking down at the Strip below. Even this early, when half the city was sleeping off its hangover, it was still too bright. I'd forgotten what it was like to be home. It was giving me a headache.

"Do you think we'll be all right?" I kept my voice small, so Beth wouldn't hear. Beth would only worry more if she knew that I was worried too. That, and she'd lie. Beth would never admit there was something she couldn't fix through sheer willpower. She and Mom had that in common, even if Beth didn't want to admit it.

But Kerry had never had to be Mom when Mom wasn't around or when Dad was being himself. Sometimes I thought Kerry didn't know how to lie, but it seemed more likely that she just didn't see the point. Maybe after growing up in a city of glitter and glamour, she just wanted to be something real.

She met my look and gave me a lopsided smile. She nudged me with her elbow, probably the closest thing we'd get to a hug while Beth was around to make a big deal out of it. That made me wary more than anything else. If Kerry was getting sentimental, it meant that this was serious. "C'mon," Kerry said. "Were we ever really all right to begin with?"

♠

Aileen Shannon and Robbie Castle were not a love story. She was a casino heiress. He was the lead singer in a Queen cover band trying to make it big in the Las Vegas circuit. They never married but managed to have three children, each born three years apart. Aileen inherited her father's hotel and casino, and Robbie's band never once played at the Golden Age, though he did enjoy free drinks at the bar.

Sometimes I wondered if our births were a transaction, the way things with Mom tended to be. She wanted kids, and she got them, the other half of the equation more or less incidental. If cloning had been an option, she would have seriously considered it.

Kerry and I inherited her fair hair, though Kerry had colored hers purple at the ends since the last time I saw her. Beth, meanwhile, looked like the spitting image of Dad, with his dark hair and darker eyes. Sometimes it was scary, seeing them side by side. It was a weird reminder that he was actually our dad and not just a weird guy we were obligated to spend time with every now and then.

Fortunately, none of us inherited the gaudy shirt covered in parrots, nor the tendency to have a colorful frozen drink sweating in one hand. Dad sat crookedly with his ankle resting on one knee, his foot jiggling impatiently. I couldn't stop watching it bounce, my eyes stuck on a dirty piece of gum wedged in the tread.

"Miami again, Dad?" I asked when the silence got too thick. Kerry had to reach her leg across the couch to stomp on my foot. Starting a conversation with Dad was dangerous, because you never knew how, why, or if it would end. Dad, in typical Dad fashion, didn't notice her hint.

Instead his eyes lit up. "Yeah!" He lounged back in his chair as if it wasn't designed to be as uncomfortable as possible, his hands folded over his gut. The living room was unfriendly around us, like it didn't approve of us actually using the furniture instead of admiring it from a safe distance. "Great place. The water? God, like sapphires. Have you ever been?"

I shifted uncomfortably in my seat. "You took us for Kerry's sixteenth birthday, Dad."

And I had somehow ended up lost in the club his band was playing at, where I was informally adopted by a bachelorette party. They'd delivered me to Dad's condo via limo at the end of the night, luckily, or else I might have spent the rest of my life with a maid-of-honor sash tied around my forehead. Beth had arrived the next afternoon to collect us after Kerry called to tell her I was missing.

Our family, I was realizing, spent a lot of time on planes.

"Oh."

Kerry's foot mashed my toes into the carpet.

I elbowed her in the side. "Stop it," I hissed.

"*You* stop it."

"I'm just trying to make conversation—"

The door opened, and we all hushed, except for the gentle swish of crushed ice as Dad stirred his drink. Beth appeared at the end of the entrance hall first, her hair swept up again. Suddenly she looked a lot like Mom instead.

"Mom's lawyers are here," she said unnecessarily, seeing as though she went down to the lobby to collect them in the first place. She fixed us each with a stern look in turn. "*Behave*," she mouthed.

Doherty & Doherty were a husband-and-wife team of equally hawkish-looking lawyers. It was like they both came out of the same mold at Yale, where one was given a tie and a receding hairline and the other was given a jewel-tone pantsuit. Beth herded them onto the snowy-white loveseat that faced the view overlooking the Strip. The best seat in the house, though neither Doherty looked fazed. They'd been on retainer since before I was born, and the Golden Age wasn't the only casino they represented. They'd forgotten how to be impressed a long time ago.

Mr. Doherty leaned forward, his elbows resting on his knees. His gold-rimmed glasses slipped down his nose. "Let me be frank," he started gravely.

"I thought your name was David." Dad laughed at himself. The joke landed so badly that we could all feel the impact. I winced.

Mrs. Doherty's lips thinned. "I hope you all understand the weight of the situation," she said. "There's the very real possibility that Aileen is going to prison for a very long time."

"Yeah?" Kerry said, pulling her legs up to her chest, her shoes planted firmly on the white cushion. She rested her chin on her knees. "Aren't we paying you a lot of money to stop that from happening?"

Beth shot her a warning look.

"And we will certainly try our best," Mr. Doherty said sharply, "but we need to be realistic. The FBI have been after the Shannon family since your grandfather first shook hands with Gavino Carlevaro." He hesitated, his mustache quivering. I stared at it, fixated on a piece of his breakfast still stuck among the hair. What was that? Scrambled egg? All I could do was watch it tremble. "We're afraid that due to her assets and ties to the international community, Aileen has been determined to be a flight risk. The judge has refused bail."

I'd seen videos of mushroom clouds before—the way they rose and expanded as devastation swept across the ground below in every direction. I imagined the roar—like a hurricane, like the end of the world. Mr. Doherty had just dropped a bomb, and I couldn't understand why the room was so quiet.

Mrs. Doherty cleared her throat in the middle of the awkward silence. "We've been working closely with her to ensure that the impact on you and your family will be as minimal as possible, but the effects will be wide reaching . . ."

Her voice faded into white noise, distant and annoying, like a gnat. My eyes wandered the room. Beth was quiet, her eyes turned down. She knew. At least before this moment; the Dohertys probably warned her in the elevator. Kerry didn't. She'd gone completely still, her hands curled tight around her knees. Dad definitely didn't. Not that that meant much.

Here's the thing—we always knew something like this could happen. I mean, when you grew up in a criminally rich family, it was just kind of a given. But (and this sounds bad) it never felt like it would mean that much. At least at first. The Shannon family had made a career of throwing money at our problems until they went away, and that was literally what bail was. Mom was going to be under penthouse arrest like every other Wall Street crook you saw on the news, and it was going to be fine. Or so I thought.

Suddenly things were not very fine.

"Why?" I didn't realize I'd spoken until I caught the Dohertys' dirty looks aimed in my direction. "I mean—that's a little extreme, isn't it? She didn't kill anyone." Did she? No, probably not. Maybe.

The Dohertys exchanged a sideways look. "There was . . . ," Mr. Doherty started.

"Compelling evidence," Mrs. Doherty finished.

Compelling evidence. Favors. Greased palms. We all knew what that meant. The realization was like a spike of adrenaline injected directly into my heart, and I couldn't stop myself from saying, "You know who did this, right?"

Every eye turned to me, some harder than others. Dad kept stirring his drink.

"It was Peter Carlevaro."

Aileen Shannon and Peter Carlevaro were also not a love story, as much as Peter wanted to believe they were. She was a casino heiress, and he was a crime boss's son, brought together by their fathers' friendship. To Peter, the medieval idea of marrying the two families together was obvious. To Aileen, less so.

I barely got the name out before Kerry groaned.

"Not Uncle Peter again," she sighed, tipping her head back. She kept her eyes fixed on the ceiling, but I could tell they were glassy. "You sound just like Mom."

"He's not our uncle," I snapped. He liked to pretend he was part of the family before Mom cut ties with him, but that didn't make it true. The Carlevaro and the Shannon families were tied together through decades of increasingly illicit activity, but not blood. Thank God. The Carlevaros had a tendency toward heart disease that I wasn't interested in. Rest in peace, Gavino Carlevaro. It had only been a year since he croaked, and "Uncle" Peter took his place as the head of the family, but it seemed like he wasn't wasting any time in exacting petty revenge now that his dad wasn't around to stop him. "He's always been jealous of us. Mom always said so."

"Your mom says a lot of things," Dad said with a shrug. "Doesn't he have his own place now? The Imperium?"

Of all the times for Dad to choose to pay attention, it would be that one. "It's not about the Golden Age, it's about Mom," I said. "He never got over that she had kids with . . . *you* instead of him." I almost said *a washed-up Freddie Mercury impersonator,* but that seemed too personal. "He can't stand to see her successful without him. He thought they'd rule the Golden Age together." Like some sort of king and queen of the Strip. What a freak.

I was just parroting back what Mom had told me, but it *sounded* true. It made sense. And now he wanted to take her down, and everything our family had built with her.

"I think that's best for your family to discuss privately," Mrs. Doherty said awkwardly, neatly sidestepping my conspiracy theories. "At present, we should discuss the logistics of the situation at hand. Pending investigation, most of your mother's assets have been frozen. Fortunately, the hotel is a public company, so the day-to-day operation of it should go on uninterrupted. However—"

"Excuse me," Beth said. She'd yet to sit. Instead, she hovered behind her chair, her hands plucking at the cushion.

Mrs. Doherty's mouth twitched. "Yes?"

"That's all very important," Beth said without really meaning it. She hadn't touched the family money since she turned eighteen, including her trust fund. She'd rather scrape by as a dental assistant in Phoenix than give in, especially if Mom was there to gloat about it. "But I think we should talk about . . . Jack."

My head jerked up, and I was suddenly very aware of my breathing. What did I usually do with my arms? They had to go somewhere when I wasn't paying attention. My elbow dug awkwardly into the unrelenting arm of the couch. "What about me?"

"I've talked it over with Dad," Beth said without actually looking at him, "and I would like to become Jack's legal guardian."

My stomach dropped to my feet. Oh.

I should have expected it. Beth was half a mom already sometimes, and she'd taken control of the situation before any of us were even in the city. But until that moment—despite the impromptu family reunion, despite the lawyers—a part of me had still expected Mom to walk through the front door and pour herself a glass of red wine. At any moment, this whole charade would fall apart, and I could get on a plane and go back to normal. Or at least as normal as things got.

"Nothing would change," Beth said hastily. "You could still go to Elkhollow. They can take your tuition out of your trust. I know this is hard, but . . ." Her eyes darted toward Kerry, but our sister had her nose tucked in the collar of her hoodie, her eyes fixed determinedly at the ground. "I think this could be good. For all of us. Mom messed up, and she's paying for it. We can learn something from that. We can change the Shannon family. We can be normal."

"I don't want to be normal. I want Mom!" My voice cracked like an iceberg that just figured out that climate change is real. Embarrassing. Compounded by the fact that I was on my feet now without any knowledge of how I got there. "Stop acting like she's not coming back. She's not dead! *Jesus.*"

The pressure in my chest was out of control now, a hurricane in miniature, tearing at my ribcage and threatening to pull it apart. Hot tears pricked at my eyes, even more embarrassing than my outburst. They were all staring at me now. The Dohertys were as stoic as before. Dad with the straw still hanging out of his mouth. Kerry looked like she wanted to say something, but she couldn't quite do it. Beth just looked sad.

I couldn't breathe. The living room was too white, its corners too perfect. The Las Vegas Strip burned gold against the pink sky. I turned away from it, emotion stuck in my throat. Las Vegas was a place set apart from the rest of the world, one foot in reality and the other somewhere else. It was home, but it wasn't. It was real, but it wasn't. I grew up in the Shannon penthouse before I was sent away to school, but it still always felt like I was just another guest at the Golden Age.

"Do whatever you want," I muttered. "I need some air."

IMPERIOUS

I DID WHAT YOU MIGHT EXPECT: I MADE ANOTHER BAD decision.

For those keeping track at home—don't.

I couldn't stay in the Golden Age. There was too much Mom there, too many Shannon family values built into the foundation. Work smart, not hard. If they won't give it to you, then take it. Don't let a challenge go unanswered.

My head pounded like my brain was trying to leap out of my skull and onto the hot pavement. I had to do something. Didn't I? Mom was a lot of things—cutthroat and ambitious and impeccably dressed—but those were all things she needed to be, being a powerful woman on the Strip. I knew she was frustrated with Beth's rebellion and Kerry's disinterest, but I was different. I was the one who was going to grow up in her image, the way she did her father's, and take over the Golden Age someday. If anyone was going to fix this, it should be me. At least, I was the only person who seemed interested in doing anything besides damage control.

Personally, I was a little more interested in doing some damage.

I stopped and looked up at the Imperium Hotel and Casino.

In a city of glamour and glitz, the Imperium was like a black hole. It rose fifty-three stories into the sky, like a needle, built entirely from black steel, black stone, and tinted glass. Only the accents were gilded—flecks of gold in the black-marble floor in the lobby and an elegant metal grate laid over the wall like a thousand fish scales, or maybe palm fronds. The Imperium looked like the architect wanted it to be classic art deco, but didn't want to compete with the MGM Grand, so they aimed for art deco two hundred years in the future instead.

It was, simply put, *a little much*. And I grew up in a hotel meant to invoke the ghosts of Fifth Avenue robber barons with Gatsby-style grace. There was a speakeasy in the basement, for God's sake.

This was Peter Carlevaro's hotel, only opened about five years earlier, the rotten heart of his whole enterprise. It stared back at me like the gate to hell, and, like metal against metal, my mind started giving off sparks.

Another question. What do you think Peter Carlevaro cared about?

a) My mom

b) His family

c) Money

Now to review the results:

a)   He got her arrested. Next.

b)   His father? Dead. His wife? Divorced. His daughter? All I knew was that she didn't live in the city, and I'd met her maybe once. Overall? Doubtful.

c)   Ding, ding, ding. We have a winner.

That was the bad-decision part, and probably the petty part too, but I didn't care. Carlevaro had gone after what *I* cared about, I knew he had, and at the moment, I wasn't really concerned about anything except for hurting him back.

I stepped into the Imperium.

When Gavino Carlevaro was the head of the family, he'd mostly ruled from an estate north of the city. I remembered it like a castle in the desert, whitewashed walls and abstract art, the sharp smell of lemon floor polish and men with handguns casually sitting on their hips. We stopped going after Granddad died. In retrospect, I couldn't believe Mom let us go at all, but Granddad and Gavino had been like brothers. Peter Carlevaro really had been *Uncle Peter*, before Mom realized he was a slimeball.

But Granddad was dead and now so was Gavino, and evidently all good manners had gone out the window. Fine. If Carlevaro wanted to play dirty, then so could I.

My phone buzzed as if Beth got an alert every time I made a bad decision. I didn't know where she found the time to tread between *I'm trying not to be overbearing* and *I don't care if I'm being overbearing*, but it must have been exhausting. It certainly was for me.

Beth Shannon

Where did you go?

The front desk said they saw you leave.
I thought you were going to the floating
gardens?

I rolled my eyes. Because I was upset, and I always went to the floating gardens when I was upset. The Golden Age had three floating gardens that jutted out from the side of the building at different floors, each cultivated into miniature parks. They weren't exceptionally popular, which meant they were quiet, the foliage easy to lose yourself in, which is why I enjoyed them when I didn't want to be found. I couldn't believe she remembered that. We hadn't lived together in years.

Beth Shannon

Jack, I'm serious.

I'll report you missing.

Oh my God, as if we didn't have enough problems with the police.

Jack Shannon

I'm fine.

I'm at the library.

The library? I didn't even know where the nearest library was, but it sounded tame enough that Beth wouldn't send out a search party. I was seventeen years old. If I could fly across the country three times a year without major incident, I think I could manage the Las Vegas Strip. The Golden

Age was pretty easy to find, considering the part where it's fifty-two stories tall and topped with a golden angel wielding a whole sword.

Beth must have read my annoyance in the subtext, because she didn't argue.

Beth Shannon
Be home in time for dinner.

Was she really making us do family dinner too? Was bearing witness to Dad's day drinking not enough of a bonding activity? I didn't bother to respond. I checked on the Hullabaloo conversation instead.

[remy]: stop. STOP.
[gabe]: stop trying to HIDE FROM THE TRUTH
[lucky]: wait hold up
[lucky]: so these were like your old star wars original characters right
[lucky]: so how did she have two lightsabers? gotta be against the rules right
[remy]: LOTS of jedi had two lightsabers ok
[remy]: it's NORMAL
[georgia]: Jedi rules
[gabe]: jedi law
[jack]: no hold on
[jack]: if I remember correctly one was blue and the other was red
[jack]: because she was a genetic chimera
[remy]: JACK NO
[jack]: and only half of her was evil

[remy]: listen I never claimed to be a space scientist

[remy]: also nothing twelve-year-old remy could come up with is sillier than canon star wars so fuck you george lucas

I darkened the screen of my phone, tapping my finger contemplatively against the case. Granddad always said that the best offense was reconnaissance, and as much as that sounded like it belonged on a camo-print mug, he was right. I needed to observe. To find the faults in Carlevaro's armor and figure out what was happening in that bald little head of his. My eyes swept the lobby.

There. The lobby café. The only thing I needed right now besides petty vengeance was an iced coffee.

Which should have been the easiest part of the plan, until I was standing in front of the register, watching the pin pad flash red as my card was rejected for the third time.

"Oh," I said, staring down at my card. My stomach dropped to my feet. Right. Mom was in police custody. Her assets were frozen. I guess I should have listened to the Dohertys a little more carefully.

"Hey," the barista said. "Just take it. Don't worry about it."

She felt bad for me. A kid staring at his credit card like he'd never seen it before, my ears going red. I clenched my jaw. "No, no, it's fine," I said, fishing a crumpled twenty-dollar bill out of my wallet. I always carried cash since I started Blackjack Club. I paid for the coffee and stuffed the change in the tip jar without counting it, trying not to see the look on the barista's face. This was going great. Leave it to Carlevaro's palace of evil to be the scene of my latest humiliation. I should probably have quit while I was ahead.

But a door caught my eye.

I almost tripped over a display of chips, but my mind was already moving at a thousand miles an hour. It was a service door, tucked to one side of the café kiosk, painted so that it blended in with the walls, except for the stern *EMPLOYEES ONLY* sign square in the middle of it.

I sidled over to it. No keypad by the handle. I assumed, like the Golden Age, that the Imperium had parts that were only accessible if you had a keycard to prove you had paid for a room and weren't just there for the casino or other attractions, but management hadn't seen the point in handing out employee-access cards to every pimply barista they hired off the street. I tested the handle. Unlocked.

I chose to take the sign as a suggestion.

I darted inside and closed the door behind me. The hallway beyond the door was devastatingly dull, beige painted-over cinder block and squeaky linoleum flooring, but this was the important part of the hotel. The casino floor might have all the glamor, but the back hallways and service doors were where the real magic happened. And I was starting to figure out exactly how to use a little bit of that magic for my own purposes.

Listen, I knew I wasn't going to ruin Carlevaro's whole life and get my mom back and solve world hunger in the course of a morning, but I had to do *something*. Carlevaro cared about money more than anything. So I'd hit him where it hurt.

According to the University of Nevada, Las Vegas, in 2018 the average Las Vegas casino made over $1,900,000 a day. $76,166 an hour, $1,319 a minute. Eleven thirty in the morning wasn't exactly peak time, but if I flipped the circuit breakers and cut off electricity to the casino, Carlevaro and the Imperium would be losing money until they realized what had happened and flipped it back on. Maybe not Elkhollow-tuition levels of cash, but not an insignificant amount.

Not stunning, I know. Metaphorically speaking, I had lost a limb, and I was using the fingers I had left to poke Carlevaro in the eye, but desperate times called for desperate measures.

I needed to find a stairwell. I couldn't hack the Imperium's mainframe or whatever and pull up the blueprints, but common sense said the circuit breakers were probably in the basement. I put on a bored look, trying to embody a teenage barista as much as possible, and set off down the hall.

I barely made it fifteen feet before I heard voices echoing off the beige walls. Actually, one voice, and one half of the conversation that seemed to imply he was on the phone. I panicked for a second, my iced coffee sweating in one hand. What was more suspicious—playing it cool or trying to hide?

Easy decision: always go for the path of least resistance, and the least amount of eyeballs, if possible. I ducked sideways, down a hall that seemed a little darker than the others. There was a shallow alcove housing the door to a custodian's closet, just enough to flatten myself against it like a cockroach and try not to breathe too loudly.

Something scratched at the back of my mind as the voice approached, accompanied by the shuffle of footsteps. Something familiar.

"I don't have time for this," the man huffed. "I've got a meeting with Carlevaro. I'm already late."

I tilted my head, shifting infinitesimally closer. Carlevaro? Do go on.

A pause. "*Yes*, it's important," he snapped. "Are you kidding me? Everything is important right now. The man stands to own more than half the Strip without Shannon keeping him in check." He paused, listening. "Well, clearly you picked the wrong side. I suggest you change your mind. And soon."

My nerves jumped. He was meeting with Carlevaro. He was talking about Mom. Did he know something?

I had to look.

I peeked around the corner of the alcove and jerked back again. The guy was standing right where the two hallways intersected, and for an instant I thought he'd seen me. I stood frozen, but he never came down the hall or peeked back at me. I stole another glance. He was still standing there, grumbling something under his breath. He held the phone between his ear and his shoulder as he dug through his wallet.

I knew him.

I sank back against the door. *I knew him.* Or at least I thought I did. He was a short man, built like the last pick at the pumpkin patch. But it was his hat that bothered me. It was a flat cap, like you might wear if you were a golfer or a 1920s newsboy, red-and-black plaid. I knew that hat. I knew that man.

The memories were old and jumbled, relics from before Elkhollow. Before Granddad died, even. I remembered muffled voices and cigar smoke that made my nose burn, the thump of chips on felt, and the soft *thwip-thwip-thwip* of playing cards. I remembered Mom laughing.

And I remembered *him.* He was there, playing cards with Mom and a cast of blurry faces I couldn't remember, sipping on expensive amber liquor and patting me on the head with a hand heavy with rings. All of Mom's friends were the same to me then, but suddenly the difference between them was much more important. Especially now that this one was wandering through the back of the Imperium, on his way to a meeting with Peter Carlevaro about the future of the Strip.

He was moving again, and I was torn. Could I follow him? Maybe. Probably. Right? My fledgling revenge felt amateur now that I had something much more real in front of me. If I could follow Flat Cap to Carlevaro's inner sanctum without getting caught—well, it was a whole new array of possibilities.

Bigger stakes. Bigger reward. I made a quick assessment of the risks.

The *play it cool* option, then.

I waited a beat, just long enough for his footsteps to start to fade, and then followed after him. The act was easier than I expected. I nursed my iced coffee and pretended to be absorbed in my phone while I kept one eye on Flat Cap ahead of me. I stuck close to the wall to avoid collisions as we passed delivery men pushing dollies and harried poker dealers straightening their vests. No one gave me a second glance. They didn't get paid enough to notice me. Maybe Carlevaro should consider giving them a raise.

Flat Cap didn't notice me either. As much as I studied the back of his head, I couldn't remember his name. Mom had a lot of friends—well, business associates—and even more enemies. In her business, there wasn't much of a difference. Mom and Carlevaro fell out years ago, but we were still supposed to call him *Uncle Peter*. Sometimes even I couldn't keep up with the politics of it.

Flat Cap crossed some kind of delivery bay, and I spotted his destination across the room. A service elevator, the kind used by maids and room-service staff, tucked away from the public eye. I wasn't surprised. We'd used private elevators in the Golden Age my entire life, though usually ones a little nicer than this. Clearly Carlevaro didn't think very highly of his associates. A keycard flashed in his hand.

Pickpocketing isn't necessarily a skill that pairs naturally with card counting and blackjack dealing—I was never a Victorian street urchin, pinching shillings or whatever out of dandies' pockets—but Kerry and I used to make a game out of it, lifting keycards from tourists' pockets and seeing how much we could charge to their room before we got caught. Actually, a bit opposite from the Victorian-street-urchin thing, but try not to hold it against me. I was ten.

The point was, I was going to pick Flat Cap's pocket. Get the keycard. Infiltrate the Imperium hotel and bring down Peter Carlevaro from the inside. Easy. I could do that. The details were a little fuzzy, but I'd figure it out as I went along.

Spoiler alert: I did not do that.

"Hey!" I jogged across the delivery bay. "Hey, sorry, do you know where the, uh, air-conditioning unit is? My dad's a contractor and—"

Flat Cap turned the same moment I started to pretend to stumble into him. In the moment immediately after that, he stepped in a puddle of oily water and actually slipped, sending him toppling forward like a majestic California redwood.

I know what you're thinking—OSHA violation. I'd worry about the workplace legal ramifications later. For the moment, I was worried about staying upright. He fell forward, which made me stagger, where my foot slipped in the same dirty puddle and sent me backward onto my ass. Flat Cap managed to keep his feet but lost just about everything else. His phone went spinning across the concrete floor, bouncing off of a stack of crates. The keycard flew in the opposite direction. My iced coffee landed squarely in the middle, splattering us both with a fountain of cold liquid.

There's a concept in aviation called decision height: the height at which point a decision must be made to either continue a landing attempt or to abort. That was the point where I should have aborted, bailed out, enacted a tactical retreat. I was covered in coffee, standing out like a sore thumb in the middle of the delivery bay. Whatever delirious dream of stealth I'd been holding on to was far away now.

As you might be able to guess, that was not the decision I made.

Time to pivot on the act a little.

"Sorry!" I squeaked, flapping my hands in a way that was meant to distract him from my face. I didn't need him recognizing me. Not exactly what I'd been planning for *play it cool*, but God laughs when men make plans or whatever. "Sorry, sorry! Let me help!"

Flat Cap decided his phone, or whoever was on the other end of it, was most important the same moment I decided on the keycard. We dove for them from opposite sides and a sickly crack rang through the bay as our skulls collided. I could hear inside my brain. The cap flopped sadly to the ground into a puddle of coffee.

I inhaled sharply and exhaled a string of curses so colorful that I expected Beth to rise up from the floor and scold me. I clutched my head as stars danced in front of my eyes. New decision height, new reason to get the hell out of there, but I'd sustained too much brain damage to give up now. I could still swap it for the Golden Age keycard in my pocket and hope Flat Cap was too frazzled to notice the difference until I was already gone. I staggered across the bay and grabbed the keycard off the floor. It was metallic gold plastic with a little white crown at the center. Not for the Imperium—the Imperium's room cards were black. I flipped it over. There were only two words in an elegant, looping script.

Avalon Club. I paused, just for an instant, my insides going cold. That name. I knew that name.

That was where I was—hunched over on the ground like an unhinged goblin, covered with coffee and clutching the growing bruise on my head—when the elevator doors opened with a *ding!*

"Ah," Peter Carlevaro said mildly, looking down his nose. "Isn't this a surprise?"

ONYX? IT'S FUCKING BLACK

THE SECURITY BOOTH AT THE IMPERIUM HOTEL AND Casino was less impressive than the rest of the building. Not that I got to really see it. What I actually saw was the break room to the security booth at the Imperium Hotel and Casino.

Still. It wasn't impressive.

I looked up at the security guard with raised eyebrows, clearly a little annoyed. Unfortunately, I played a shitty teenager better than a sweet and innocent one. "I told you, my dad is a contractor," I said, sitting at the break table like it was in a jail cell. The room was certainly as friendly as one. "Seriously, do you want me to call him?" Dad did a stint in an improv troupe that meant he was willing to *yes, and* just about anything. I had doubts about a lot of his skills, but not his willingness to play an air-conditioner repairman on the fly.

The security guard gave me a flat look. "Your sister will be here to pick you up soon," he said. He plunked a can of Coke on the table in front of me. "You just sit tight."

Ahaha. Fuck. "Have you considered arresting me?" I asked hopefully.

I could spend the night in jail if it meant avoiding Beth's wrath. Probably. It was quickly becoming a Shannon family tradition. The security guard ignored me.

Not that there was any point in trying to talk my way out of this one. Not when Peter Carlevaro found me himself. I'd really just been banking on Carlevaro's security team being particularly gullible. Clearly not one of my better bets.

I hunkered down in the hard plastic chair and put my phone on silent, flipping it over so I couldn't see the notifications pop up on the screen. Beth was going to kill me, if she even had time in between juggling every other problem our family had. Annoyance and guilt hit me in a sharp one-two punch. It wasn't my fault all of this had fallen on her shoulders. But it was my fault it just got a little heavier. I pressed my fingertips against the Coke, making invisible patterns in the condensation.

I hadn't just gotten caught. I'd gotten caught *at the Imperium*. There was really no upside to the situation, except that Carlevaro himself hadn't come back to gloat. Yet.

By the time the security guard came back for me, I was well marinated in my own misery. I tried not to let it show as he led me down another beige-brick hall that ran like an artery behind the scenes of the hotel's glamorous façade. That was all Vegas was—that's all that *we* were. A glittering face to mask the ugly inner workings. That's what Beth always said, but I'd never believed her before. Las Vegas was a terrible city, but at least it was home. Now, with Mom behind bars, I wasn't sure what was left.

Beth stood at the end of the hall, her lips tightly pressed together and her hands wrapped around the strap of her purse, listening intently to whatever Peter Carlevaro was saying to her.

Of course. I struggled to school my face into something appropriately impassive despite the stab of hatred that cut through me like a knife. God, he even looked evil. Carlevaro was a tall man, built like a vulture with a shaved head to match. The only new addition since my childhood was the slight gut, stuck awkwardly to his otherwise scarecrow-adjacent frame.

Beth spared me a flickering glance but didn't say a word, which was somehow worse. "Thank you for looking out for my brother, Mr. Carlevaro," she said. I wanted to gag. *Mr. Carlevaro.* What was she doing? Being mad at me was one thing, but sucking up to Carlevaro was just unnecessary. "It's been hard on all of us lately, with everything going on."

"Please," Carlevaro said with a thin smile. "We've known each other too long for that. Call me Peter, Bethany. We're all friends here. I don't want any more trouble for your family."

Was she hearing this? I fumed silently, my teeth clenched so hard they hurt, but Beth smiled, her whole body slack with relief. "Thank you, Peter," she said. "I—*we* really appreciate it."

"Miss," the security guard said, "if you could just sign some paperwork here in the office, you can be on your way."

"Of course," Beth said. Her eyes flickered toward me as she passed, the warning clear enough. *Behave.*

I scowled in response, guilt evaporating under the heat of my anger. I folded my arms across my chest and leaned against the wall, my eyes burning holes into the ugly beige cinder block to keep me from looking at Carlevaro. I didn't want to see the smug look on his face, knowing Beth was just through the open door. I didn't want him to know he'd won.

Again. My heart twisted. He'd won *again*.

"You're going to have to try a little harder, Arthur."

I looked up, my eyes going wide. It took me a second to realize who he was even talking to. No one called me by my first name, not even Mom. I was convinced she'd forgotten she wrote *Arthur Jack Shannon* on my birth certificate. I certainly tried to. People had called me Jack all my life, except for the first day of school when the teachers were still reading off the roster. Jack Shannon sounded like someone who ran underground gambling rings. Arthur Shannon probably wore cardigans and wrote sad poetry for fun.

Besides, it was called blackjack, not blackarthur. It was a branding thing.

"I know what happens in my hotel," Carlevaro continued, his voice low and actually a little dangerous for a man who looked like an off-brand Lex Luthor. "Who enters it. Who leaves it. Who overstays their welcome. I would have expected a little better from you." I could feel his eyes studying me, making my skin crawl. His head tilted condescendingly. "What was your plan, then? To disrupt the power? You have to know there are backup generators."

My heart lodged in my throat. Had he been watching me? For how long? Either he could read minds, or I was just that obvious. Embarrassment burned in my cheeks.

Still, it was as good as a confession, wasn't it? I wanted to grab him by the lapels and demand to know what he did to Mom, what he told the police that could make this happen. But I was rooted in place. As much as I hated him, as much as he looked like a wilted piece of celery cursed with human form, he was still the head of a crime family, and Beth was still in the other room. I didn't have a next step. I didn't know what to do.

Carlevaro looked me up and down and made an unimpressed sound. "Aileen ruined you, didn't she?" he said almost thoughtfully. "She just couldn't stand for you to end up like your father."

It was like flipping a switch, and I could move again, my hands tightening into fists. He didn't get to insult Dad. *I* got to insult Dad. "That's why I have hair," I said, the very first thing to come to mind. Low-hanging fruit, especially since that wasn't how male-pattern baldness worked, but Carlevaro's lips twisted unpleasantly as the shot landed.

There was a rustle of movement from the security office. Beth was coming back.

Carlevaro pushed his shoulders back and ran one hand over his smooth head. Ha. "Come back when you can impress me, Arthur," he said, his voice serrated, "or don't come back at all."

He turned on his heel and left, his shiny black shoes clicking smartly against the tile floor. Beth appeared not even a moment later, the security guard trailing behind her. I could feel her at my elbow, but I couldn't look away from Carlevaro's retreating back.

No, not retreating. I was the one who was retreating, my tail between my legs.

Carlevaro was issuing a challenge.

"Jack," Beth said tersely. I blinked. I didn't know how many times she had to say my name for me to hear it, but going by the look she was giving me, it was more than once. "Let's go."

"Yeah," I said faintly. "Okay." But my eyes still slid back to the space where Carlevaro had been standing when he said those magic words. *Come back when you can impress me.*

Oh, I would.

I let Flat Cap's golden keycard slip out of my sleeve as I followed Beth out, palming it like a magic trick. I twisted it there, pressing my thumb against the hard edge. Carlevaro might feel safe in his castle, but now I had a key to the kingdom.

♠

The snap of the car doors echoed in my ears as we sat in the gray light of the Imperium parking garage. Beth didn't make a move to put on her seatbelt, so I didn't either. We just sat, letting the silence congeal between us. Finally, I made a decision.

"If you try to ground me," I said, "I'm going to live with Dad."

And I'd probably end up busking outside of a nightclub in Miami if I did, but my pride was worth it. All my doubts had been burned up in the light of Carlevaro's challenge. Maybe Beth was right (she wasn't), maybe I'd messed up (I hadn't, except for getting caught), but she wasn't Mom. She could pretend, but she didn't get to punish me like I was a child.

"I'm not going to try to ground you," Beth said quietly, her eyes still fixed forward. "I don't want to replace Mom, Jack. I never wanted to replace Mom." *But I've had to.* The truth went unspoken.

Oh. I exhaled, leaning back in the passenger seat. I rubbed my thumb against the faux-leather seat of the rental car. Was Beth paying for it herself? I remembered the credit card getting denied at the hotel café. Did she pay for my flight too? I hadn't even thought about where the money came from. I'd never had to before.

"Jack," Beth said. "You knew that not everything Mom did was legal."

Of course I knew. I wasn't an idiot, and after one too many nights dragged to Dad's shows, I sure as hell wasn't naïve. "Yeah," I said dully, the barest acknowledgement possible. So? What was she trying to prove?

That I should have expected this someday? That it made it okay? She was still my mom.

"I've done everything I can to try to protect you guys," Beth said. "It was my idea to send you and Kerry away to school. This place—this city—it's toxic. Especially with Mom barely around and Dad being . . . Dad. I couldn't stay to protect you, but I couldn't leave you here either. Does that make sense?"

"Yeah," I said again. "Yeah, I guess." I didn't know that. I had been twelve, and at the time it had felt like everything was happening all at once. Beth's fight with Mom, Beth moving out. Being pulled out of middle school and sent to the East Coast, where everything was redbrick and colonial history and *cold*.

I squeezed my eyes shut and scrubbed at them with the back of my hand. My sleepless night was catching up with me. "None of this should have happened," I said fiercely, grasping desperately for the last place I saw my righteous fury. "Mom was too good to get caught. It was Uncle Peter. Beth, I swear—"

"Forget about Peter Carlevaro," she said, just as fierce. "Forget about Mom and the Golden Age and Vegas. Live for *you*. Be a kid, for God's sake. Let the Dohertys worry about Mom. We pay them a lot of money to."

Beth would never understand. In her mind, she left the Golden Age behind once and for all five years ago, and it didn't hold any sway over her anymore. The glitter and lights that brought people from all corners of the world, the money and old power that'd been rooted in our family since our grandfather stepped on American soil. It didn't mean anything to her.

Come back when you can impress me. Carlevaro wasn't done with us. He wouldn't be until Mom was ruined and the Golden Age was *in* ruins.

I couldn't let him do that to us. I couldn't let him win. Why couldn't she see that? It wasn't just about pride, it was about survival. Maybe the Golden Age was just a building to her, but to me it was family.

Beth shifted in her seat and dug through her purse. "Here," she said. "I want you to take this." She held a bank card in one hand, matte black with an electric-blue edge. I didn't recognize the bank logo embossed on the front. It just said *ONYX* in a stylish, slanting font. They must have run out of precious metals after platinum.

I stared at it. "You hate using Mom's money." She didn't just hate to, she refused to. Not her trust fund, not anything. She didn't even accept gifts from Mom at Christmas, which inevitably devolved into a fight. Beth always closed the door, and Kerry and I always pretended like we couldn't hear words like *blood money* and *extortion*. It was easier that way. Some families baked cookies, we explored the practical application of moral relativity.

"I do," Beth said seriously, "but it's not for me, it's for you. The Dohertys said that most of Mom's assets have been seized or frozen. The penthouse is fine, and so is this." She held out the card until I was forced to take it. "For now. Mom

52

had a lot of fail-safes. The Dohertys think we have a little while before anyone finds this one."

I turned the Onyx card over in my hand. "I don't understand," I said honestly. Beth was supposed to rip me a new one, not hand me a blank check. If her goal was to throw me off, it was definitely working.

"Things are going to be rough for the next couple of weeks," she said. "I'm going to be staying in the city to work with the Dohertys and get our affairs in order as much as I can. I don't know what Kerry's going to do yet, but she has access to her trust. You don't. That's why I want you to have this." She nodded at the card. "Go back to Elkhollow, if that's what you want. Or invite your friends here. Something to take your mind off of things. But stay away from all this. Stay away from Peter Carlevaro and the Imperium and whatever else you've got in your head. You can't fix this, Jack. And you shouldn't have to. It's not your mess to deal with."

She was trying to get rid of me. No—she was trying to take care of me, that's what Beth did, but that's not what it felt like. It felt like being sent to the playground while the grown-ups did important work, so I wouldn't get in the way.

I frowned down at the Onyx. Who would I invite? My blackjack dealers? Hardly. Despite Blackjack Club's runaway popularity with the student body, none of it really extended to me. I was friend*ly* with some of my classmates, but *friends* was a stretch. I couldn't go back to Elkhollow either, no matter what Beth said. I couldn't run away from this.

"I don't really . . ." I stopped, staring down at the Onyx. How much money was on it? A sizable number of digits, if this was Mom we were talking about. *All it takes is a little bit of money and a lot of sense to be dangerous*, Granddad used to say.

I flipped the card over between my fingers like I was holding the ace of hearts again, admiring the bright blue edge. *A little bit of money*. Imagine what I could do with a lot of it. I might not even need the sense part at all.

Come back when you can impress me.

"Yeah," I said, a thought tugging at the back of my head. The corner of my mouth tilted upward, almost a smile. "Yeah, maybe you're right."

SOME ASSEMBLY REQUIRED

[jack]: hey guys
[jack]: question
[georgia]: Wait, Jack, you never told us how the plane movie was
[gabe]: did the dog die?
[lucky]: it's john wick stupid the dog dying is like the plot
[remy]: omg guys shut up I want to hear it
[lucky]: if it's about the pineapple on pizza thing again i'm divorcing all of you
[georgia]: I think we've already talked about your lack of taste ad nauseum, Lucky
[jack]: all right maybe i'll just ask remy
[remy]: (:
[gabe]: WAIT!!

I smirked quietly to myself, letting them squabble at one another for a minute because that was half the fun, for all of us. I already felt lighter, my heart less like a clenched fist. The Onyx card burned a hole in my pocket next to the Avalon

Club keycard, my skeleton keys. I could do this. I could move forward. The only thing I wasn't good at was standing still.

Whatever family dinner Beth had in mind mercifully became pizza in the living room. It was almost normal, in a TV-family kind of way, sitting on the ground next to open pizza boxes, watching red sauce drip perilously close to the white carpet as Dad tried to negotiate with the long strings of cheese. It was worse, somehow, that the room didn't feel empty without Mom. We didn't really do things like that. We certainly didn't do them in the penthouse.

I had escaped to my childhood bedroom as soon as I could. It still smelled like dust and lemon floor polish. It felt weird to be there again, even weirder to think of it as my *childhood bedroom*, as if I'd already grown up and gotten a mortgage and a 401(k). I had been staying at Elkhollow over the summer since I started there, only flying home for special occasions.

Now I sat at my desk, one leg pushed up against the arm of my battered old desk chair, spinning idly as I considered the Hullabaloo app. It was getting late, especially on the East Coast, three hours ahead of Vegas, but they were all awake anyway. Summer meant no early wake-up call the next morning, which meant plenty of opportunity to stay up until ill-advised hours of the night.

[jack]: anyway
[jack]: what are you guys doing this summer?
[gabe]: sleeping
[remy]: ¯_(ツ)_/¯

[georgia]: suffering
[lucky]: why? You got a suggestion?

I hesitated, my thumb hovering over the Send button. I couldn't wait too long. They could all see the *[jack] is typing* . . . and they'd start making fun of me if I didn't say something soon. Which might have been for the best. We could still laugh this off. I could go back to Elkhollow, back to my blackjack and slightly clever cheaters and waiting until I turned eighteen and could access my trust. That was what Beth would want me to do.

The moment felt like a domino, teetering on the edge. I hit Send.

[jack]: what do you guys think of las vegas?

♠

I know what you're thinking. Stranger danger, Internet safety, and so on.

I get it. Catfishing, MTV, etc., etc.—I already made that joke. It's very easy to lie about who you are on the Internet. But sometimes the people on the other side of the screen are who you need to figure out who you are in the first place.

I first discovered the word *asexual* at age fifteen, on a *Star Wars* fan forum.

The advice board, more specifically. I'm not sure what made any of us think that a very tenuous shared interest in space wizards qualified us to be dispensing advice, but we never questioned it. I didn't give advice, or particularly take it, but I liked reading the board to keep track of what the other people on the forum were saying. Aside from role-playing original characters with dark pasts and convoluted relationships, there was an intricate web of social drama underneath. Keeping track of the players was like watching live updates on a presidential debate.

That, and I liked reading about problems that weren't mine. In retrospect, I was lonely. It was my first year at Elkhollow, and I wasn't connecting with my classmates the way I claimed to be when I was lying to Beth on the phone. I didn't have Blackjack Club yet, and the things we had in common were few and far between. Somehow in the time it took me to go from the West Coast to the East Coast, dating had risen to the top of everyone's mind, and I didn't get the same memo they did. It felt like being plunked in the middle of a nature documentary, only I wasn't quite the same species as the rest of them. They flashed their plumage and danced around one another in intricate rituals, and I shuffled cards and tried to decide which faculty adviser could be most easily bribed.

I missed Mom. I missed the Golden Age. I even missed Kerry. But it was hard to feel neglected when I was going to a school that costs more per year than most mortgages. I liked reading the advice board and seeing all those problems that I could say were worse than mine. I liked the idea that it meant my problems weren't worth thinking about.

And then I met sithskywalker13.

Thread: *What Am I?*
Author: sithskywalker13
Post:

Hello, friends! I could use a little advice if you've got the time . . . I'm just not really sure what to do. I'm a sophomore in high school, and I keep thinking that I'll end up dating, but it hasn't happened yet? I thought it would happen when I went to middle school, and then high school, but it hasn't, and I'm not sure if that's a problem. Am I doing something wrong? Do I just pick someone and ask? I don't really know if it should be a boy or a girl. I guess it doesn't really matter.

The problem is that I don't really know if I'm straight or gay. I don't really feel like either, I think? Honestly I'm not really sure if I'm a boy or a girl either, ha ha, so I guess that doesn't help. But I don't know what it's supposed to feel like. Everyone else just seems to know who they like. Are they making it up? Or is something wrong with me?

The responses had mostly been along the line of *be patient* and *there's no rush* and *you'll know them when you meet them* (: which bothered me in a way I didn't fully understand. *But what if you don't?* I almost typed. What happened then? Was that when you knew something was wrong with you? sithskywalker13's post was like a punch to the chest. I'd never read something like that before, something that felt like it'd been pulled from my own mind and put into words. Almost unreadable green text on a black background, but still.

I read every response, but I didn't find anything useful until I got to the bottom of the thread.

x_jarjarblinks: sounds like you might be ace, buddy

It took me three solid days to work up the courage to direct message either of them, until I finally hit Send and then left my phone across my dorm room for another two hours. Those early days were terrifying, but at some point, fate took over and everything changed.

sithskywalker13 was Remy and x_jarjarblinks was Gabe. *Ace* meant asexual, which meant the lack of sexual attraction, which made things make a lot more sense. I felt like a puzzle, mostly put together but with a piece missing, waiting to be filled. There were plenty of pieces to fill it—gay, straight, bisexual—but none fit quite right. Sometimes I thought I could make one fit if I pressed hard enough, but it would never lie flat.

The word *asexual* took the puzzle piece and turned it, letting it click into place where before it'd been better to just leave the space empty. I wasn't broken. I wasn't empty. I wasn't nothing at all. Just a little differently shaped.

Remy, Gabe, and I eventually moved away from the forum and onto Hullabaloo, which was a newer chatting platform and, frankly, much cooler. We picked up Georgia and eventually Lucky about a year ago, until we formed an informal little asexual support group. Support group was probably a strong phrase for people who mostly talked about anything but, but it was nice to have people who got it when it did come up. It could get lonely.

We were all from the United States, but that's where the similarities ended. Georgia was from the South, but Florida, not Georgia the state, which was minorly confusing. Remy was from North Carolina; Lucky was in California. Gabe lived in Pennsylvania. I was in Massachusetts or Nevada or whatever locale my family decided to use as neutral ground for holidays that year.

They were my best friends, no matter how geographically scattered we were. We couldn't go to lunch together or compare notes from class, but that didn't matter, however much I wished we could. They knew me, the pieces of me that I could barely acknowledge sometimes, and they accepted it. It was the universally accepted truth that we would support one another through anything.

So yeah, I needed them, now more than ever. Just maybe not exactly in the way they expected.

A PLAN SET IN MOTION TENDS TO STAY IN MOTION

TO BE CLEAR: I DIDN'T INTEND TO INVOLVE MY friends in the mess that was Shannon v. Carlevaro. Peter Carlevaro may look like garbage slime stuffed into a three-piece suit, but he was still the head of a crime family, and while that was normal in *my* life, I had enough sense to know it wasn't really something I should introduce to *theirs*. Flying my friends out to Las Vegas was only a part of the mess that was Shannon v. Shannon.

Because Beth was watching me.

It was very nice of her to give me the Onyx card and tell me to run wild with it, but Beth was a Shannon just as much as I was, and I knew better than to think it was really that simple. I'd messed up by getting caught at the Imperium, and now I'd shown my hand. I had no doubt that Beth was monitoring the charges to the Onyx card and spying on me in between meetings with the lawyers. I had some of my own money, winnings from Blackjack Club squirreled away for a rainy day, but not doing anything with the Onyx card would be just as suspicious as using it to put a hit out on Peter Carlevaro. I didn't need that kind of attention.

What I needed was an alibi, so I could do what I needed without being noticed. That was where my friends came in.

In related news, it was surprisingly easy to fake an invitation to a youth academic conference.

Elkhollow's elite student body came from around the world, so Beth wouldn't blink an eye at flights from all over the country charged to the Onyx card, but my friends' families might have a few more questions about a sudden, all-expenses-paid vacation, especially to a Las Vegas casino under federal investigation. Questions that I didn't really trust Beth to answer without revealing too much about my sad, oh-poor-Jack circumstances. I wanted to see my friends—I *needed* to see my friends—but what I didn't need was anyone feeling bad for me. If I pulled this off, no one would need to pity me in the first place.

Besides, it was kind of fun. The secrecy of it all. Lucky put together a website in two hours. Georgia designed a brochure. The next day, I tested out my new Onyx card and had four copies printed out on glossy, trifold paper and sent via priority mail. All the others had to do was fake an envelope postmarked three months earlier and pretend that they had forgotten about it until now, the week before the program was set to begin. It was any bright young student's dream: a fully funded opportunity to meet with other academically gifted and like-minded youth in the beautiful and bustling

Las Vegas. Sponsored by the Samuel McNabb Foundation and the Academic Center of Excellence.

[georgia]: ACE? Really?
[lucky]: (;

I found using my grandfather's real name funnier, but I kept that to myself. I told them . . . a degree of the truth. My mom was the CEO of a major hotel and casino, the family was all in town for this impromptu get-together, and I'd been gifted her bank card in order to invite my friends over and enjoy myself for the summer.

I didn't like lying to them, but lying came pretty easily to the Shannon family, so bad feelings didn't exactly stop me. I was afraid the whole truth might scare them off or make them look at me differently. Aside from a quick introduction to Beth to prove that they were real, I didn't intend to let them be around my family for more than ten seconds at a time anyway. Kerry wouldn't care, and Dad would keep them trapped listening to a story about the time he got lost at sea for three days off the coast of Boca Raton. No one wanted that.

[remy]: dad
[remy]: can we go to a magic show
[jack]: somehow I think we'll be able to find a magic show in las vegas, yes
[remy]: yisss
[gabe]: rems you know I have a fragile constitution

i'm not sure I can handle chris angle mindfreaking me and come back the same person
[georgia]: chris angle
[lucky]: I luv chris angle
[georgia]: he's so acute
[jack]: guys don't be obtuse
[remy]: no she's . . . right . . . angle.
[remy]: itried.png
[gabe]: sorry I thought remy wanted to see a magic show not amateur hour at the comedy open-mic night MY MISTAKE

Okay, they weren't *just* an alibi. They were my best friends in the entire world, and I'd never seen them in person, so yeah, I wanted to see them, even if I also wanted to save my mom and screw over a crime boss in the process. I was surprised to find how much I actually *wanted* to show them the city. I wanted to show them the Strip and the Fountains of Bellagio and the Golden Age. I wanted them to know who I really was, even if I was still hiding the uglier parts.

Soon, but not yet. In the meantime, I still had thinking to do.

I leaned back in my chair, my laptop screen casting my room in harsh white light. I flipped the trusty ace of hearts that had followed me all the way from Elkhollow between two fingers, almost soothed by the familiar *thwip-thwip* of a playing card. Flat Cap's stolen keycard sat in front of me, glittering tauntingly. The Avalon Club. I knew that name. It was stitched into my childhood almost as deeply as *the*

Golden Age or *Carlevaro*. My mom used to play poker there, because I guess that's the way casino owners unwind. I had fuzzy memories of tagging along as a kid, before life started to get complicated and I was sent away to school. Memories that could have belonged to any poker table I probably wasn't supposed to be at, but the name stuck in my brain more than the sound of shuffled cards or clinking glasses did.

And yet I couldn't actually *find* it. I'd googled every iteration of *Avalon Club* I could think of, but I could only find Hollywood nightclubs and condo rentals. Nothing to do with the Imperium Hotel and Casino or even Las Vegas. But I knew it was a lead, even if I didn't know where it led to just yet. The Avalon Club was a connection between Carlevaro and Mom. It had to mean something.

It *all* meant something. It was all connected in a sticky web that I had inherited when Mom went to jail. Peter Carlevaro smiled back at me from an article pulled up on my laptop about opening day at the Imperium. I felt like he could see me through the screen, smirking. His last words still scraped against my ears. Beth didn't want to see it, and Kerry just didn't want to hear it, but I knew better. I knew this hotel, this city, this *business*. We were in Las Vegas, the city of sin. Of high risk and higher reward. Of course Mom's business dealings were dirty. They all were. But no one was leading Peter Carlevaro out of the Imperium in handcuffs.

Not yet.

There was a knock at my bedroom door.

I flipped over my phone, hiding the Hullabaloo notifications. I quickly pulled up a more innocuous tab on my computer and scanned my desk for incriminating evidence.

"Come in," I said, slouching in my desk chair for good measure. Casual.

The door opened, but it wasn't Beth on the other side. Kerry leaned against the doorframe, her hands buried in the pocket of her hoodie. She had the hood pulled up, turning her curls into a lion's mane.

"Hey," I said awkwardly. I'd been expecting Beth. My *I'm well-adjusted and not scheming at all* look felt more performative knowing that Kerry could see right through it.

"Hey," she said back, kicking at the hardwood floor with the toe of her shoe. "Beth says you're having some friends over. To show them the hotel and stuff."

That was definitely not what Kerry came to say, but I didn't want to talk about what was eating at her any more than she did. That's the difference between us and Beth. A healthy sense of avoidance. "Yeah," I said.

"Cool." She was definitely scuffing the floor now. "The Dohertys said we can visit mom tomorrow. If we want."

My heart squeezed. Oh.

"Are you going to go?" Kerry asked.

I swallowed loud enough that we could both hear it. My stomach turned like I was lost at sea, the ground unsteady beneath my feet. "I don't . . ." My voice faltered. "I don't want to see her like that."

Did that make me a coward? A bad son? Or just weak? I wasn't sure what Mom would say if I asked her.

I could imagine Mom in a prison jumpsuit, her hair pulled back, her hands shackled together, just like a scene out of a movie. But only barely. The image always fell apart after a moment, before I could look at it too closely.

I wanted to keep it that way. If I saw her like that, I'd never be able to forget it. When I closed my eyes, that would be all I'd see. Not vacations on the beach. Not following at her heels across the casino floor. Not the warm pressure of her hand on top of my head, before I grew too tall for her to reach.

That would be the moment this all became real.

"Is that . . . bad?" I asked tentatively. Kerry didn't lie, I reminded myself. She'd tell me if it was.

Kerry chewed on her bottom lip. "I don't know," she said. "I feel like we're all, like . . . in survival mode, you know? Beth is mothering. Dad is drinking. You're trying to find some kind of meaning in it." Well, that wasn't how *I* would put it, but okay. She shrugged. "We're all doing what we have to in order to get through the day. It's what Mom would do too."

"She would fix it." She'd never met a problem she couldn't force into submission, one way or another.

"Mom's way of fixing things is what got her arrested," Kerry said. I winced, but it wasn't a rebuke like it would have been if Beth was the one saying it. With Beth it was always personal, but Kerry seemed to understand the way

I felt without me having to say it. We could see what Mom did was wrong but convinced ourselves that it was normal. That we could resent her for when she was gone and love her for when she was there at the same time. Kerry picked at her hoodie sleeve. "I'll tell her you got a stomach bug on the flight. You know she thinks commercial flights are disgusting."

Relief hit in a wave, stronger than I expected. "Thanks."

I could have said more, but that wasn't how we worked. I could tell her how I felt—like the whole world was on the verge of collapse, and all I had was a roll of Scotch tape—but that wasn't how we worked either. I'd only be embarrassed, and Kerry would be awkward, and we'd just have to pretend like it never happened anyway.

"So," I said instead. "What's your survival mode?"

Are you okay? Kerry and I didn't say a lot of things to each other, but we still found a way to say what mattered.

"Oh, you know." She shrugged exaggeratedly, her toe scuffing the floor again. Her hair almost obscured her face, but I could see a funny little smile. "I'm just bottling it up so when I get a therapist someday, I'll have enough trauma to get my money's worth out of it."

I laughed. "That shouldn't take long."

Kerry smiled for real this time. "You're telling me." Her eyes flickered downward. "What's that?"

"What? Oh." I looked down to find the ace of hearts in my hand again, the bottom corner creased where I kept worrying at it with my thumb. It was becoming a strange kind of comfort blanket. "Just a playing card." Shit. The keycard. I twisted my chair, obscuring the gold keycard with my back. But it sparked an idea.

"Hey," I said, "do you remember the Avalon Club?"

"Yeah," she said without missing a beat. "What about it?"

"Where was it? I can't find it online."

Kerry gave me a weird look, one that made me bite my tongue. The thing about gambling was that you were always taking a risk, no matter how good the odds. I might have already shown my hand too soon, but if she knew something, I needed to know it too.

Finally, Kerry shrugged. "It wasn't a real place, it was Mom's gambling club, the one with all the CEOs and high rollers," she said. "She stopped going when she had the falling out with Uncle Peter. I guess he probably runs it now."

♠

Peter Carlevaro was running a high-stakes, probably-most-likely-illegal gambling club out of his Las Vegas Strip hotel and casino. In retrospect, not that surprising.

Not surprising that Mom was involved either. I could almost remember it, if I closed my eyes—or pieces of it, at least. Cigar smoke and shuffling cards, standing at Mom's elbow when she talked over my head, one hand resting in my hair. I was young, back before Granddad died, when Mom still had time for doing things for fun instead of profit. Before she realized that Carlevaro was a human cockroach wearing an expensive watch. Not exactly the kind of person you want to hang around, much less commit crimes with.

Because the Avalon Club *was* less than legal, I was certain about that. When people had too much money, it stopped having meaning to them, except for the fact that they wanted more. At that point, it wasn't about the money; it was about the *game*. It was about getting away with it, and I could only imagine how the movers and shakers of the Las Vegas Strip enjoyed moving large sums of money around without having to give Uncle Sam his cut.

It was the in I needed, something soft and vulnerable beneath the plates of Carlevaro's armor. I needed to know more, but I couldn't exactly ask Mom. Even asking Kerry had been treading dangerous water.

Luckily, I did have one family member I could always rely on to be unreliable.

I stood outside the Imperium, leaning against the wall built from glossy black stone. I flipped the Avalon Club card restlessly between my fingers, the gold flashing in the sunlight with every rotation. I'd be back inside the Imperium soon enough, but I didn't want to risk showing my face in there right now. Not when there were a few more pieces to slide into place.

I pushed my sunglasses farther up my nose, ducking my head even though at this time of day, I was well hidden by the flow of foot traffic. That was the good thing about the Las Vegas Strip. Something was always moving, someone was always talking. Or in Dad's case, laughing.

Robbie Castle swaggered out of the double doors to the Imperium like he owned the place, an image that probably would have given Peter Carlevaro an aneurysm if he were watching. A part of me hoped that he was. I could only imagine how Dad's gold pineapple-patterned Hawaiian shirt looked over CCTV.

"Hey, kid," Dad said, ruffling my hair before I could duck out from under his hand. "Got the goods." He tossed the battered old backpack I'd given him.

I caught it, swinging it over one shoulder. The $5,000 in Imperium poker chips was lighter than I expected it to be, considering how important it was to my plan to infiltrate the Avalon Club. And the fact that it was, you know, $5,000. As much as I hated giving money directly to Carlevaro, sometimes you had to break a few ethical standards to make an omelet.

"Thanks, Dad," I said, plucking my bank card from his hand before it could conveniently disappear. That was a bit of a chunk now taken from my Blackjack Club funds, separate from anything that the federal government would be interesting in freezing *and* separate from anything my sister knew about. There wasn't much left now, but I had to believe it was worth the investment. I hadn't loved trusting Dad with it, but there weren't many other ways for a seventeen-year-old to get what I needed. I was lucky enough to have a parental figure that accepted "just for fun" as a reasonable explanation to need thousands of dollars in poker chips.

I hesitated. My plan had been to buy my dad lunch for his trouble and call it a day—the less he was involved in any of this (or in most things), the better. But I couldn't help my curiosity, especially as we walked away from the Imperium, lurking behind us like an oversize shadow. I couldn't ask Mom about the Avalon Club, but I have two parents.

"Dad," I said lightly, holding the backpack a little tighter as we shouldered our way through a knot of people surrounding a performer wearing not nearly enough clothes. "Do you remember when Mom stopped going to the Avalon Club?"

Honestly, I expected him to say no. The Avalon Club was obviously highly secretive, at least to those outside of the right circles, and Dad was decidedly *not* in the right circles. Sometimes I thought that was what Mom liked about him. On the days that she liked anything about him.

"Oh, yeah," he said, gesturing casually. "It was a big thing between Peter and your mom. Don't you remember the time I took you kids to San Francisco?"

I frowned. "You made me go to the beach even though I'd just ruptured an appendix," I said. "And Kerry got lost on the cable car for two hours." Really not that notable for a trip with our father. "*That's* why we went?"

Dad shrugged and slapped the button for the crosswalk. A herd of tourists coalesced around us, waiting to cross. A brave few eyed the road like they might be willing to risk it. "Your mom wanted to keep you out of it," he said. "It wasn't just the club. It was everything with Peter. And the business—"

"The business?" I stopped short. "What business?" The Golden Age? Mom never would have let Carlevaro get his greasy fingers on the Golden Age, even before they fell out. The Golden Age belonged to the Shannon family. Period.

Dad seemed to realize that he was getting into dangerous territory—maybe he had a Beth that lived in the back of his head too, though clearly he was a little better at listening to her. "Oh . . . business," he said with an exaggerated shrug. "You know those types . . . all about the business."

The light turned red, and the crosswalk flashed invitingly. The crowd surged forward, but I spun on my heel, planting my hand on the crosswalk pole to cut Dad off at the pass. I raised my eyebrows. "What kind of business?" I asked sweetly. Or threateningly. It was a fine line to walk.

Dad grimaced and shook his head, waving his hands defensively. "Aw, Jack, I don't know. You know I like to stay out of that crap." That was a nice way of putting it. Dad didn't even do business for his own band, and everyone was better off for it. Fortunately, that also meant he was an exceedingly bad negotiator. I didn't even have to say anything for him to cave.

He sighed dramatically, as if I'd twisted his arm instead of stared at him in the middle of the sidewalk. "It wasn't that big of a deal," he said, directly contradicting himself. "Peter and your mom had some investments together. Places on the Strip, companies with stock in different casinos. Some whole crazy idea about a . . . ah, what's it called? The board game?"

"Monopoly," I said. I dropped my hand but didn't move— traffic was already moving again, and a new crowd was drifting into place around us. It didn't matter. My mind was running faster than my feet ever could. "Mom and Peter were trying to monopolize the Strip?"

"Something like that." Dad shrugged, helpless. "Anyway, they split it all up when Aileen left Avalon. Better not to ask her about it. At least don't mention me," he said hastily.

All I can think about is Flat Cap in the bowels of the Imperium, muttering about Carlevaro taking over the Strip without my mom there to stop him. I hadn't realized that he'd meant it so literally. Mom would never sell her investments to Carlevaro, but if she went to jail . . .

Well. Carlevaro might be hard to get to now, but with the Strip under his control? It'd become impossible.

I tightened my grip on the backpack strap, feeling every chip weighing it down. I needed to get to work. And fast.

"Didn't it bother you?" I said, emerging from my own thoughts to look up at Dad. He was fussing with a stain on his shirt collar. "That Mom and Carlevaro spent all that time together?" Everyone knew that Carlevaro was grossly in love with her—even I knew, and I'd been a kid. Not that I ever really understood what my parents had going on, because it certainly wasn't marriage, but it still had to be . . . weird, right? Probably?

Dad actually looked thoughtful for a second. "Not really," he said. "Aileen is always going to do what Aileen is going to do. You can't stop it. It's either what you love about her or it's what you hate." He shrugged, straightening his shirt collar. "I guess that's what finally caught up with her, huh?"

KNIGHTS OF AVALON

TIME PRESSED AGAINST ME LIKE A THUMB, REMINDING me that it was a limited resource. Carlevaro wouldn't be satisfied to throw my mom in jail and be done with it—he was in the middle of his own grander plan, which meant I couldn't dawdle. I knew what my next step would be. After all, I had the key to Carlevaro's kingdom.

But first I had to go to the airport.

Which I wasn't nervous about. It was perfectly reasonable to be this sweaty in Nevada, even as the airport pumped air-conditioning directly into my face. It was summer. Of course it was going to be a little warm.

I checked my phone for the twentieth time since arriving. No messages, except for Lucky complaining about how quiet the group chat was. She had family in the city, so she'd already arrived yesterday. Which was a little weird—I never knew Lucky had a connection to Vegas too, but Lucky had always been a little mysterious. I think she liked it that way, and I could hardly complain, considering how many holes

I'd purposefully left in my own story. The rest of them were still on their planes. It was Monday afternoon, almost a week since I'd flown in myself. It felt more like a lifetime.

I was starting to have second thoughts about not telling them the whole truth, now that I was standing there, waiting for them to appear in front of me. The last thing I wanted was for them to pity me for the whole mom-in-jail situation, but the second-to-last thing I wanted was for them be pissed that I *didn't* tell them. It occurred to me, rather too late, that it might have been easier to tell them over text than to their faces. At least then I wouldn't have to say the words out loud.

Oh well.

I exhaled slowly, puffing out my cheeks. Huge screens dominated the wall space, displaying rotating advertise-ments for the very concept of Las Vegas. You would think by the time someone made it to that side of arrivals, they'd already been convinced to stop and visit, but the Strip wasn't taking any chances.

A TV screen over a cluster of chairs played CNN on silent, subtitles rolling in black and white along the bottom of the screen. The footage of the FBI leading Aileen Shannon out of the Golden Age played, so familiar by then that I could pinpoint the exact moment I should look away before Mom's eyes met the camera.

I'd tell them later, then. Not in the airport, which was hardly impressive, though it certainly tried to be. At the Golden Age. That would work. I'd throw it out casually— *oh, by the way*—and it would be fine, because they'd have already seen enough of the beautiful parts of my life to not be scared away by the ugly ones. Perfect. Flawless. Assuming they didn't see the news on their flights in.

I sighed. Yeah, genius. If I were really smart, I would have left them out of this entirely and tricked Dad into being some sort of alibi. It might have been simpler, though it was always hard to tell with Dad.

But . . . I didn't want to. I told myself they were an easy excuse so Beth wouldn't wonder what I was up to, but the truth was that I was tired of being alone. I was tired of having my friends scattered to every corner of the country. I wanted to see them, and I wanted to ruin Peter Carlevaro's life, and I didn't see why I couldn't kill two birds with one stone.

Besides, it was a good plan. I mean, it was an amazingly, spectacularly stupid plan, but it was all a matter of perspective. It would be fine. I'd run the numbers, and there wasn't much to lose. I would only ever be putting myself at risk, and it wasn't like life could get much worse. It would be totally, perfectly fine.

Probably.

[lucky]: are they there yet
[jack]: not yet
[jack]: remy should be in any minute now but I think gabe's connection got delayed
[lucky]: boooooo
[lucky]: are you guys still meeting me for dinner

[lucky]: it's literally so boring here my mom won't let me gamble lmao
[jack]: it's the law that won't let you gamble
[lucky]: i've always thought that the law was more like a suggestion
[jack]: but yeah we'll be there
[jack]: the favreau right?
[lucky]: u got it

I still thought the Favreau Spectaculaire was a weird choice in restaurants, especially coming from Lucky, who subsisted more or less off of grilled cheese and Diet Coke, but whatever. It was touristy enough that everyone should be happy, and the Onyx card would cover the tab. According to the Facebook page, Chef Favreau was supposed to be cooking live.

And then there would be the Golden Age. I'd gone back and forth on whether to put a different hotel on the Onyx card or not, but in the end, I had given into temptation. The simple fact was that I didn't like any hotel on the Strip so much as I liked the Golden Age, even if its name was in far too many headlines at the moment. I wanted them to see it. It felt like having friends over for a sleepover for the first time and showing them your room, if your room were a multimillion-dollar hotel and casino under federal investigation.

I took a sip of my iced coffee, swirling the ice around with the straw. As if meeting your best friends in person for the first time weren't stressful enough, I had to throw in a healthy dose of subterfuge and criminality. Typical Shannon. Couldn't I be normal for, like, five minutes?

"Jack?"

I would love to tell you that I reacted calmly and rationally. I would really love to tell you that.

In reality, I froze like a meerkat, accidentally jamming my straw into the roof my mouth so hard that my eyes watered.

We should pause for a moment, because I haven't been entirely honest. Please don't act surprised. I told you this wasn't a love story, and that's true, but that doesn't mean I wasn't a little in love with Remy Brotz.

Remy was, objectively, the coolest person I knew—person, like, in general, out of all people, but also because they were nonbinary and used they/them pronouns. Remy was my best friend basically since we met. The *love* thing was a little newer, and still made me vaguely nauseous to think about, so I just did my best not to think about it.

The thing about asexuality was that it was complicated in ways I was still figuring out. Just because you didn't experience sexual attraction didn't mean you didn't experience romantic feelings. But those romantic feelings didn't look like they did in the movies because, well, Hollywood didn't make movies about ace people. Period. So they could be a little hard to figure out.

Which is why it took me so long to figure it out. Why it might have been different from the way I felt about my other friends, and what that meant, and what I was supposed to do about it. Which, I'd decided, was nothing. Because Remy lived hundreds of miles away, even when I was in Massachusetts; because I was asexual, and they were asexual, and I didn't know what that was supposed to mean; because . . . because it just didn't matter, okay? Shannons weren't good at love, any kind of it. We really weren't good at anything that didn't involve dollar signs.

Anyway. I was in the middle of embarrassing myself in the airport. Iced coffee, flying. Remy, witnessing. Me, mortified. And . . . *action*.

I whipped around, as if Remy were going to disappear if I hesitated for a moment longer. Fortunately, they didn't. Unfortunately, they were standing closer than I expected, and we more or less collided.

We sprang apart again, the iced coffee barely caught by my fingertips. I had flashbacks to the incident with Flat Cap back at the Imperium. If I thought about it too much, my head ached all over again.

"Fuck!" Remy said, just loud enough that it rang out across the arrivals lobby, over the heads of tourists in fanny packs and what looked to be a girls volleyball team. Remy's eyes went wide, and they slapped a hand over their mouth a moment too late. "Fuck," they whispered.

"Sorry," I choked, clutching my iced coffee to my chest like I'd never let it go. Jesus, I was going to lose every ounce of cool factor I'd ever begged, borrowed, or stolen. I needed to stop carrying iced coffee. Or maybe just have a little more spatial awareness.

I knew what Remy looked like. I knew everything about Remy, the way you knew your favorite character—familiar but in a way you never got tired of, predictable but in a way that still caught you by surprise. I knew they were almost seventeen and their birthday was July 24, which meant they were a Leo—which explained a lot, according to Georgia. I knew they had an ancient golden retriever named Barley that featured in most of their profile pictures, who would steal blueberries straight from the bush. I knew their mom was Vietnamese American, their dad was German, and theirs was a disgustingly romantic love story that involved five different countries, Yale, and a couple of PhDs, and yet they now lived on a farm in the heart of North Carolina for some reason. I didn't know why.

I knew a lot. But it was a little different in three dimensions.

We locked eyes, and I searched for something to salvage this interaction even a little bit. "I'm actually just the valet," I said. "For someone else."

Remy squinted. "Shouldn't you have a big sign with their name on it?"

"That's only in movies."

They laughed, their shoulders shaking with the effort to stay quiet. Remy was so short, I could see the top of their head, their black hair shorn short on the back and left to curl wildly on top, a kind of messy casual that was just the right side of ambiguously intentional. There were artful rips in the knees of their jeans, and the backpack slung over their shoulder was so heavy with enamel pins, I couldn't believe the TSA let it through.

This is a problem, I thought. *This is a very big problem.* My heart did a sort of drunken backflip. Was that normal? That couldn't be normal.

"Really," I said, fighting a smile. My mouth twisted and battled against the laughter bubbling up from my chest. *Play it cool, Jack. Pretend you at least know the definition of the word* cool. "I don't know what you're laughing at. I was just assaulted."

"Oh, yeah? Do you always tackle people to say hello?" Remy asked. Security hadn't swept down to throw us out by our collars, so that was a good sign. Good thing too. Georgia's plane would be landing any minute.

"I don't know if I'd call that a *tackle*." I fought the urge to check the Hullabaloo app, like I usually did when I was bored, or awkward, or about to take an impromptu poll about whether pineapple on pizza was valid (it was not). But Remy wouldn't be there. Remy was *right here*. Oh God, Remy was looking at me with their real, human eyes. I was beginning to realize that I definitely did not emotionally prepare myself for any of this. "How were you sure it was me?"

Remy raised their eyebrows, and maybe they were a little nervous too. They worked their thumb into a hole on their backpack strap, still grinning. "Well," Remy said, "it was either you or a random kid really into the WNBA."

"Wha— Oh." I touched my hat belatedly. Wearing a ball-cap displaying the stylized diamond for the Las Vegas Aces women's basketball team had been wildly funny when I saw it on the way into the airport. Now I felt a bit more like an idiot. "The WNBA is a really underappreciated league."

"So you've heard."

"So I've heard," I said with a nod, and it was like something clicking into place. I wasn't quite used to their soft southern drawl, but otherwise it could have been any conversation we'd had before. I swiped at the condensation on my drink, ducking my head to hide the goofy smile threatening to take over.

Remy noticed anyway. Remy always noticed. "What?" they asked suspiciously. "Do I still have crumbs on my shirt? They only give you like six Doritos to a bag, but they were all crushed up. I think I got them in my binder." They fussed with the collar of their shirt, trying to find orange crumbs against red plaid.

"No." Well, maybe a little, but they mostly got them anyway. "It's going to sound stupid."

"When's that ever stopped you before?"

"It's just kind of weird," I said. "That you guys are real. You know. Like on the physical plane." As opposed to the metaphysical plane? I was starting to sound like Dad. "Instead of just names on Hullabaloo."

But Remy mirrored my smile, small and crooked like they were trying to hold it back as much as I was, like the sun cutting through a cloudy day despite what the meteorologist said. We'd all talked about this before—how hard it was, being so far apart. What we'd do if we were closer.

Where we'd go. Every so often, I would follow a daydream into imagining if they went to Elkhollow, but it always fell apart before I got too far. My friends were too colorful— too vibrant, too *real*—to be in a monochrome place like Elkhollow Prep, playing blackjack in the library basement with lacrosse jocks and future business majors.

"And not an axe murderer," I added quickly.

"Well," Remy said, "*I'm* not an axe murderer, and *you're* not an axe murderer, but we can't rule out the others yet. My money's on Georgia. It's always the nice ones."

"That definitely rules you out then."

Remy laughed and swiped the cap off my head. "I'm glad you're real too, Jack." They put it on backward, carefully tugging a lock of hair out the hole in the back before giving the curls an artful ruffle. "Gabe is going to be so fucking jealous."

DINNER AND A SHOW

"I'M SO FUCKING JEALOUS," GABE SAID. HE LEANED over the center console and into the front of the car, like a very lanky dog with very sharp elbows. "Why didn't you get me a cool hat?"

"I didn't get anyone a cool hat," I said defensively. "Remy stole it."

Gabe's eyes went wide, and he inhaled dramatically.

"From me," I amended. "They stole it from me."

Gabe deflated. "Oh."

Remy turned all the way around in the passenger seat just to stick out their tongue.

Two more friends and another iced coffee later, I was getting used to the idea of seeing them in three dimensions instead of just text on a screen. Like Remy, Gabe and Georgia had managed to meet my expectations and defy them at the same time.

Let's break it down real quick:

NAME: Gabriel "Gabe" Gutiérrez

ORIGIN: Hershey, PA

BIGGEST STRENGTH: The ability to pull off a green crushed-velvet bomber without looking like he lost a bet.

BIGGEST WEAKNESS: Six foot three with a high center of gravity, easy to tip over if necessary.

FIRST IMPRESSION: Dropped everything he was carrying and grabbed the nearest victim—Remy, thank God—and swung them around like a doll. Followed by a headlock and a hair ruffle for me before security shooed us away.

And:

NAME: Georgia Anastopoulos

ORIGIN: Tarpon Springs, FL

FAVORITE COLOR: Yellow

SKILLS: Oil painting, remembering every embarrassing thing you've ever said, confining voluminous weaves of black curls into a bun the size of an orange.

FIRST IMPRESSION: Stepped off the plane and nearly threw up on the luggage belt from motion sickness. Took one look at my car and hung a Greek evil eye from the review mirror. I couldn't tell if it was meant to ward off my bad driving or everyone else's.

"Can't hurt," Georgia had said, with a doubtful look at the cherry-red 1996 Honda Civic that Dad kept insisting was a "classic." It smelled like stale cigarette smoke and feet, but it was my only option. Mom hadn't driven herself anywhere in over a decade, and you had to be twenty-one to rent a car. It was almost old enough to be cool in a vintage way, until you turned the key and the whole thing started to shake.

We were still missing Lucky, but I was grateful not to have another person crammed into the Civic. There were already enough opinions on the situation to go around.

Georgia yanked Gabe back by the collar of his shirt before he could join me in the driver's seat. "Hey, Jack," she piped up. "Quick question."

"Yes?"

"Do you, like, actually know where you're going, or . . . ?"

I couldn't look back to glare, so I settled for staring flatly at the rearview mirror instead. Georgia smiled sweetly from the back seat.

It wasn't that I *wanted* to be driving through five o'clock traffic down Las Vegas Boulevard. The Civic's ancient air conditioner wheezed, struggling to keep up with the sun baking the asphalt outside. I desperately wished we'd taken an Uber instead. I didn't know what I was thinking when I convinced myself that driving together would be a good bonding activity.

Dying in a fiery crash would be a good bonding activity if Gabe didn't stop *elbowing me in the face*.

"Yes," I said, tightening my grip on the wheel. It was the Las Vegas Strip. It was a little hard to miss. Especially considering it was practically around the corner from the airport.

"Okay," Georgia said. "Follow-up question. Do you actually know how to drive?"

Elkhollow didn't even allow their students to keep cars on campus, not that there was anything to see in western Massachusetts except for maybe the Yankee Candle Village. But I *could* drive. In theory. "Okay, listen—"

"Do you want me to drive?" Remy interjected.

"Yes, let me just hop out in the middle of traffic—*Gabriel, I swear to God*—"

"It's important this time!" Gabe squawked, falling into his seat as Georgia yanked him back again. He smacked her arm with the back of his hand. "Look! That's it, isn't it? Where we're staying?"

I looked up, past the sea of cars vying for position. It was easy to forget what the Strip must look like to other people. Even after so many years away from it, it was familiar. Gaudy and artificial, for sure, but that was why people came to Vegas. They wanted artificial, they wanted larger than life. The Golden Age rose up along the boulevard, one more hotel scraping the clear blue sky. The golden angel sat on its top with her sword thrust upward, like she might cut open the sky and look inward toward heaven. Remy whistled softly from the passenger seat, and even Georgia leaned forward to get a better look.

As I watched them from the corner of my eye, my breath caught in my chest. Did they know? I waited for someone to mention the news story, even in passing, whether they'd connected the dots to me or not. No one had said anything so far, but things had been a bit of a whirlwind since the baggage claim.

I waited for them to look confused, or reproachful, or even just sheepish. But they were only starstruck, their eyes trained on the Golden Age like they didn't want to look away.

I knew the feeling, though it had been a long time since I thought about it. The Golden Age was always something I took for granted, so completely ordinary that I hardly even noticed it. But now, sitting in traffic, surrounded by three out of four of my closest friends, I saw it how they saw it. Fifty-two floors of cream, gold, and mirrored glass, speckled with green where the aerial gardens looked out over the city.

I forgot, sometimes, that it was beautiful. It was a sharp reminder of what was at stake—not just Mom but the entire Shannon family legacy. It was a big thing for one kid to save, but if I could pull it off, it would be worth it.

"Yeah," I said, my eyes dazzled by the late-afternoon sun off the angel's wings. "That's the one."

♠

Now all we needed was Lucky.

The Favreau Spectaculaire existed in the space between fine dining and Cirque du Soleil. The restaurant was built like a sunken dais, entirely circular and tiered like a colosseum.

Definitely a fire hazard, considering all the flames dancing on the stage kitchen at the center of the restaurant. The tables were arranged like bleachers, forcing us to awkwardly shuffle in a sloppy line, like kindergarten all over again. And no one wanted to sit on the end next to a stranger. The ensuing dance concluded with Gabe on one end, next to Lucky's empty seat, and me on the other.

I frowned down at my plate. How did I get stuck with the worst seat? I swore I was between Remy and Georgia when we started to sit down.

The restaurant was dark except for bright blue spotlights that rotated around the room as the show began, splashing the walls and occasionally blinding an audience member. Acrobats twisted themselves around thick panels of fabric hanging from the ceiling. The *Spectaculaire* part. A rotating cast of celebrity chefs cooked in the kitchen below. The *Favreau* part. Some of the time.

Tonight, Chef Favreau herself slung delicate-looking sausages onto a flat-top grill, filling the air with the sizzle of cooking meat. The menu was more like a proclamation of what we'd be eating tonight, with caveats for vegetarians and those with food allergies written in tiny print all the way at the bottom. According to it, Favreau specialized in Cajun-French fusion, which seemed like a pretty obvious combination, but she made it look like an art form. Her hair was pulled back in a bright red wrap that matched her apron. Sweat beaded her forehead as she chopped an onion so fast the knife became a silver blur.

"I'm just saying"—Gabe was haggling with a harried-looking waiter—"there are things besides salad that are vegetarian." An acrobat in a frilled blue jumpsuit rolled around in a ball on a platform suspended from the ceiling. "I just don't like salad. It's not a crime."

Remy leaned over Georgia, practically in her lap to be heard over the electronic beat shuddering from the speakers. "Where's Lucky?"

"I'm not sure," I yelled back. As fun as bleacher-style seating was for, say, a soccer game or a Medieval Times performance, it was less than convenient for just about any other function. I had to lean into my plate to see anyone, stuck between Georgia and a preteen more interested in her phone than Favreau's fancy knifework. Not that I could get too high and mighty. I'd already spent most of the first course trying to placate Beth, including a couple of group pictures to satisfy her (actually pretty justified) paranoia. For someone who specifically told me to do my own thing and enjoy himself, she was astoundingly nosy.

But I'd been deflecting Beth's quasi-mothering for years. What was weird was Lucky's failure to appear. We all usually lived in the eastern time zone—at least when I was at Elkhollow, which was most of the time—except for Lucky, who was from California. Somehow, she managed to be an almost permanent fixture in the group chat regardless of the time of day. She *was* online, the dot under her icon glowed green, but if she was checking her messages she certainly wasn't saying anything. Which was strange. Lucky rarely let an opportunity slide where she could have injected her opinion.

"She's got to be here somewhere," Gabe said as the waiter finally escaped. "She's the one who suggested this place. It's not like she got *lost*."

Remy frowned. "Why did she suggest this place anyway? All Lucky eats is chicken nuggets and Diet Coke."

"She said her mom goes here a lot or something," I said without looking up from my phone. "I don't know why. It's a little much." A woman in a silver leotard went cartwheeling down the aisle in front of our table.

"Guys, I have a weird question," Georgia said, a peculiar note to her voice. "Does anyone know what Lucky looks like?"

There was a palpable pause.

Remy spoke first. "We could look her up—"

"Actually," Gabe interjected. "Do we know her last name?"

Another pause.

"Jack?" Georgia prompted.

I shook my head. "I didn't book her flight," I said. "She said she has family in Vegas; she came on her own." Why did Georgia have to look at me like that? What was I supposed to do, make Lucky submit her family tree for consideration? Mine certainly wouldn't pass inspection. I considered the information I had on hand:

NAME: ??? "Lucky" ???
ORIGIN: San Jose, CA

PERSONALITY: Gremlin
FAVORITE GAME: The Sims
FIRST IMPRESSION: ???

Hm. Significantly less than the others. I hadn't really held them up side by side before.

"I don't think she even has a Facebook," Remy said. "Her dad doesn't let her have one, remember? He's some Silicon Valley tech guru."

Georgia had her phone open, scrolling through what Lucky called her secret Twitter. Tech-guru Dad didn't want her having a Twitter either, which seemed a bit strict for sixteen years old, but that didn't stop @luckyducky6 from retweeting memes, funny dog videos, and scathing political commentary in equal measure. But I couldn't remember ever seeing any pictures of Lucky herself posted there. Even her icon was just a cat wearing sunglasses and holding a knife.

"Unless she's a puppy who keeps tipping over every time it tries to eat, I don't think she's posted any pictures," Georgia reported.

"That *would* be cool," Remy said.

"I would love that, actually," Gabe added.

"That's so weird," Georgia went on. "I guess I never really thought about it. That I didn't know what she looked like."

"It didn't really seem important," I said, fiddling with my fork. At the center of the stage, Chef Favreau swept into a bow, a knife in each hand. It made her look like an assassin moonlighting as a celebrity chef. The restaurant erupted in applause as the acrobats struck their final poses. Only the energy at our table was off, all of us shifting awkwardly in our seats.

"Do you think that little gremlin catfished us?" Gabe said, loud enough that the middle-aged couple sitting in the next tier down turned their heads to look.

There was a soft sigh from my left, barely audible even as the applause died down and the waitstaff swept back through the aisles. I looked over only to lock eyes with the girl sitting next to me, her stare distinctly and powerfully unimpressed.

"You guys are, like, *really* dumb," she said with so much preteen condescension that something inside of me quaked. It wasn't right to be afraid of a girl with a cartoon dog on her shirt and her hair pulled back into two puffy pigtails, but I couldn't shake the feeling that she was about to say something so devastating that I would look down and find myself in a Nathaniel Hawthorne novel, a red L pinned to my chest.

Georgia was only the only close enough to catch it. She frowned. "That's not very nice."

"What's not very nice?" Gabe leaned over his plate to try to get a better look.

Remy took the opportunity to steal back the Aces hat Gabe had nabbed outside the restaurant. "Who are you talking to?"

I frowned at the girl. I definitely didn't know her. I'd never been exceptional at mingling with my peers in settings that didn't involve a deck of cards, much less people several grades below me. But there was something about her that I just couldn't shake.

The girl smirked.

The gears in my head ground against one another, kicking up sparks, and reluctantly clicked into place.

"You—"

The girl snapped her fingers, and a waiter appeared practically out of nowhere.

"Yes, miss?" The waiter bent forward at the waist. Either to hear over the clatter of plates or to actually get on eye level. No way the girl was an inch taller than four foot eight.

"I'll have the chicken tenders, please. And not the kid's menu trash. Veronica knows how I like them," the girl—the *very Lucky-esque girl*—said blithely. "And tell her to throw together some tofu jambalaya for the tall one on the end here. No salads. Quinoa or otherwise."

"Yes, miss," the waiter said.

Lucky caught his attention again as he started to escape. "Tell her that if she doesn't, I'll come back there and do it myself. That'll make her laugh."

The waiter bobbed his head. "Yes, miss."

"I love them," Lucky said with a little self-satisfied sigh. "They always act like I'm going to chop off their heads. I don't know where they got that idea."

I was definitely staring, my mouth hanging open wide enough to probably catch flies. The pieces were all there, packed into a smug-looking package staring back at me.

Okay. All right. There was a girl sitting next to me, saying things that Lucky would say, giving me what I imagined was a Lucky look. She didn't look like a cat wearing sunglasses and carrying a knife, but she definitely embodied the vibe. That was all unsurprising.

What was really tripping me up was the fact that she was *thirteen years old*. Maybe fourteen. It was hard to tell.

"And a half," she said.

I blinked. "Excuse me?"

"Fourteen and a half," Lucky said. "You were giving me that look."

"I think it's a pretty reasonable look," I said through gritted teeth. That wasn't going to work. How was that supposed to work? Beth wasn't going to buy that I was friends with the world's tiniest freshman—or she was at least going to *mention* it, and while it turned out there was a lot about Lucky I didn't know, I *was* confident that she'd open her smart mouth and say something that wouldn't help. I wasn't even sure if we could take her around the Strip. Navigating Vegas was difficult enough when the rest of us could pass for eighteen—Lucky looked like she was passing seventh grade and not much else. God, we'd probably get stopped for . . . corrupting a minor. Or keeping her up past her bedtime.

Lucky narrowed her eyes like she could read my mind.

"Wait." Georgia leaned around me, finally starting to catch on that something was up. "What's going on? Do you know her?"

"Thanks for the tofu, though," Gabe piped up from the

end. I suspected he could barely even hear what was going on, judging from the fact that he'd already folded his cloth napkin into a swan. "You're cool for a little girl."

Lucky scowled. "Call me little girl again, and I'll pull your lungs out through your nostrils." All bark and no bite, in true Lucky fashion. Lucky and Gabe always snipped at each other, but only because they had the exact same sense of humor. Even then it was hardly arguing as much as it was riffing off of each other.

"Lucky?" Remy's eyes went wide.

"Lucky?" Gabe repeated incredulously.

"Lucky," I said faintly.

Lucky \ˈlə-kē\.

Noun. A fourteen-year-old who convinced us that she was sixteen, though in retrospect I wasn't sure I could remember her saying those words. But they'd certainly been implied.

Adjective. The exact opposite of what I was feeling at the present moment.

"*Lucky.*" The girl in question rolled her eyes. "Why is *that* the sentence that clued you in? I'm not that mean, am I?"

"A bit," Gabe teeter-tottered his hand. "You did catfish us, you—I repeat—fucking gremlin."

"Gabe," Georgia hissed. "You can't say that around her."

"She's said way worse!" Gabe squawked. "Once she told me to—well, I don't want to say it out loud."

"Coward," Lucky countered.

"Okay, everyone shut up." I said, planting both hands on the table. A headache was growing behind my eyes, and Remy was about the only one I wasn't ready to minorly strangle. They sat quietly, their face scrunched like they were trying to work out a puzzle. If only we could all be so quietly contemplative. "I think there are a couple of things we need to discuss." I turned to Lucky. "You're fourteen."

"And a half."

I narrowed my eyes.

Lucky sighed, but she wasn't as impervious to nerves as she tried to make herself out to be. She was leaning forward with her elbows on the table. One hand toyed restlessly with the little yellow plastic balls on her hair ties, clacking them together rhythmically. "What's the big deal?"

"You told us you were sixteen," I said. "To start." What was I doing when I was fourteen? Definitely not crafting elaborate lies to hang out with my friends. It took me a few years to work up to that.

"I *implied* I was sixteen," Lucky said defensively.

"You said you could drive."

"I didn't say it was *legal*," she said. "What does it matter? You're all teenagers too, even Old Man Gabe. It's all the same. It's not like you're going to have to leave me at daycare while you gamble. You're not old enough."

"Hey!" Gabe protested. "I'm eighteen, not eighty-five."

"I can drive," I said stiffly, ignoring him. "*Legally*. It's a big difference."

"Barely," Lucky countered, "if Georgia's liveblogging is anything to go by."

I shot Georgia a glare. She raised her eyebrows innocently, as if I hadn't seen it all in the group chat once I parked the car. Traitor.

"I'm not the first person to fudge the truth." Lucky narrowed her eyes. She lowered her voice. "Am I, Jack?"

My mouth snapped shut with a click. Did she know about Mom, or was she just guessing? It was impossible to tell with Lucky, even staring her right in the face. If she knew Vegas better than she let on, she might know about the Shannon family too. Or at least well enough to connect the dots. She raised an eyebrow. I couldn't risk it. Lucky was not sliding out of the spotlight by sticking it on me instead.

"It doesn't matter," I said. Maybe. Hopefully. After all, Lucky hadn't lied any more than I had. "At least she's not eighty," I added, desperate to inject some levity into the moment. I could feel the mood that had been lurking over me since the news about Mom broke, dark tendrils threatening to drag me down. If I let it grab me now I'd have to fake a smile all night. "Like Gabe."

"Oh, *ha ha*," Gabe groused. "It was eighty-five, thank you very much."

"We can discuss it back at the hotel," Georgia said neutrally. "I think we've caused enough of a scene here."

Remy snorted. "Are you kidding? This whole place is a scene." There were still acrobats with red-and-gold frilled leotards taking selfies with diners on the bottom tier. "Anyway," they added, their chin balanced on their knuckles. "She's still Lucky. That hasn't changed."

"*Anyway*," Lucky agreed. "Try to act cool for, like, five seconds okay? Don't ruin this for me, assholes."

My stomach dropped. Please, God, no more surprises. Not tonight.

"Ruin what—" The words were halfway out of Georgia's mouth when her eyes widened. "Oh."

I turned my head just in time to see Chef Favreau herself come up to the table, her forehead still beaded with sweat from the heat of the kitchen. She was grinning, her hands on her hips. She looked a lot more real standing in front of our table than she did in the middle of the stage, breaking an egg with the blade of a knife.

"Hi, Butterfly," Chef Favreau said, leaning her hip against our table. Up close, she also looked a lot more like Lucky. Lucky's skin was a shade darker, her eyes brown instead of green, but they had the same smile, though Lucky's was significantly more evil and, God, I was going to kill her if we got out of this restaurant without getting caught.

What exactly about this situation said, *Yeah, we'd love to meet your mom?*

"Are these your friends?" Chef Favreau said, turning her thousand-watt smile on us. I swear I saw Remy actually squint under the full force of it.

We chorused the most awkward set of hellos possible.

"I've got to go check on the kitchen, but have fun, all right, Butterfly? I hope you all enjoyed the show." Chef

Favreau was already looking over her shoulder. Something about it was too familiar. I'd seen that I'm-distracted-but-pretending-not-to-be glance more than a few times before. "Do I need to sign you in or anything for this conference?"

"No, Mama," Lucky—or the spirit of a significantly sweeter, more docile girl who briefly possessed Lucky's body—said. "Daddy took care of it."

"Perfect. Let me know how it goes." She leaned forward to give Lucky a kiss on the head before disappearing with the red flutter of her apron. Lucky's eyes tracked her as she went, something soft and vulnerable on her face that I wasn't sure if only I could see. I glanced at Georgia, but she still just seemed mildly starstruck.

Lucky blinked, and she was back again, her mask clicking comfortably into place. "So," she said, holding out her hand. The waiter who had nervously been waiting for Chef Favreau to exit put a can of Diet Coke in her hand, a bendy straw sticking out the top. "See any good movies on the flight?"

NOT THE SEXY KIND OF SLEEPOVER

WHEN SAMUEL SHANNON ESTABLISHED THE GOLDEN Age Hotel and Casino, he did it with one thing in mind: greatness. When it first opened its doors in 1968, it had been modeled after the Gilded Age, the tail end of the nineteenth century as rapid industrialization drove society forward at breakneck speed. *Golden* in every meaning of the word, from the gold-streaked marble in the lobby to the gilt cages around the hexagonal glass elevators that looked out over the atrium.

Later, they'd introduced other decades—the speakeasy in the basement for the 1920s and the 24-7 disco on the fourth floor for the 1970s. The best of American history pulled out and preserved like butterflies under glass—or at least approximated in a glossy, plasticky kind of way. People wanted flapper dresses and poodle skirts and guitar-heavy rock songs, not war and poverty and all the things they came to the Golden Age to forget.

And I loved it. As weird as my relationship with my family could be sometimes, it was still home. It was still *mine*.

I slapped the keycard against the sensor like I owned the place, because I kind of did. At least for the moment. This was the part I was looking forward to. Maybe not everything had gone exactly according to plan so far, with the whole Lucky thing, but I would figure it out. I always did. I just needed a little confidence boost, and the Golden Age was my ace in the hole. They couldn't *not* be impressed. I was impressed, and I'd grown up there.

If they were impressed, they'd forgive me for lying. More than that, they'd see that they didn't need to feel sorry for me. It was a twisted, Elkhollow kind of logic, but it came to me easily—how could I be lonely, I told myself then, when I could afford to go to a place like Elkhollow Prep? It was a game I learned quickly, and one that I could still play just as well. Why would you pity someone who had all of this? They didn't need to know that it meant more to me than just the glitter and gold plating, and they definitely didn't need to know how afraid I was to lose it. Those things were harder words to say.

"Welcome," I said, pushing open the heavy door, "to the Golden Age."

The suite looked like a place out of time. Mint-green carpeting went as far as the eye could see, the walls cotton candy pink. The furniture was spindly legged and delight-fully rounded, representing every pastel shade commercially available. No one said a single word as they all shuffled inside, their suitcases trailing behind them.

All right, not exactly the reaction I'd been hoping for.

I'd booked one of the 1950s suites because I thought it was the most fun, but maybe I'd missed the mark. I should have gone with one of the more modern rooms. Or maybe one of the 1920s suites. I was starting to suspect that maybe what I found delightfully ugly was really just normally ugly to anyone else.

Remy spoke first.

"Oh my God," they said, throwing their backpack onto the mustard-yellow couch. "This is so cool."

It was like a starting gun. Suddenly they were all racing off in every direction, shedding their luggage as they went. Lucky bounced between rooms while Remy decimated the bowl of mint chocolates by the couch. Gabe stared out the tall windows on the western wall, his hands in his pockets, uncharacteristically quiet as he looked out over the dark sky and glittering city. My eyes caught on his turned back, but I let him be. After the noise at the Favreau and trying to pile all five of us into the Civic, I could have used a quiet moment too.

Instead, I found Georgia inspecting the olive-green mini fridge. Beth had cleared out all the little bottles of liquor. I rolled my eyes. Of course she checked which room I booked. I'd be surprised if she didn't swing by for a surprise inspection to make sure nothing untoward was happening. That wouldn't be a problem, but I couldn't really tell my sister that we were housing a mini convention for asexuality. She didn't really know about the asexual thing at all, which wasn't something I was interested in discussing . . . ever. Discussing the concept of sex with your sister was not a fun thing to do, even when the point was a lack thereof. I'd so far managed to dodge every "Do you have a girlfriend yet? Or boyfriend. I'm open-minded and supportive" conversation like my life depended on it.

"You can have one." I gestured to the rows of candy bars and sodas.

Georgia gave me a sideways look. "And take out a loan to afford a Snickers bar? These places are as bad as the movie theater."

"You don't have to pay for anything," I said automatically. Georgia's response had been swift and immediate when I first pitched the Vegas idea—she couldn't afford it. I still felt irreparably stupid for not leading with the Onyx card thing. I'd never had to think about it before.

Besides, at the Golden Age we didn't actually have to pay for anything. I'd spent most my life flashing my name like a credit card here. On the weekends, Kerry and I would hop through suites like time travelers. Half our visits with Dad were just trips to different floors, which was probably why we were still alive.

A whole life that my friends didn't know about. I watched Georgia gleefully discover the ice cream freezer, aware of the rest of them moving throughout the suite like tremors at the edge of a spider's web. Somewhere behind me, Remy laughed. I flexed my hands and exhaled slowly, running through my hastily prepared speech again in my head. We'd had dinner, they'd seen the Golden Age. Now they were perfectly primed for a crash course in the life and lies of Jack Shannon. Better to rip the Band-Aid off now before they figured it out for themselves.

They were my friends, my best friends in the entire world, all in the same place for the first time. My life was falling apart, and I was desperately trying to hold it together with both hands. If there was ever a time to be honest, it was now. I bit the tip of my tongue and took a deep breath—

"Hey, guys?" Gabe said, strangely tentative. I exhaled again, deflating just a bit. Fine, I could wait. Gabe turned away from the window, his hands sunk in the pockets of his bomber jacket. "Can we talk? I mean really talk."

Unless, of course, Gabe was about to call me out right then and there. My eyes slid sideways and met Remy's, exchanging a look before I really realized that was what we were doing. Or maybe we had bigger problems than my near-miss with honest living. Gabe didn't really do serious. He went out of his way not to do serious. Seeing Gabe frowning like that was like seeing a cryptid. My nerves prickled in warning. At that moment, I would have preferred Mothman over whatever was about to come out of his mouth.

"Yeah," Georgia said when no one else would. "Yeah, of course. What's up?"

Gabe stood on one leg, scratching his calf with his foot. "I don't want to be an ass," he said, ducking his head. "That's a first, ha ha, I know, but—I feel weird about this Lucky thing."

Lucky stood in the doorway to one of the rooms, her hand on the doorframe. I saw the moment her face fell. "I'm not a *thing*," she spat.

"You know that's not what I meant," Gabe said, and even I could tell his tone was condescending. I winced. Remy raised their hand, as if to intervene, but Gabe kept going. "I mean that you lied to us. All this time."

Ah, shit. I really had to say something now, or else I was the asshole who let her take all the heat for playing a lying game. "Gabriel—"

"Let me finish," he snapped, and I balked. Gabe didn't snap either. He swallowed and looked away guiltily, like he was realizing that he wasn't acting very Gabe-like. "Listen. I love you, Lucky. You're one of my best friends. That hasn't changed. But I told you everything, thinking that you were someone else. I don't know how I'm supposed to know what was true and what was the act." He paused. "Are you even asexual? Was that a lie too?"

"*Yes*," Lucky said, the word clipped like she bit off the end of it. She folded her arms across her chest, gripping her elbows tight. "*No*. I mean—I am."

"How can you be sure? I mean—you're fourteen years old."

The tension in the room skyrocketed.

"What are you even saying?" Remy said. Their voice stayed even, but spots of color appeared on their cheeks. "She's too young to know for sure? That's bullshit, and you know it."

"I'm saying what if she changes her mind?" Gabe demanded. "What if—"

"So what if she does? Does it matter?" They countered. "Sorry, will you have to go personally revoke her ace card? I didn't know that was your responsibility."

Gabe looked flustered, his hands moving like he didn't know what to do with them. "And she was what? Thirteen when we started talking? Are we just going to forget about that part too? I was sixteen. I think I should have gotten a say in who I was talking to."

He wasn't *wrong*, exactly—it was something I was still working on wrapping my head around, recontextualizing the last year that we'd known Lucky—but he definitely hadn't chosen the right way to go about it. Lucky had gone entirely still, her shoulder pressed against the doorframe, and I was rapidly losing control of the situation. This wasn't anything I had planned for. These were my friends. We didn't fight. We rarely even disagreed, and when we did, it was easy to shuffle the conversation toward a different, safer topic. This wasn't supposed to happen.

"It took me a long time to figure out who I was. And way longer to be okay with it," Gabe said, his voice shaking. Gabe was always the most open about his sexuality—he kind of had to be. Being both asexual and aromantic made him functionally invisible in a world where everything seemed to be built around settling down with a romantic partner and getting a white picket fence, two-point-five kids, etc. "So yeah, it matters. It matters if this is all just some—some game to her, because it's not to me. This is who I am. I can't just shrug it off and become someone else when I decide I want new friends."

"That's not fair." The words pried themselves out of my mouth. It felt strange. This wasn't me playing pit boss in the library basement, bullying amateur dealers into admitting they've cheated. That was a different Jack, one who had a bottom line to protect and didn't really care what anyone at Elkhollow thought of him. This one had a lot more to lose.

"You don't get to tell someone they're too young to know who they are." Remy moved closer to Lucky protectively, their eyes still burning holes into Gabe. "Jesus. Do you even know what you sound like right now?"

I winced. Remy was right, even if there might have been a better way of saying it. Sexuality can be fluid, or at the very least a journey, not to mention personal. If someone said they were ace or gay or whatever, you believed them. Assuming that you were straight until you "know for sure" only implied that it was better to be straight until you had no other choice.

"It's how he feels," Georgia said, stepping forward. She held out a hand toward either side of the room. She was trying to play peacekeeper, but it felt like we were drawing lines in the sand. "He's allowed to feel things, all right? Everyone, calm down. He's not saying he doesn't want Lucky to be here."

"Maybe I shouldn't be." Lucky looked up, her eyes steely, but I could see her bottom lip trembling. Remy definitely could too. They went to put a hand on her shoulder, but she shrugged it off. "Maybe I should just leave."

"*No*," we all said at once, with varying degrees of emotion. Lucky posed her own complications, but if she left now, we would all fall apart. I could see it as plainly as if it had already happened, and I didn't know if I could handle that. My friends were supposed to be my rock. As much as I thought I was outsmarting Beth by using them as a distraction, she was at least a little bit right—I did feel better with them here. At least before they all started fighting.

If we couldn't stay together, if *this* couldn't work, how was I supposed to do everything else? It only got harder from here.

Gabe dropped his hand from where he'd reached out, as if to stop her. He stuffed it back into his pocket. "You don't have to do that," he mumbled, his eyes on the ground.

But if it was an apology, or even just an olive branch, Lucky wasn't taking it. She blinked and her face twisted. "I thought you guys were different, but you're just the same as anyone else. It's all some stupid fucking club I have to prove I can be a part of." She spit like a cat, her voice thick with tears that refused to fall. "Whatever. I won't stay somewhere I'm not wanted."

But she turned around and disappeared into one of the bedrooms instead of the front door, Remy hot on her heels. They threw a look over their shoulder at me and raised their eyebrows.

I blinked, startled. *What? What am I supposed to do?* A little more instruction than a pointed look would have been nice.

Remy closed the door behind them, so I could only assume it was *leave us alone*. Done. Easy. The very last thing I wanted to do was see Lucky cry.

I exhaled, my shoulders dropping. "Well, that could have gone better."

"Shut up, Jack." Gabe stalked into a bedroom on the opposite side of the suite.

Georgia sighed, pushing a hand through her hair. "He's not mad at you," she said. "He's mad at himself."

"So he yelled at *me*?"

Georgia rolled her eyes. "Don't be an asshole, Jack," she said. "I'll try to talk him off the ledge." She grabbed a Snickers bar off the top of the mini fridge and followed Gabe. Was that supposed to help? He's not himself when he's hungry? Maybe if we lived in a stupid commercial.

I looked around. The room was unchanged, their luggage where they left it, but my friends might as well have been taken by the Rapture. I almost expected to see scorch marks on the carpet where they stood, before I realized that I didn't really know all that much about the Bible. Less than twenty-four hours since they'd arrived, less than *twelve*, and I was alone again.

I sighed, and the Golden Age swallowed the sound.

IT'S GO TIME

NOTHING HAD CHANGED.

Well, a few things had changed—like how all my friends were at one another's throats and things were falling apart even worse than they were before—but the plan remained the same. It had to.

I splashed water on my face and scrubbed until fireworks bloomed behind my eyelids. I dragged my hands down my face, like I might pull off Jack Shannon and find someone else underneath. Maybe someone with better luck.

I checked the time. My phone looked empty without any Hullabaloo messages. My thumb hovered over the app anyway, like if I opened it, I might find my friends there. They were the ones I talked to when things went wrong. I didn't know what to do when they were the problem.

Or maybe I was the problem. I was the one who brought them here. I was the one who hadn't told them the truth. Maybe if I had, Lucky would have been inspired to have her reveal someplace besides a crowded restaurant. Then again, I sure as hell wasn't feeling very inspired after the reaction back there. If Gabe was upset that Lucky had lied about her age, he'd have kittens when he discovered that I'd dragged them all out to Las Vegas so I could exact revenge on a crime boss.

I looked back up at my reflection. Granddad always said I looked like Mom. Normally I couldn't see it—Mom was poised, unshakeable. Even in the video of her in handcuffs she didn't flinch. My eyes roamed my face, looking for pieces of her. My hair, my nose, my eyes. I suppressed a sigh, even if I was the only one around to hear it. I wished she was here. She'd tell me what to do next.

But she wasn't. I gripped the edge of the counter, hard. Peter Carlevaro would be having a good laugh about that right about now.

I swept back my hair, my damp hands patting it back into place just like Mom would, and straightened the collar of my shirt. I don't know what Mom would tell me to do, but she never stood around waiting for anyone else. I was a Shannon, and I had a job to do.

It was time to find the Avalon Club.

♠

I closed the door to the suite gently, wincing as the latch clicked. Originally, I'd been planning on sneaking out, using Beth as an excuse if necessary. Which probably would have worked, but with all my friends licking their wounds in their separate corners, I didn't have to find out. I held my backpack under one armpit, the poker chips courtesy of Dad clicking and sliding around inside. If anyone looked, they'd see the door to one of the bedrooms closed and assume I went to sleep. Or at least that was the plan. I'd be back well before morning, if I made it back at all.

Hm. Grim. I didn't think Peter Carlevaro would kill me, but I guessed I couldn't be sure. Crime boss and all. I rolled the thought over in my head as I stepped into the elevator at the end of the hall, my thumb pressed against the edge of the gold Avalon Club card I swiped from Flat Cap. The truth was, there were more unknown variables than I cared to admit. Had Flat Cap noticed his missing keycard? Did Carlevaro know? Would Carlevaro be there at all tonight? They weren't questions I could answer from the safety of the Golden Age. *Risk and reward*, I reminded myself. In this town, you didn't have one without the other.

The elevator doors dinged and stuttered as someone stepped through them last minute. I braced myself for my best tourist small talk.

Instead I looked up to find Remy.

"Hey," they said, coming to stand next to me, my Aces hat now in their hands. My eyes shifted past them, down the hall. It remained empty as the doors slid shut.

"Hey," I repeated lamely. "How's Lucky?"

"Asleep," Remy said. "She'll be all right. She doesn't have any siblings, so this is kind of new for her." They cracked a grin at my baffled look. "Wanting to kill each other one minute and being best friends the next. The usual."

I hadn't thought about it like that, but Remy had a point. Kerry and I going to different schools across the country cut down on our fighting considerably, but we still said things to each other that would make Beth's hair go gray.

"So," Remy said. "What are we doing?"

I blinked, remembering that we were in the elevator and I had an old backpack slung over one shoulder with $5,000 worth of Imperium poker chips weighing it down.

We're not doing anything. I bit back the words, but the instinct was still there. Remy heard it somehow, because they met my eyes and raised one eyebrow. I hadn't said a single word, and Remy already saw right through it. They always did.

I closed my mouth, and reevaluated quickly.

Fact: I trusted my friends more than anyone else.

Fact: But I didn't want to put them in danger.

Fact: Standing in the elevator with Remy made my mouth dry and my heart beat too fast, which was probably a symptom of something dangerous. Like cardiac arrest.

Conclusion: If I cared about Remy, I would lie. I would send them away, even if they didn't like it.

"It could be dangerous," I said.

"Sounds like fun," they said without missing a beat.

"And stupid."

"Obviously."

"I don't need help."

Remy fixed me with another look, their eyes dark even in the unflatteringly yellow elevator light.

Fact: Everything felt possible when Remy was standing next to me.

"We're going to play some blackjack," I said, plucking the Aces hat out of their hands and putting it on my head. Remy grinned.

♠

The Imperium was just as horrible as when I saw it last, but Remy gaped like a fish. "This is nuts," they said, tilting their head back to stare up at the art piece that hung from the high ceiling. It was made from thick wire contorted like a spider playing Twister and dipped in gold.

"It's something, all right," I agreed without enthusiasm. I pulled the Aces hat down farther, shadowing my face. It had been the better part of a week since Carlevaro caught me at the Imperium, and I wasn't conceited enough to think he was watching for me 24-7, but it made me feel better to have at least something of a disguise. The more I thought about it, the more I didn't expect Carlevaro to notice me at all.

He talked a big game, issuing challenges like we were some kind of rivals, but I didn't think he actually took me that seriously. I guess I hadn't exactly given him a reason to. The last time he'd seen me, I'd left with my tail between my legs, dragged out by my big sister. Not exactly very threatening. The Imperium was a big place. So long as I kept my head down, I was just another moving body. Carlevaro was probably busy doing something suitably terrible anyway. Eating caviar. Growing a mustache and then twirling it. Staring at a framed photograph of Mom like a freak.

I shuddered. Gross.

I darted into an empty elevator, Remy on my heels. It was built like a gold cage. It felt like standing in the belly of a whale, golden ribs arching around us. Numbered buttons stared back from the panel like a multitude of eyes next to a touchpad. Like the Golden Age, some of the floors were accessible to anyone. Otherwise, you needed to tap your keycard against the pad to prove you'd paid for a hotel room first.

I pulled out the Avalon Club card and tapped it against the pad. I wasn't sure if it would work, but it was either give it a shot or try to find the service elevator Flat Cap had been using. Considering that Carlevaro already caught me there, this seemed like the safer idea.

The edge of the pad flashed green and every button lit up, indicating access. The only problem was that I didn't know which floor we wanted.

Remy caught up to the dilemma immediately. "What are we looking for?" they asked, a spark in their eyes. Remy liked puzzles, sometimes to an intense degree. To them, this probably wasn't any harder than unlocking the next level in a video game.

"Someplace secret," I said. "Exclusive. Someplace you wouldn't want people stumbling into." More than likely, the entire floor was private. I couldn't imagine Carlevaro wanting his secret club to be neighbors with a nice little family vacationing from Ohio.

Remy nodded shortly, their eyes scanning the elevator buttons. After a heartbeat, they smirked. "Twenty-nine," they said, reaching forward to press the button. I tried desperately not to blush. "See most of the other numbers? They're worn down, they get pressed a lot. But twenty-nine looks practically new."

I blinked. I never would have seen it myself, but once Remy pointed it out, it was obvious.

"I guess you needed me after all," Remy said with a grin, elbowing me playfully in the ribs.

"I guess I did." The thought jarred me a bit. I was used to doing things on my own. Especially at Elkhollow, where I didn't have much of a choice, but home had never been overflowing with reliable figures either. It was weird, having Remy standing next to me, making things easier in a very real and tangible way. It wasn't even that I hadn't wanted to ask for help—I guess I kind of forgot that help might be something I needed.

"Jack," Remy said as the elevator spirited us upward, "is this about your mom?"

My whole body tensed, and my mouth went dry. I stared at the LED screen displaying the floor numbers as we climbed, but I could feel Remy's eyes on me. Finally, as the elevator neared the twenty-ninth floor, I summoned enough courage to meet them.

I probably should have known if they could figure out the elevator button thing, they could figure out the thing that was national news.

Remy looked sheepish. "I read the news," they said, sounding almost apologetic to have caught me in my—I didn't want to call it a *lie*. "Jack Shannon. Aileen Shannon. Big Vegas hotel. It wasn't much of a leap."

Well, when you put it that way. "No one else figured it out," I said quietly. Well, except maybe Lucky, back at the restaurant. Not that her threat had been enough for me to prevent the ensuing fight anyway.

"To be fair, they probably have better things to do than read the news," they said. "It's not your fault the world's a nightmare and I like to keep up with it."

"But you came anyway." But they were still *here* anyway. At every opportunity they went forward with me, where they could have easily turned back. A wave of emotion threatened to take me down. I should say something. *Thank you*, maybe. *I love you*, definitely not. I settled for an uncertain smile.

"Are you kidding me?" They shot me an incredulous look. "We're in a swanky elevator headed toward an illegal poker game. This is the coolest thing to ever happen to me." They paused. "It is about your mom, though, isn't it? Somehow."

"Yeah," I said, thinking about Carlevaro, about Mom being led out of the Golden Age in handcuffs, about words like *legacy* and *destiny* and *responsibility*. "Yeah, it is."

"All right," Remy said with a nod. "Details can wait. Just making sure it's important."

The elevator doors slid open with a chime.

The Avalon Club was . . .

A waiting room.

Maybe we didn't have the right floor after all.

The bank of elevators opened up into what could have been a dentist's office if there were a few more pictures of teeth. The walls were a neutral sort of beige, the chairs stiff and unattractive. A half circle of a desk sat against one wall, a bored-looking woman staring at a computer screen, her chin on her hand. There were no windows in the room. Outside it was getting closer to 11:00 p.m., but here it could easily be the middle of the afternoon, lit by yellow fluorescent light.

Not exactly what I had been expecting, but I was beginning to understand that *what I expected* was the same thing as *wrong*.

Only one way to find out.

"Excuse me," I said, stepping up to the desk. I took the dial on my charm and cranked it up to an eleven, stepping into the role of the *polite young man* like a pair of shoes I broke in a long time ago. "I . . ."

I faltered as the receptionist held out her hand without even looking up. Okay. Unsure what else to do, I set the gold card in her hand. She tapped it against a pad on the desk and again it flashed green. This time, her eyes went up.

"John Fairfield?"

I froze. Flat Cap, obviously. I considered lying (well, I was going to lie either way) and stealing his identity on top of his keycard, but that posed its own set of risks. Namely that I didn't know what other information the receptionist had on her computer screen. Too big a risk.

"My dad," I said, and I tilted my head with a grin that was equal parts sheepish and mischievous. Like she'd caught me but was also in on the same joke. If it could get me out of detention, it could get me out of this. "He might not know I have it," I added conspiratorially. And I winked.

All right, the wink was dicey, but worth it if I could pull it off. The receptionist stared.

And then she huffed a soft laugh, shaking her head.

"I didn't hear you say that," she said sternly, but she was smirking as she handed me back the keycard. She hit a button under the desk, and a door on the opposite side of the office unlocked with a click.

Oh, thank God. I grinned to hide my relief and held up the card in a faux cheers. "Your secret is safe with me," I said. I pocketed the card again and adjusted the strap over one of my shoulders. Suddenly the chips in the backpack felt like they weighed a thousand pounds. Our footsteps echoed against the thin industrial carpeting as Remy and I crossed the room.

"I thought you were about to ask her to dinner," they said in an undertone, smirking.

"It's called acting," I said, hoping they couldn't see my cheeks go pink. "Just like in the movies."

"That's definitely not how it goes in the movies," Remy muttered with a backward glance. The receptionist was already engrossed in her computer screen again. "I thought there'd be more secret codes. Maybe some guns."

"Welcome to the twenty-first century," I muttered back. It was slightly anticlimactic. So far, getting into an illegal high-stakes gambling den didn't feel much different than going through the lunch line at school.

The receptionist cleared her throat, and we froze like we'd been caught red-handed. I fought the animal urge to run, which actually wasn't all that different from the lunch line either. She pointed to a bin at the end of the desk, gray plastic like a TSA checkpoint.

"Phones and any electronic devices," she said, like it should be obvious. Remy and I reluctantly dropped our phones into the bin. I half expected a comment about kids these days and their phones, but the receptionist only made a semi-approving noise.

Trading one last look with Remy, I pushed the door open.

The Avalon Club greeted me with a wave of cigar smoke and the low rumble of voices. I stopped short so suddenly that Remy bumped into me, but neither of us really noticed. We stared.

The Avalon Club was, for once, exactly what I expected it to be. It was like a scene from an old movie: dim lighting and plush carpet, the heady sting of cigar smoke and the clatter of poker chips hitting felt tabletops. Air purifiers whirred softly in the corners, sucking up the smoke before it could get too thick, and TV screens glowed along the back wall, racehorses and greyhounds streaking across the screen. Otherwise the scene was timeless. I had expected people to be dressed nice, and some were. Half looked like they came here straight from the office. Dark suits, tie pins, and eyeliner so sharp it could cut.

But the other half looked entirely normal, or in some cases a little *too* casual. I saw a man, wearing a traffic-cone-orange Hawaiian shirt, sitting at the bar tucked into the back corner, hunched over a radioactive-green cocktail. I almost expected to see Dad sitting next to him. Between the Aces cap still on my head and Remy's beat-up jeans, we didn't stand out nearly as much as we should have. A couple more years and I could have been the tech start-up genius staring religiously at one of the races, furiously scribbling lines of code on a pad of paper without even looking down.

Remy hovered over my shoulder, so close that their curls tickled my ear. They gave a low whistle, and I could hear them grin. "This is more like it."

HIGH ROLLER

THERE WERE A VARIETY OF TABLES—TEXAS HOLD'EM, blackjack, craps. Another cluster of people in the corner watched a horse race being broadcast in another language, the track as bright as day despite the night stretching outside of the wide bay windows that made up the back wall.

There was a booth by the front where you cashed in your winnings, but I saw a man in a suit trading chips as well. I suspected that the club had its own chips—every casino had a unique set, and most had extra security like RFID or other scanned tags to prevent counterfeits. Obtaining the Imperium chips had been a gamble, but it was paying off. Unlike the receptionist, the man behind the booth didn't even blink as we exchanged $5,000 worth of Imperium tokens for the Avalon Club's custom poker chips.

"What are we looking for?" Remy asked, their eyes sweeping the club. It was a lot to take in—colors, lights, and the constant drone of hushed voices, cut through with the occasional shout or burst of laughter. There had to be something useful here, something I could work with. The amount of alcohol, money, and important people in one room all but assured it.

"Anything to do with the name Peter Carlevaro," I said in an undertone, careful not to advertise the name. I didn't see any sign of the man himself, but he'd already proven to be sneakier than a man of his unimpressive physique should be.

"Okay." Remy nodded, determined. And then faltered. "Where do we start?"

My eyes settled onto one of the poker tables—a smirk pulled on the corner of my mouth. "I've got an idea."

The blackjack table drew me forward like a fish on a line. We couldn't waltz into a poker club and not play any poker, after all, and the familiarity was like a breath of fresh air. At Elkhollow we played on old study tables with gum stuck to the bottom and a few yards of felt from JOANN Fabrics to keep the cards from sliding. Avalon, as much as it wanted to recall the glory days of old, was just like the rest of the Imperium. Top of the line.

The dealer evaluated us in a two-second glance. The fact that we were both seventeen barely even registered. Evidently if you had the card, you were in, no questions asked. I had a feeling no one here was asking a lot of questions about anything, considering the kind of money trading hands. Looking around, we weren't the only people under Vegas's usual hard twenty-one minimum.

"Buy-in is five hundred," the dealer said.

Remy sucked in a breath, but I only smiled. That I could

do. I dropped a neat stack of hundred-dollar chips on the felt and reached for another one when Remy shook their head.

"I'll just . . . watch," they said, clearly a bit nervous about jumping into triple-digit bets. I probably should have been, considering my limited options for funds, but I'd spent too much time in places like this to be scared off. Big risk, big reward. That was how it worked. I wouldn't be there in the first place if I wasn't willing to gamble everything.

I settled for sliding my stack of chips forward. The Avalon Club chips were the opposite of the dark Imperium ones, white and gold against the green felt. There was no name, only denomination numbers on one side and a minimalist logo on the other. A sword through a crown. Avalon. Excalibur. Yeah, I got the idea. How very Arthurian.

Any anxiety leftover slipped off me like an outgrown coat as the dealer started a new hand, the cards flashing as they hit the table. If I had an element, it was this one.

The hands went quickly, the click of chips and the scrape of cards soft beneath the loud rumble of conversation that filled the club like white noise. Blackjack moved fast and didn't involve bluffing, so it tended to be a more sociable game, but this wasn't a table of tourists talking about their flight from Omaha. The table consisted of the two of us and two businessmen having an animated conversation in Mandarin. They seemed more interested in their bourbon than the cards. Not a good lead on what we were looking for, unless Remy decided to reveal they'd been studying Mandarin.

I played conservatively, quietly keeping track of the count with one half of my mind but not acting on it so much that the dealer would notice a winning streak. Card counting got complicated with casino-level decks, where the shoes could hold up to eight decks specifically to discourage card counting, but I was a Shannon. Circumnavigating the rules came pretty easily to me.

I kept the other eye on the club, aware of Remy watching over my shoulder, occasionally wandering away to observe nearby tables with the pretty convincing air of someone just killing time until they got to leave. The rest of the club, what I could see of it from the blackjack table, was filled with half-familiar faces. A short woman with hair that almost doubled her height, a pouchy man wearing a bow tie with fashion sense almost as bad as Flat Cap's. There was the skinny Silicon Valley mogul who dressed like he was still twenty-two and liked to call me *kiddo* every time we crossed paths. They were Mom's friends. Or whatever passed for friends in circles like this.

And they were still here. Laughing, drinking, tossing money around like it meant nothing at all. There was no doubt in my mind that their hands were all as dirty as Mom's, if not Carlevaro's, but while she was sleeping behind bars tonight, they were here on the outside. Carlevaro was sleeping on silk sheets, most likely. Just his name made my blood simmer.

"Jack." Remy appeared at my shoulder. They tugged at the sleeves of their jacket, fidgeting. "Come check this out, it's really cool."

Meaning they had something to tell me that they didn't want the dealer or my tablemates to hear. My heart leaped in anticipation, and not just because Remy was leaning against my shoulder.

I folded my hand—a three and a five, not great anyway—and collected my winnings. I'd have to count it later, but I was pretty sure I was a thousand dollars ahead of where I started. A nice, small victory, but not the kind I was interested in. I slung the backpack back over my shoulder and followed Remy across the club, where a floor-to-ceiling painting dominated one dark red wall. It was annoyingly modern, a unicorn made from a chaotic collection of geometric shapes, kneeling in three-dimensional grass made from some sort of snarled yarn. I frowned at it, trying to imagine what disgusting amount of money Carlevaro paid to hang it up there.

Remy touched my elbow, yanking me back to reality. "There's some kind of high-roller table over by the windows," they said out of the corner of their mouth, looking up appreciatively at the unicorn. "Over there. I heard one of the old-guy-CEO types say the name 'Carlevaro' a lot. Think that's anything?"

They tilted their head toward the back of the club, and I followed the line of sight to where a poker table overlooked the view of the city, just like Remy said. Even at a glance, I knew they were on to something. I'd seen half the players seated at the Golden Age before, all CEOs and real estate magnates, the kind of people who controlled the ebb and flow of money though the city from behind the scenes. It was the kind of table my mom would have been at, if she were here.

I could hardly just waltz right up and ask to be dealt in, though I doubted anyone at that table cared enough about Aileen Shannon's snot-nosed kids to recognize me. That was assuming I had enough to buy into the high-rollers' table to begin with, which was optimistic. I was going to have to be a little smarter if I wanted to get close.

"You're pretty good at this spy stuff," I said, as I considered my options. Better think quickly. We couldn't stand here admiring the dumb painting forever.

Remy raised their eyebrows. "Remember that theater camp my mom made me go to last summer?"

"I thought you hated that camp."

"I did, because it was stupid." They shrugged. "This is more fun."

Theater camp. That was it.

"I'm going in," I said before I could change my mind. "Watch my back."

"And tip over a table if things go bad, got it." I wasn't entirely sure if they were joking. I guess I'd find out if things went bad.

I took a circuitous route to the high-rollers' table, ducking sideways along the wall, where I picked up an empty server's tray. I didn't look like much of a server, though at least I was wearing a dark jacket that made my outfit at least semi-ambiguous. If there was one thing I knew about rich people—one thing I could count on with absolute confidence—it was that no one paid attention to the help.

I straightened my back and held the serving tray in my best approximation of professionalism.

The high-rollers' table was swathed with a cloud of cigar smoke, heavy despite the air purifiers working hard above it. Four men and two women sat around the table beside the dealer, almost as anonymous as I was, each only half-way considering their cards. The chips in front of them were black, probably denoting increments that were higher than I could afford.

They all had drinks too. I slipped in between a man with a bristling mustache and a woman with long, red fingernails, testing the waters as I took her empty glass and set it on my tray. Neither so much as blinked. Or broke their conversation.

"It's just uncomfortable business," the woman said in a sharp English accent, tapping her nail against one of her chips. "What's the difference between Aileen Shannon and any of us?"

I almost fumbled with the glass, stepping back out of their line of sight. Some spy I was, getting tripped up at the sound of Mom's name as if that wasn't exactly what I'd been listening for.

Mustache man snorted. "Quite a bit, unless there's some-thing you'd like to tell us, Margot," he drawled. It took the innuendo a second to hit me. I nearly gagged. Did everyone know about Carlevaro's weird thing for my mom? Was that just industry knowledge?

Margot's smile was drawn and poisonous. "Hardly."

Even Carlevaro's own friends didn't like him. Figured.

I circled the table, eyeing another basically empty glass. Probably not what a good server would do, but I couldn't afford to go out of earshot now.

"I'm saying we should consider our options," Margot said, dropping her voice to an undertone. I could see the dealer pretending not to listen, her eyes down as she shuffled the cards. I didn't know if they were stupid or arrogant, but they were something if they thought that Carlevaro's dealers weren't reporting interesting table talk back to him. It was what I would have done. "Things are changing. Quickly. If the food chain around here is getting a good shuffle, I'd like to make the most of it." She shrugged. "Aileen might be feeling more generous now that she's in a tight spot."

"You don't have any options," the other woman cut in. She was older, her neck glittering with a necklace so big and intricate it was more like chainmail. Her mouth curved down in a harsh frown. "You wouldn't be here if you did."

One of the men laughed. "She's not wrong, Margot."

"Carlevaro owns you, same as the rest of us. Best get used to it, dear," the older woman continued sourly, shifting her weight just as I was going for her glass. I flinched back, the first glass sliding perilously across the tray. "So long as he's got that little black book of his, you can get comfortable doing as you're told."

My heart leaped. A little black book full of the secrets on the movers and shakers of the Las Vegas Strip? The leash

Carlevaro used to keep them all at heel? That was certainly what it sounded like.

And that was exactly what I needed. Without it, Carlevaro's entire empire would fall apart. Probably starting with red-nailed Margot there.

I got what I needed, and I was pretty sure I'd overstayed my welcome too. Waitstaff weren't exactly supposed to hang around and watch them play. I grabbed the glass and started to beat a hasty retreat.

The woman's hand snapped out, grabbing me by the wrist. I froze, my heart in my throat. For a single, perilous moment nothing happened.

"Another one of those, would you?" she said imperiously, dropping my wrist.

"Yes, ma'am," I said, my voice cracking. Embarrassing. She didn't even look back at me.

I had no idea what she'd been drinking, nor did I intend to find out. As casually as possible, I walked away from the high-rollers' table, tray still in hand. I left it on the bar, not even breaking stride, and rendezvoused with Remy where they were observing a particularly rowdy game of craps.

They looked up, their eyebrows raised in a silent question. *Got it?*

I nodded. *Got it.* Or at least as much as I was going to get tonight.

Remy winked. "Let's get out of here," they said, affecting a yawn. "I'm falling asleep."

"Good idea," I said, smothering a grin. For the first time

in a long time, things had gone right. The problem wasn't solved, but I was moving in the right direction—I was *doing* something. And Remy was right there with me.

I looked back at the Avalon Club, swathed in dusky light and mystery, looking like a scene out of a painting. In the corner, the bettors whooped as the racehorses on the screen crossed the finish line. Remy was saying something, but I could hardly hear over the buzz of adrenaline. This was why people came to Las Vegas. To find things they couldn't do anywhere else.

My eyes skipped forward and then back again, toward one of the Texas Hold'em tables tucked away to the left. A girl sat facing the door, her face partly hidden by the fan of her cards. Half of her head was shaved, the rest dyed bright pink and almost obscured by the hood of her jacket. She was our age, maybe a year older, but in a place like the Avalon Club, none of that was remarkable. Sitting between a man wearing a bolo tie and a woman wrapped in a leopard-print shawl, there was no reason for her to stand out.

Except for the fact that she was watching me.

The girl winked and pushed a stack of chips into the center of the table. Remy and I were out of the door before I could see if her bet paid off.

♠

Our good mood carried us all the way back to the Golden Age. Technically there was a curfew for anyone under eighteen on the Strip, but it wasn't that hard to get around if you knew what you were doing. I'd been away from the city for a good five years, but I'd spent enough time sneaking around Elkhollow to keep the rust off me.

"This way," I said, tugging on Remy's sleeve and ducking to the left, around the side of the Golden Age. Enough of the front-desk staff could recognize my face that I didn't want to risk it. Seeing me waltz in at this time of night would definitely get back to Beth sooner rather than later.

We skirted around to one of the staff entrances instead, between topiaries and dumpsters. This part of the Golden Age, admittedly, was less impressive.

You needed a keycard to get into the staff entrances, but you could always count on someone being on their smoke break.

"Long night, Little Jack?" Marian said, exhaling smoke out into the pool of yellow light surrounding the staff door. Marian was a relic of a human being, built like a turnip and chronically unimpressed, but out of any member of the staff, I was glad to run into her. Mainly because she had the amazing quality of not giving a single shit about anything, including what I may or may not have been doing.

"Sure was," I agreed, and on a whim, I tossed her one of the Golden Age poker chips I carried around like a token of good luck. She caught it with more dexterity than a woman her age should be capable of.

Marian wheezed a laugh. "Just like your dad," she said and slapped her keycard against the pad without question.

Remy snorted as we moved down the staff hall. Plain and beige, disturbingly identical to the guts of the Imperium. I found them smirking in my direction. "You think you're so cool," they said, jostling me with their elbow. "I saw that poker chip. Do you charm all the old ladies like that?"

"I *am* so cool." I elbowed them back, a little embarrassed, but in a way that felt pleasantly warm in my chest. It made me feel like a kid again, when Granddad would hide Golden Age chips in Easter eggs for us to find. We *had* felt devastatingly cool, swaggering up to the counter to exchange them for ten-dollar bills. Even Beth.

We were still laughing, giddy with the sheer unlikelihood that we'd made it to the Imperium and back again both alive and undetected, when we got back to the room. I *shh*'d Remy and they *shh*'d me back as I keyed open the door. I released the doorknob slowly, careful not to let it click as we shuffled into the room. The lights were still on, just like we left them. Somehow that just made it feel even later, like the hotel was waiting up for us, looking at its watch and tapping its foot.

It made me feel weightless, like I was flying, or maybe just about to fall, my feet on the edge of a precipice. That was the thing about bad decisions. Once you got to like the taste of them, it was hard to stop.

"Remy," I said, my heart in my throat. They turned back, their cheeks still flushed from laughing, their dark curls turned to a frizzy mess. Was this when I was supposed to tell them? In a hotel-room foyer, still wearing that stupid hat? It was a dangerous hour of the morning, when the entire world was a little surreal. I would say, *Hey, I'm in love with you, just thought you should know*, and Remy would laugh, and we'd both wake up in the morning, unsure if it really happened or if it was just a weird dream.

That'd be okay. I'd be okay with that. The words fluttered like butterflies in my chest.

"Young man."

I froze. Remy rocked backward, backpedaling into me. I grabbed their shoulders.

"Young person of unfathomable and undefinable gender."

"Shit," Remy whispered. They cleared their throat. "Hey, Gabe."

We peeked around the corner, where the foyer led to the rest of the room. The rest of our friends sat collected in the living room in their pajamas, surrounded by enough wrappers and open laptops to suggest that they'd been having a grand old time since we'd been gone. I scowled. Good to know they'd all gotten over the whole catfishing thing when I was busy being convinced they'd never speak to one another again. Or me.

Gabe stood in the middle of the living room with his arms crossed over his chest, wearing one of the plush Golden Age bathrobes over his pajamas. He was even tapping his foot. He looked more motherly in that single moment than my real mom was even capable of.

He raised his eyebrows. "Where have you been?"

Georgia rolled her eyes. "Indulge him," she said, turning to me. "He's been rehearsing this."

"Just be glad he decided against doing the voice." Lucky had a haunted look in her eyes. I didn't want to know what *the voice* meant.

"You guys were supposed to be sleeping," I accused. I belatedly released Remy's shoulders.

"We were going to," Lucky said. She was wearing slippers with pink pom-poms on the toes. The sight was so un-Lucky, I almost thought I was hallucinating. She really *was* a fourteen-year-old girl underneath the sharp tongue and propensity for lying. "But then we noticed you two were gone, and one thing led to another."

Led to them resolving their differences, evidently. Great. Fantastic. I wished we could have done all that in the morning. The long day was rapidly bullying past the adrenaline high and catching up with me.

"I'm glad we could inspire you to talk it out," I said dryly.

Gabe gestured impatiently. "So where were you? I'd accuse you two of something untoward, but I don't think that's of much concern around here."

"Well." I considered it. "I guess it depends on your definition of untoward."

"*Excuse me?*" Georgia choked the same time Gabriel made an incomprehensible sound. Lucky just looked confused over the top of her laptop screen.

"Oh my God, not like that," Remy said, exasperated, but their ears went red.

"I didn't *mean*—I hate you guys." There was no reason to be so embarrassed. The whole asexual thing—asexual *times two* thing—really covered the worst of it, but I still minorly wanted to die. I'd almost told Remy I loved them. I'd almost told Remy I loved them *while the rest of our friends were right around the corner*. I imagined that was what it felt like to have a near-death experience.

Gabe raised his hands defensively. "I didn't say anything, dude."

Remy elbowed me in the ribs. "Just tell them already," they said.

Lucky leaned forward, closing her laptop and resting her elbows on top of it. "Yeah, Jack," she said. "Tell us."

I hesitated. The cat came out of the bag the moment I took Remy to the Avalon Club. The right decision, as it turned out. It occurred to me that maybe I should have told the truth from the start. Funny how that worked.

But I could still make up for lost time.

I was proud to say that, out of the Shannon children, I took after Mom the most. Something about Shannon blood just makes you want to break a few laws and make some cash doing it, I guess. But Marian had a point. There was unmistakably a little bit of Robbie Castle in me. I didn't, as a rule, dress up in sequin bodysuits and sing "Bohemian Rhapsody" for tipsy tourists, but I knew a little bit about dramatic flair.

I swung the backpack off my shoulder and tugged at the zipper, loosening it just enough so that when I dropped the backpack onto the coffee table it slumped over. Poker chips slid through the zipper's teeth and across the lacquered white surface.

I put my hands in my pockets, affecting casual as they all stared down at the chips—even Remy, who had helped me shovel them into the backpack in the first place.

Gabe reached out and picked up one of the chips. An elegant *100* flashed gold on the back.

"This is—" he started.

"Seven thousand dollars. Give or take."

"Where did you—" Georgia attempted.

"Illegal high-stakes blackjack."

"How?" Lucky said, looking up. Her eyes were wide, but there was something hungry in them that didn't quite line up with her puffy pigtails or pink polka-dot pajamas.

I grinned, flashing my teeth. I knew that look. It was exactly what I'd been hoping to see. "It's a long story."

CAFFEINATION STATION

WE ENDED UP WITH EVERY LIGHT ON IN THE SUITE, camped out in the middle of the living room wearing our pajamas and draped in blankets. My eyes itched with exhaustion, but no one was about to go to sleep any time soon, and that was before room service arrived with the coffee tray. I accepted it at the door, and someone shoved the fallen poker chips aside to make room for it.

I hesitated as I handed a mug to Lucky. "Are you allowed to drink this?" I said. "Or will it stunt your growth?"

"I'll stunt your growth," she muttered threateningly. She took the mug and proceeded to dump an unholy amount of sugar in it.

Georgia was sitting cross-legged on an ottoman, her laptop perched on one knee, watching the news coverage of Mom's arrest. She had an earbud dangling from one ear, and I was quietly grateful. I'd already seen all the footage. I didn't need to hear it again.

She hit Pause, chewing contemplatively on her coffee

stirrer. "Run through it with me again," she said, pulling the earbud out. She'd taken out her contacts. Her red cat-eye glasses made her look something like a cross between a secretary from the 1950s and an overworked fashion designer.

I wrapped my hands around my own coffee mug and paced the length of the living room. "My mom shouldn't have been arrested," I said. It was a small relief, to say the words out loud and have them nod like they believed me. "Not to sugarcoat it, but the Shannon family isn't known for being morally upright. We've been at this for a long time. The police wouldn't have gotten enough evidence to arrest her unless someone gave it to them."

"Peter Carlevaro," Georgia filled in.

"Because he has the hots for your mom," Remy added, consulting their notes. Okay, I didn't really want that part written down, because gross, but I had to respect their work ethic.

"You don't have to say it like that," I said, grimacing.

"But she's not into him, and he's a little bitch about it," Lucky finished, taking a long sip of what must have been coffee-flavored sugar at that point.

"Exactly," I said before Georgia could interject about Lucky swearing again. I couldn't tell if it was supposed to be a joke or not, but we didn't need another fight. We were finally all on the same page.

"And we're sure it was Carlevaro?" Gabe asked. "The head of a crime family? Not someone that sounds a little less scary?"

"It *has* to be him," I said viciously. "I mean"—I gestured vaguely—"our family has enemies, yeah." Business rivals, people Granddad screwed over, people who just didn't like Mom because she was a successful woman who didn't put up with their bullshit. But those things were so mundane, almost routine. This was clearly personal. "But no one knows more about our family than the Carlevaros, and no one stands to gain more than Peter. My mom was the last thing keeping him from taking over the Las Vegas Strip."

Because she'd changed her mind about taking it over *with* him, but that was an unimportant detail. At least she hadn't sent Carlevaro to jail when she decided to break ties with him, though clearly she should have. It would have saved us all a lot of trouble right about now.

"All right," Georgia said. I had the feeling I wasn't selling her on the idea as much as she was orienting herself, getting the lay of the land before she stepped out onto it. Georgia lived for detail. "So how does this work? How does the Avalon Club come into play?"

"And how are we going to get back into it?" Remy asked, their chin propped up on their hands. They were sitting on the back of the couch, their bare feet planted on the cushion next to Lucky. It was hard to look at them head-on, thinking about my close call in the foyer. I needed to keep better control of myself if we were going to do this. I couldn't be distracted. "Jack only got in because he impersonated some guy's son, and I wasn't sure they were gonna let me in at all. Four guests might be pushing our luck."

"Don't worry about that," Lucky said, her eyes fixed on her laptop screen. She looked small but serious behind it, her face lit up by the glow of the screen. "You don't need luck. When you've got me." She shot Gabe a pointed look, and I tensed, but he only stuck his tongue at her. Lucky smirked and I rolled my eyes. Remy was right, they were just like siblings. Was this what Kerry and I looked like from the outside?

"I overheard a bunch of the club's high rollers talking about him—Carlevaro keeps a little black book filled with all the dirty laundry of the Strip's most influential people," I went on. "When money can't get him what he wants, he uses blackmail to control people. I'm sure that's how he got my mom arrested. If we can get our hands on that, suddenly *we* control *him*."

"A little black book?" Gabe drawled. "Easy. This place got a library?"

"I'm not sure there's a Dewey decimal number for *evil book of secrets*," Georgia said.

"Very funny," I said dryly. "Maybe the black book is there, maybe it's not, but I think the Avalon Club is the best place to start. It's the closest thing we've got to his inner sanctum. We can get a better look at the place, maybe get close enough to the high-rollers' table again to see if they have anything else interesting to say. They all seem pretty eager to bitch about him." We'd been shooting from the hip on our first excursion, and we were lucky to have uncovered as much as we did. With a little more focus and preparation, we stood a better chance at finding Carlevaro's secrets.

"Real quick, let's be clear," Gabe said, gesturing like he was giving a symposium. He was still wearing the fluffy white robe, and at some point, he'd stolen Lucky's pom-pom slippers. They dangled off his toes as he bounced his foot. "This is definitely a crime. This might not go well for us. Especially those of us that aren't rich white guys."

No, that was exclusively me. "No one has to do anything," I said fervently. "Say the word, and you can go home." I wasn't going to hold anyone hostage here. I didn't know how long the Onyx card would go undetected by the authorities, but I would make it work, preferably without Beth's intervention. "Or stay here, whichever. This is my problem. No one else's."

"That's not the same thing as calling it off," Remy pointed out, raising their eyebrows, their chin resting on their interlocked fingers now. "You're still going to do it."

I hesitated, tripping over my own tongue. I wasn't sure what the right answer was. "Ah," I said carefully. "Yeah." It was too late to turn back now. Maybe if our first journey into the Avalon Club had gone badly. Maybe if Peter Carlevaro hadn't looked me in the eyes and thrown a challenge down at my feet. Maybe if I could think about anything besides Mom sitting in a jail cell. But those possibilities were far away now, and I knew playing blackjack in the library basement would never live up to what I'd seen at the Avalon Club. It was a basic rule of gambling, one that ruined as many people as it made. Once you knew what it was like to win, once you'd tasted it, you only wanted more.

Remy shrugged. "Then I'm in," they said. "You're not getting rid of me that easily."

"Hey!" Gabe interjected. "I never said I wasn't *in*. I'm ride or die, baby. Just that we should maybe try not to get caught."

"Damn!" Georgia snapped her fingers. "Don't get caught. I almost forgot that part."

"Oh, you're *so* funny."

"I thought so."

Remy scoffed. "Aw, I thought getting caught might be fun—"

"All right," Lucky said, raising her voice to be heard. She closed her laptop, resting her hands on top of it. "I'll be the one to say it. I guess I deserve it." Her eyes swept the room. The only sound was the repetitive click of Remy's poker chip against their knuckles. "If we're going to do this, we've got to be a hundred percent honest with one another. No more secrets. We're a team."

Lucky met my eyes, looking sheepish. All right, so we were the offenders there, but it was a good reminder. I'd only left them out of the whole truth to protect them, with maybe a dash of cowardice too, but I was also the one who brought them to Vegas in the first place. Honesty, I was learning, wasn't something you could do halfway.

"We're a team," I agreed.

"Aw, all right, come on," Gabe said, jumping to his feet. "I know a group hug coming on when I see it."

Okay, I was being sappy, but not that sappy. "I don't think that's necess— *Hnkk.*" Gabe hooked one arm around my neck and roped Georgia in with the other, an unholy chain reaction of people grabbing and being grabbed until we were all piled together like a litter of puppies.

I didn't know why I had to be the one squashed in the middle.

"We should have a name," Remy mumbled from where their face was pressed against Georgia's shoulder. Lucky's hair was tickling my nose. "Teams have names."

"What do you call people about to infiltrate an underground gambling ring?" I asked right before I sneezed.

Remy's elbow somehow found my ribs through the tangle of humanity. "You named your secret blackjack club *Blackjack Club*," they said. "No one is expecting you to be the creative one."

"Hey!"

Their laugh vibrated through our knot of limbs.

"Asexuals against Peter Carlevaro," Georgia suggested.

"Ace Scandal Syndicate," Lucky chimed in.

"All right, I think you just want it to spell *ass*—"

"What's it they say in five-card stud?" Gabe said, cutting through the chatter. Coincidentally, right in my ear. "When the twos are wild cards?"

"Deuces wild," I supplied. I wrinkled my nose. "Are you saying we're five studs? Because I think you missed the mark."

"No," Georgia said, nodding her head like something was making sense. "Five aces."

I smirked, hidden by the group hug I couldn't believe was still going on. All I could think about was Magic Bryan and Blackjack Club, playing sleight of hand with the duplicate ace of hearts. I still had it in my wallet next to the Onyx and the Avalon Club keycard, a little good-luck charm. The corners were starting to crease. "Five aces," I agreed. "So, basically, cheating." Unless one of us was supposed to be a joker. There was no such thing as five of a kind without a wild card.

"I'm good with cheating," Lucky said.

"Cheating sounds good," Remy said over the top of her head. Barely.

"Cheating it is!" Gabe said, releasing us from the hug in order to clap his hands over our heads. "So, let's see: Break in"—he ticked off each point on a finger—"get revenge, don't get caught." He put his hand in the middle of us, clearly gunning for something out of a sports movie. "Aces Wild."

Remy rolled their eyes. "It's supposed to be a team name, not a catchphrase."

"Aces! Wild!" He wiggled his fingers insistently.

Remy snorted. "Aces Wild," they agreed. They put their hand over Gabe's.

"Aces Wild." Georgia went next, grinning.

"Aces Wild." Lucky slapped her hand on top. "I like that."

Gabe raised his eyebrows at me, and the same unstoppable smile that first assaulted me at the airport returned, bullying its way into reality. It tried to squash it, but somehow that just made it stronger. Finally, I gave in.

"Aces Wild," I said, putting my hand in, grinning like an idiot. It wasn't really what I imagined when I first sent them that message, the one I couldn't take back, even if I wanted to. It wasn't really how I imagined this would be like at all.

But it was pretty damn good.

START COUNTING

AS GABE SO SUCCINCTLY PUT IT, WE HAD THREE objectives: get in, get what we were looking for, and get out without getting caught. Easy.

Sort of.

First: getting in. Fortunately, as she reminded us often, we had Lucky.

"Keycards are easy," she said the next night, after we'd crashed in the living room more or less where we fell, some of us still cradling coffee mugs. Gabe complained endlessly about the ensuing crick in his neck, until Georgia reminded him how old it made him sound. "They're mostly RFID these days. You just have to duplicate the information transmitted by radio frequency." She sighed, rubbing contemplatively at her chin. "If the keycard was the only obstacle, it'd be even easier than that. Most keypads can be hacked with, like, a ten-dollar machine. I might have my dad send me one, just in case."

"I thought your dad was some Silicon Valley tech guy,"

Georgia said. "Where did all this hacker-spy stuff come from?"

"He is," Lucky said, clearly enjoying the attention. She sat at the end of the couch, in what was rapidly being established as her spot, the rest of us listening with varying degrees of attention. Remy, for instance, was building a tower out of poker chips. "You have to know how to break tech if you're going to make tech. That's why they hire hackers to test their programs for weaknesses at Google or the Pentagon or whatever. My dad has been teaching me this stuff since I was, like, five."

"So not that long ago," Gabe stage-whispered to Georgia. He squawked as Lucky flicked him on the nose.

I frowned. "Is that how you knew who I was?" I hadn't forgotten her little threat in the restaurant. "Did you hack me?"

Oh God, did she see the fan fiction?

Lucky gave me a pitying look. "No, Jack," she said. "I just have a brain that I choose to use every once in a while."

I scowled. All right, it hadn't been the best lie in the world, even for a lie of omission. But still. I waited for the cries of indignance to rise. Certainly the others would take offense to the way she put it, at least.

They never came. I frowned deeper, glancing suspiciously around our loose little circle. "Did *everyone* know?" What the hell?

Remy smiled sheepishly, offering me a little shrug. Okay, I knew that. But the others?

"Kinda," Georgia said gently. She wrapped a stray curl around her finger. Unwound it. Wound it up again. "I mean, I didn't *know*, but . . . once I saw which hotel we were staying at, I had a few suspicions."

I cringed. Yeah, that was a bit of a giveaway.

Gabe scratched the back of his head awkwardly, glancing sidelong at the rest of them for support. They dutifully averted their eyes. "I, uh"—he hemmed and hawed—"thought you just didn't want to talk about it?" Somehow, he made it a question.

"You were correct," I deadpanned. I felt stupid for worrying how they would react to it now—I should have trusted them to know me well enough to know what I needed, or at least I should have been brave enough to ask for it. Good to know for next time. I was still a bit new at this whole crisis-mode thing. "You could have said something and put me out of my misery."

"We knew you'd get to it eventually," Remy said. "The cool spy stuff was a surprise, though."

"Yeah, really didn't see that one coming," Georgia chimed in.

"I wasn't surprised," Lucky said.

"Shut up, yes, you were." Gabe leaned over to flick her ear.

"*But* the keycard isn't the only obstacle," I said, eager to move away from the subject. "There was a whole receptionist situation. All she had to do was tap the card to find out whom it belonged to." I didn't know if John Fairfield even had a son. Maybe I should have worn a flat cap, to fake family resemblance.

"Exactly," Lucky said. "I said it'd be *easier* if it was. Not that the alternative is hard." She smiled in a way that implied *at least not for me.* "Each keycard is probably linked to a profile of the user. You said it was pretty diverse in there, right? Not just a bunch of old billionaires built like sacks of tapioca pudding?"

Evocative. "Yeah," I said, thinking about the girl with the pink hair who had watched us on our way out. Watched me. The Avalon Club was hardly a high-school prom, but we hadn't stuck out as much as I'd expected to.

"So," Lucky continued, "we just need to duplicate the keycard, hack Carlevaro's system, and create fake profiles. Jack will have to maintain the act as Fairfield's son. I'll see what I can do about changing how it'll appear on their logs, in case anyone connects the guy's missing keycard to you. As for the rest of us, no one has to know that we've ever even met."

"We?" Gabe raised his eyebrows. "*We* have to hack Carlevaro's system?"

"Well," Lucky said, straight-up preening now, "*me*, but you guys can pretend you were moral support if you want."

"Nope," Remy said, draping themself over the back of the couch. "We'll be busy. Right, Jack?"

"Right," I said, pulling a crisp deck of cards out of my pocket. I'd grabbed it from the gift shop on the second floor. It had the Golden Age logo on the back of every card, surrounded by shiny gold filigree. I usually preferred a deck that was broken in, but this one would see plenty of work before we were through with it. I tapped the cards out into my hand and started shuffling them, my hands falling into the familiar motion.

We were skipping ahead a bit to the *not getting caught* part. Once we got in, it was important that we didn't stand out. Everyone in the Avalon Club shared a common goal: They were gambling. While that came naturally to me in a way that should probably be concerning, my friends needed a little work.

"All right," I said, eyeing the others as Lucky buried her head back in her laptop. "So how do we feel about math?"

♠

The idea behind counting cards wasn't necessarily hard, at least not any harder than tenth-grade math. Much like the mathematicians and philosophers of old, someone else had already done the hard work for you. You kept your eyes open, and probability did the rest. I had been doing it for so long, I didn't even think about it anymore, as evidenced by the $7,000 in chips still sitting on the coffee table.

In blackjack, each card had a value. Numbered cards were worth exactly what it said; face cards like kings, queens, and jacks were worth ten; and aces could be worth either one or eleven, depending on what you chose to get the best score. Simple.

Card counting operated under a similar principle. Each card had a number correlating with how valuable it was to draw. You kept a running count of the deck's total value in order to predict which card would be drawn next. Two through six had a value of plus one. Seven through nine were zero. Tens, the face cards, and aces were minus one. The higher the number, the hotter the deck, the better the odds.

As long as you kept track of which cards had been played and what that meant for the value of the deck, you were as good as gold. Easy.

Card counting is what I did. I just wanted to teach them how to play blackjack. Period.

"Can we take a break?" Remy asked for the fifth time, face-planting in the cards. "My brain is going to start leaking out of my ears."

"Careful with the carpet, I think brain juice stains," Gabe said, his tongue sticking out between his teeth as he considered the numbers he had written on a piece of hotel stationery. Evidently it was easier to keep track of his cards' values that way. It was also a good way to keep track of just how many busted hands he'd had. Gabe seemed to think blackjack was more of a *gotta catch 'em all* sort of situation.

"This is only with one deck," I said, trying and only half-way succeeding to hide my exasperation. It was a bit of a crash course, okay, but it wasn't *that* hard. It'd be a hell of a lot harder when the lights were low and there were several thousands of dollars in poker chips on the table. So a little more effort would have been appreciated. Lucky was busy with the keycard situation, which was fine, but Georgia was too busy playing with her phone to even be paying attention. "A professional table can have up to—"

"Eight decks in a shoe," Remy filled in, looking down their nose dramatically. Was that supposed to be what I sounded like? I scowled, but Remy only tossed their head. A five of diamonds was stuck to their cheek. "Who even knows what an underground table might have. Ten decks! Fifteen! *Mmph—*"

I shoved a pillow in their face, careful not to disturb the cards. God, I could finally understand every lesson Mom had ever tried to teach me. You really did have to learn by doing. Though the time Granddad left me in front of the Fountains of Bellagio and told me to find my way home still seemed like overkill. Particularly because I was only nine when Granddad died.

Gabe sighed dramatically. "What does it matter? We know how to play. You want to get to twenty-one. Easy. Got it."

"Is that why you keep losing?" I said dryly. "Because it's that easy? You're going to burn through our chips in five minutes and then get kicked out for sucking so bad just because you like saying 'hit me.'"

"It's fun," Gabe whined, his shoulders slumping. "How am I supposed to know which card you're going to hit me with? I keep getting high ones."

"Just keep track of the ones you've already seen," Georgia said. "Like he said at the beginning."

I blinked. Georgia sat cross-legged on a pillow next to the coffee table, one hand holding up her cheek as she played some sort of cutesy cat game on her phone. She didn't even look up.

Okay, yeah, I'd given the whole speech about card counting, but I didn't expect any of them to actually absorb any of it. I was really just showing off. I cleared my throat. "What's the count?"

"Six."

She really *was* counting. Holy shit. "Which means . . ."

"Which means there are a lot of aces and tens still in the deck. So, a good time to increase your bet." Georgia looked up to find us staring at her. Remy sat up, looking like they'd just found religion. Gabe was frowning so hard I could almost see the numbers floating around his head. "What? It's just math."

"I . . ." I faltered. "Have you ever played blackjack before?"

Georgia blinked, her eyes darting between us like she'd only just realized she should be self-conscious. "Not really," she said, fidgeting with her phone. "It's not a big deal. It's just keeping track of all the numbers."

"I can barely keep track of the numbers I *can* see," Remy said, still looking dazzled. I tried not to take it personally. I mean, I had done it at the Avalon Club, with a six-deck shoe, while I was distracted. But I guess what Georgia did was impressive too. For a newbie.

"You should be good at that, Gabe," Lucky piped up from behind her laptop screen. She swirled Mountain Dew around in a champagne glass. "How many hundreds of years has it been since you were born?"

Gabe threw a wadded-up receipt that landed in Lucky's glass.

I looked at Georgia with renewed appreciation. It *was* impressive. Really impressive, actually. I'd always known that Georgia was smart, but there were lots of kinds of smart, and math smart wasn't always one of them. I was math smart and people stupid, for instance. At least according to Kerry. Georgia was apparently a little more well-rounded.

Maybe we could fit in pretty well at the Avalon Club after all.

"What?" Georgia said as our friends devolved into chaos behind us. My staring was less subtle than I thought.

"What?" I parroted back, playing dumb. I didn't know how to tell her that I was impressed without it being either a) weird or b) condescending. I was a little less people stupid than Kerry thought.

Meanwhile, Lucky was trying to smother Gabe with a pillow. Or she would have been, if she could reach.

"All right, all right," I said, shuffling the deck. "Let's try again."

15

SURVEILLANCE STATE

ONE PROBLEM WITH THE *DON'T GET CAUGHT* PART
of the plan: Carlevaro wasn't the only person keeping both
eyes open when it came to Jack Shannon.

I wasn't stupid enough to think that Beth would be satisfied by the innocuous charges on the Onyx card and the gag-
gle of friends to keep me occupied. We were both Shannons,
for better or for worse, and we both knew that nothing was
ever that easy in this family. My problem was that Beth, as
the older sister and responsible adult, was going to have the
hotel staff side with her at any opportunity.

Some wouldn't care if I were sneaking around, but I
couldn't bet on Marian taking her smoke break every time
I needed to smuggle four other teenagers in and out of the
Golden Age unnoticed. I needed my own keycard to get into
the staff entrances.

Which was fortunately something I could handle on my
own. With the help of a coconspirator.

I chose Georgia, leaving Lucky to preside over as many

hands of blackjack as it took to get Gabe and Remy to look like they knew what they were doing. Lucky took to the task with almost sadistic glee. Georgia was the obvious choice, considering she clearly already knew how to play, but she was too nice. Lucky's particularly brand of motivation was a little more effective.

There was another reason too, besides wanting to see my friends suffer by a fourteen-year-old's hand. The card counting had led to a strange realization—Georgia was one of my best friends, but in some ways, I didn't know her as well as the others. At least one-on-one, the way I did Remy or even Gabe, to a lesser extent.

Naturally, the solution to this was to involve her in a scheme. Clearly that was how I operated.

"Is this a good idea?" Georgia wondered aloud as we crossed the Golden Age's casino floor. She said it like she was more curious than concerned.

"It's a great idea," I said, glancing over my shoulder. Normally we wouldn't be allowed on the casino floor until we were twenty-one, but we didn't exactly have time for that. Luckily, being a Shannon still had a couple of perks, including flashing my ID at security and promising that we were just cutting through. I could still feel the eyes of the security cameras tracking us, as if we were going to sneak in a hand of blackjack or a pull on the slot machine along the way.

"Trust me," I said, waving my hand. "Babs owes me a favor."

Honestly? I loved the casino floor. I loved the dim lights and the *click-shuffle-thwawp* of cards and chips being passed across felt. It wasn't like the movies anymore—so much was digital, down to the slot machines loading your winnings onto a card with a digitized jingle of coins falling—but there was still something electric in the air. The ideas of luck and chance and possibility, charging the atmosphere like the air before a storm. Like any place open twenty-four hours a day, it was set apart from time and something wholly its own.

The security office, meanwhile, was not that exciting.

Scheme was probably a big word for what we were doing. *Five-finger discount* was a little closer to the truth, though the distraction element brought it closer to scheme status. The seasonal staff were notoriously bad about losing their work badges, so the security office kept a stash of blank ones for those days a hapless employee forgot theirs. I just had to liberate one from security, and we had unfettered, unmonitored access to the Golden Age's staff entrances. Easy.

The head of security was a woman known simply as Babs—short but built like a brick wall and about as unyielding. I'd seen her throw out drunk men twice her size. She was also very into LARPing and had a sword mounted to the wall behind her desk. She contained multitudes.

"It's never a good day when a Shannon walks into my office," Babs said without looking up from her computer screen. One of them. An entire bank glowed in one corner of the office, like she didn't trust the rest of the security team to monitor the casino themselves, so she kept a backup.

She was joking about the Shannon thing. I was pretty sure.

"Babs," I said, leaning on her desk. Her eyes flickered

toward where my hands met the wood and I quickly straightened up. "Remember that favor?"

"No," she said with brutal efficiency. I was glad that Georgia was behind me so she couldn't see me wince. "But I'm curious. Go on."

"My friend Georgia lost her bracelet yesterday, and we were wondering if we could check the cameras in case anyone picked it up." I put on as much casual innocence as I knew how. "It's a family-heirloom sort of thing. It's really important to her."

I waited, holding my breath as Babs stared me down. Her eyes flickered behind me, assessing Georgia, who waved awkwardly. Another reason to drag Georgia along: Remy had turned out to be a bit of an actor, but Georgia was the one with a poker face. As head of security, no doubt Babs had gotten the full briefing from Beth.

"Hotel-security footage is privileged information," she said staunchly.

But I could see cracks in her resolve. Babs liked me. It was her fatal flaw. "Hence the favor," I said. "Please? If you could even just see where she dropped it, it would help a lot. We don't have a lot of leads here."

"I'd really appreciate it," Georgia threw in for good measure.

Finally, Babs huffed a laugh. "You're lucky I feel sorry for you, kid."

I flashed a winning smile. "Most people do."

She didn't laugh, but Georgia did.

Babs's keys jingled as she turned her chair around, toward the bank of monitors set against the wall—under the sword. Her back to me, exactly like I wanted. "All right, kid, don't be shy," she said, beckoning Georgia over. "Where did you last see it?"

I listened with one ear as Georgia took Babs on a wild-goose chase through security footage, naming locations that were so busy that Babs wouldn't be able to tell that Georgia was never there. I needed Babs distracted, not more suspicious.

For my part, it was easy. I casually paced the office, considering the different awards and photographs on the walls until it took me past a filing cabinet, a small plastic basket of numbered keycards on top of it. I ignored the clipboard with a checkout list next to it, dipping my hand into the basket of keycards. I palmed one, quick as a magic trick, and tucked it up my sleeve as I let my hand drop back to my side.

I started to move away—and stopped. The light in the security office was bleak and white, and it reflected brightly off the glass of the framed photograph, but I could still see it well enough. Babs and my mom standing shoulder to shoulder, a much younger Kerry and me playing in the background. It felt like a slap in the face, seeing Mom where I didn't expect to. I should have. She and Babs had been friends for as long as I could remember. Babs was one of those lifer employees I'd grown up with, like a distant, less fucked-up branch of the family. It was a sharp reminder of what we were doing here. This wasn't a wacky vacation, even when it might feel that way, surrounded by my friends and ordering room service past midnight. This was my life at stake.

"You all right, kid?"

I jumped. I didn't notice Georgia and Babs had given up on their proverbial needle-in-a-haystack search. Now they were both looking at me, caught in the act of displaying a raw moment of emotion. I clenched my jaw. Stupid. What was I doing, getting sentimental now? We didn't have time for that.

"Fine," I said briskly. "Did you find it?"

"No," Georgia said. "Let's hope someone turns it into the lost and found." Which was exactly what she was scripted to say, but the look on her face didn't quite match up. She was still watching me, her brow wrinkled in concern. I didn't know why. I looked at a picture and got sad—so what?

"That sucks," I said mechanically. "Thanks anyway, Babs."

Babs said something good-natured, but I wasn't really listening. Suddenly, I wanted to get out of there. I ducked out of her office, my ill-gotten goods tucked up my sleeve. It was too warm in there. I didn't know how Babs could stand it.

"Jack, wait up." I could hear Georgia hurrying to catch up, but I didn't slow my pace. Couldn't linger on the casino floor, not unless we wanted to get dragged back into Babs's office after all. *"Jack."*

She wanted to talk about it. I could practically feel it oozing off her. Thinking about it, I could see why Georgia and I had never fallen into the easy rapport that Remy or Gabe and I did. Georgia liked communication and feelings and communicating about feelings. I had been raised to do neither of those things, and I didn't particularly want to change now.

"It's fine," I said tersely as we stepped out of the casino and into the hotel lobby. Sunlight cut through the tall windows, turning the atrium to gold. I took a deep breath, like I could hold that golden air in my lungs and keep it there forever. "Really, we don't have to talk about it."

Georgia's hand hooked around my elbow. She probably intended to gently slow me down, but when I didn't cooperate, she ended up yanking me to a stop. I spun around to face her, my face flushed.

She met my gaze squarely. Tourists flowed around us like a mindless herd of gazelle, threatening to mow us down with their wheeled luggage but flinching away at the last moment. "Jack," she said firmly. "Whatever happens, it's going to be okay."

I bristled. "Wow, I've never heard that one before—"

"*Listen*," she said, and I shut my mouth. She pushed a curl back behind her ear, her mouth set in quiet determination. "I was really close to my yiayia. She basically raised me when my parents were getting divorced. When the doctors told her that she was dying, I thought it was the end of the world. I didn't know how I was supposed to do this without her. I told her that, ugly crying and everything, and she took my hand, she looked me right in the eye, and she told me—you'll live."

I blinked, startled. That wasn't exactly the wise, grandmotherly advice I was expecting.

Georgia's mouth quirked in half a smile, but her eyes were still sad. "That was my reaction too," she said. "But later, months after she died, I realized she was right. She didn't say that it would be easy, or that it wouldn't hurt—but I lived. Even when I didn't think I could do it, when I just felt sorry for myself, I figured it out, and I lived."

I swallowed, but the lump in my throat wouldn't go any-where. "You don't think we can do this," I said, connecting the dots to what she wasn't saying. She was trying to prepare me for the worst—not that my mom was dying, but that my world was changing irrevocably. That there was nothing I could do about it.

I couldn't accept that.

"I wouldn't be here if I didn't think we could do this," Georgia said with enough sincerity that I had no choice but to believe her. She shrugged awkwardly, as if realizing in the aftermath of her speech that we were still standing in the middle of the lobby. "But if we can't—you'll live, Jack. And you'll have us there to help you figure it out."

I swallowed my pride, just for a moment. This was her way of saying that she cared. I didn't have to agree with it to know that it was important. "Thanks," I said, and I looked down at the marble tile beneath our feet. "Really. Thank you. I couldn't do this without you guys." I could see that now.

"Did you get the card?" she said, and I nearly sighed with relief at the permission to change the subject. We'd had our emotions; now we could put them back in the box where they belonged. Whew.

I smirked. "Of course I did." I flashed a corner of the badge before slipping it into my pocket. "C'mon, we'd better get back before Lucky makes Remy and Gabe start running laps." I punched the button for the elevator with my knuckle.

I'd almost regained my confidence that everything was A-okay when the elevator doors slid open and reminded me that there was still one very big obstacle in my path.

"Arthur." Peter Carlevaro's eyes slid past me, and his mouth curled unpleasantly. "And friend."

I almost stepped backward, like I could backpedal out of the elevator, but we'd automatically stepped inside, and the doors were already starting to close. The only thing worse than being stuck in an elevator with Peter Carlevaro for several painful floors would be abandoning Georgia to do it solo.

Okay. Fine. We were doing this.

"Carlevaro." I made a show of looking around. "No friends, I guess."

I could practically hear Georgia's eyes darting sideways when I said his name, but she covered her shock well, casually scrolling on her phone like she didn't even notice him standing there.

Carlevaro's mouth flattened into a thin line.

I considered hitting the button for one of the lower floors just to escape the way his presence made me itch to take a shower, but I didn't want to give in. This was *my* hotel, not his. I wasn't going to run away here, especially not with the conversation with Georgia heavy on my mind. I didn't want to just live—I wanted to *win*.

That, and it all begged the question: What the hell was he doing here?

"Miss me already?" I said as the elevator started upward, trying to goad him.

"Hmm. Hardly," he said blandly. He was dressed like every other businessman in the city, a dark suit with a thin tie and a collared shirt that looked like it was strangling him. His shaved head gleamed like he waxed it.

God, I hated him. I hoped he could feel it, like fire ants under his skin. Or at least indigestion.

"What do you think of the doors?" Carlevaro said.

"What?" I was too caught off guard to even sound incredulous.

"The doors, Arthur," he said impatiently. I wished he'd stop calling me that. He nodded toward the elevator doors. When closed, they formed a mural. Each elevator sported one of the Greek muses. Ours was Thalia, the muse of comedy. She smiled coyly back at us, her head crowned with ivy, holding a trumpet in one hand and a laughing mask in the other. "What do you think of them?"

"I hope they'll open soon." I wasn't even being rude—well, not entirely. I honestly didn't know what I was supposed to say to that. Who had opinions on elevator doors?

"I think they're tacky," Carlevaro said without needing to be asked. "I think I'll have them changed."

I froze.

"I do own a significant portion of the shares of the Golden Age Hotel and Casino," he continued. "Under different companies, of course, but you'll find it's all the same in the end." He titled his head, as smug as a cat. "That's why I'm here today, actually. I do believe your sister is interested in selling her share of the company. Which would make me the majority shareholder, now that I think about it."

"You're lying." My heart thundered in my chest, nearly too loud for me to hear my own voice. "Beth wouldn't do that."

Would she? She never wanted anything to do with Mom or the Golden Age or even being a Shannon, outside of seeing Kerry and me. I didn't even know she *had* shares in the company. Even if I had, I would have assumed she'd sold them a long time ago.

"Hand over the hotel she hates to someone who might be able to run it properly? Yes, that would be so unreasonable." He smirked. It made his skin pull tight over his skull, bony in all the wrong places. "Though we'll have to make more than a few changes. Starting with these doors, I think." The elevator dinged as it reached the thirty-second floor. "Think about what color you'd like, Arthur."

He stepped out of the elevator. The thirty-second floor, I remembered distantly, was where the business offices were.

The doors slid closed again, and something warm touched my wrist, making me jump. I'd almost forgotten Georgia was there until she put her hand on my arm.

"Jack." Not a question, just my name.

I blinked hard. "Fine," I lied. "I'm fine."

She didn't believe me. Of course she didn't. I didn't believe me. I hated how easily Carlevaro managed to rattle me. How was I supposed to ruin his life if I lost my nerve over elevator doors?

"He's going to get what's coming to him," Georgia said. Quiet but firm. Even if she didn't believe it, she knew I had to. "You're going to keep these hideous elevator doors whether you like it or not."

It startled a laugh out of me, and the world snapped back into place a little. Carlevaro's appearance threw me off my rhythm, the new threat to the Golden Age even more so, but nothing had really changed. Of course Carlevaro wanted the Golden Age. I knew that, even if I hadn't quite thought it through. He wanted the whole Strip under his thumb, and the Golden Age was one of its jewels.

Nothing had changed. We still had a plan. We were still going to do this.

"Lucky me," I said with a lopsided smile.

"One more thing," Georgia said as the elevator opened on our floor. *"Arthur?"*

Oh Jesus. "Trust me," I said flatly. "You don't want to know."

♠

We returned to a riot. I had no choice but to let them take a break from blackjack.

"Pizza! Pizza! Pizza!" Gabe and Remy chanted, high-fiving over the table rhythmically.

"Pizza?" Lucky wrinkled her nose. "I took you guys to an Iron Chef–rated restaurant and now you want pizza?"

"I'm sure they'll have chicken tenders somewhere on the menu," I said, handily dodging her foot. When Beth handed me the Onyx card, I hadn't really expected to end up spending it at a Pizza Hut, but whatever. At least there (probably?) wouldn't be any acrobats involved.

And it was better than dwelling on the elevator ride with

Carlevaro. Still, I couldn't help but feel trepidation crawl up my spine as we marched toward the elevator in search of pizza. I couldn't believe that out of everything in the world, Carlevaro had decided to ruin elevator doors for me.

Speaking of. The elevator doors slid open to reveal Kerry standing inside, her hand in a bag of Cheetos. She was wearing her hoodie like it was a uniform—I couldn't tell if she was wearing the same one every day or if she just had seven identical black hoodies. With Kerry, anything was possible.

"Hey," she said. She surreptitiously pulled her hand out of the Cheetos bag.

"Hey," I said back. Gabe froze with one foot already in the elevator, shooting me a backward look. They all hung back, waiting to take my cue. I didn't particularly want to ride in an elevator with my sister and four of my closest friends, but awkwardly declining the otherwise empty elevator was a much, much worse option.

So I stepped in and the rest followed suit, clearing their throats and shuffling their feet, the conversation dead and replaced with a truly painful silence. The elevator doors slid closed again. Erato, the muse of love poetry, winked back at me.

Fine, it was up to me, then. Thanks, guys.

"Kerry, this is everyone." I gestured half-heartedly around the elevator. "Everyone, this is Kerry, my sister."

My friends chorused their hellos, and Kerry waved, sinking deeper into her hoodie. It was weird, standing between them, trying to figure out where the Jack my friends knew and the Jack that Kerry knew intersected. I wasn't sure which one was most real.

I felt bigger around my friends, more colorful in a way I never was in Elkhollow, or even in Vegas when they weren't there. It made me realize just how much better I felt since they'd arrived, even after running into Peter Carlevaro. Most of all, it made me realize how lonely Kerry looked.

Guilt settled in my stomach. I was sure Beth offered Kerry the same deal—go back to school if she wanted, invite friends to the city to take her mind off things. Kerry wasn't the problem child; I was, so to speak, but Beth worried about her too. Yet Kerry appeared to have gone with neither option, unless the Cheetos bag counted as a friend.

Beth was busy keeping things together, possible betrayal aside. I was busy breaking the law. And Kerry was alone.

"Hey," I said before I could think better of it. "We're going out for pizza, if you want to go with."

Kerry blinked owlishly. "Uh," she said, as taken aback by the olive branch as I was. I'd always been closer to Kerry than to Beth, or at least close in a different way. We fought more, but that's just what being close meant. But we didn't really hang out with each other's friends. Since we went away to schools on opposite sides of the country, we didn't really hang out at all. "Sure."

She smiled a funny little smile. I mirrored it. It was as close to a Hallmark moment as we got.

"In that case," Gabe said, throwing an arm around my shoulders, "we should *probably* tell you our names."

MYSTERIOUS-STRANGER DANGER

WE ENDED UP AT A PLACE CALLED PIZZADOME, WHICH Lucky swore up and down was her favorite place in the city. After her mom's restaurant, she qualified belatedly.

Stepping inside, I couldn't help but be unimpressed. The place was, true to its name, a domed building with a linoleum floor made to look like we were walking across the cheesy expanse of a supreme pizza. It was how I imagined it felt like to walk on the moon, except with a significantly higher risk of slipping on grease.

"How old were you the last time you came here?" I asked skeptically.

"Okay," Lucky said, "maybe it's been a while. But pizza is pizza."

"This is fun," Remy said as we all wedged ourselves into a circular booth. They gestured at the roof. "It's a dome!"

"Uh-huh." But *I* was the weird one for thinking that high-stakes math was fun.

The ensuing negotiations over pizza toppings rivaled a

United Nations General Assembly in both scale and intensity. Somehow it resulted in three large pizzas for five people, plus an order of chicken tenders for Lucky.

"Where'd the blackjack thing even start, Jack?" Remy asked after the dust had settled and we all emerged alive. They leaned forward on their elbows, between Gabe and Lucky. I had gotten stuck on the end again, Kerry squashed between me and Georgia. I shot Remy an alarmed look, very aware that my sister was sitting next to me, picking at the sleeves of her hoodie. My family didn't know about Blackjack Club back at Elkhollow. Kerry wouldn't care—not like Beth would—but it opened up a lot of conversations I didn't really want to have over a chipped Formica table while nursing a Dr Pepper.

Remy caught the look and backtracked. "I, uh, I mean, where did you learn how to play?" they asked. They winked subtly in a way that was meant to say *nailed it* but came out more like *I'm having a facial spasm*.

I rubbed my fingertips against the condensation on my glass. "My mom taught me," I said, which might as well have been inviting an elephant into the room. I kind of wished I'd let Remy spill the beans on Blackjack Club instead. Running an underground blackjack game in the basement of a prep school was weird, I could admit to that, but people did a lot of weird things in western Massachusetts. This was a little more personal.

"We used to play every night, before I went away to school," I said. "Just a couple of hands, whatever she could make time for. She was busy a lot, so it was an easy game to pick up and put down again. We'd bet stuff like—I don't know, if I won, I got to stay up an hour later or I got extra dessert. If she won, I had to clean my room or get my homework done early, or something." I knew she wouldn't really notice if I didn't uphold my end of the bargain, but I did it anyway. The stakes felt like they had weight if I did. I hadn't realized that maybe that was the reason I'd gravitated to blackjack at Elkhollow until I said the words out loud. I shrugged with one shoulder. "It was fun."

Gabe nodded, his forehead furrowed. "Not gonna lie, that sounds a bit like Baby's First Gambling Addiction. It explains a lot though."

I stuck out my tongue and stepped on his foot under the table, secretly eager to jump on the distraction.

"Shut up," Lucky said, and I looked up in surprise. Lucky wasn't really the defending type. "I think it's sweet." I remembered the way Chef Favreau breezed through our introductions at her restaurant. Lucky probably knew a little something about taking borrowed time when you could get it.

And now I was out of it. I didn't imagine the prison guards would let me bring a deck of cards into the visiting area.

"Uh, bathroom," I said quickly, glad that I'd gotten stuck on the end. I turned away and slipped out of the booth before I could do something stupid. Like cry.

I couldn't *actually* go to the bathroom. I'd experienced it enough to recognize the fragile, verge-of-tears feeling trembling inside my chest, and I didn't have twenty minutes to spend in a bathroom stall trying to get it under control. The best strategy was to just buy myself a couple of minutes to shove all those feelings back down where they belonged and compose myself again. I ducked to the left, into a mazelike arcade done up to look like a casino. Vegas was still Vegas, even when it was a domed pizza joint.

I wandered through the arcade games, sparing them a half-hearted sort of interest. They didn't even take coins but connected to an app you had to download. How modern. I fiddled with the buttons as I passed, considering who I could get to play air hockey with me later. I squinted at the instructions on the side of the table, trying to figure out how the app thing worked.

Something shifted in the periphery of my vision. Something pink.

I froze, careful not to give anything away. It could be a lot of things—a T-shirt, a backpack, anyone else in the whole world who decided to dye their hair pink. But it wasn't. A shiver crawled up my neck. I knew when I was being watched. As a third-generation criminal, it was worked into my DNA.

I took out my phone, pretending to be messing with the arcade app when I was really opening the camera. I tilted it carefully until I got her in the frame. It was the girl from the Avalon Club with the pink hair, the one who had been watching me. What was she doing *here*? I didn't expect the

Avalon Club and PizzaDome to have any overlap in clientele that wasn't, well, *us*.

The answer was that she was here to watch me, clearly, but I couldn't figure out *why*. I didn't know her, or at least I didn't think I did. Elkhollow didn't let you dye your hair unnatural colors, a policy I'd been press-ganged into signing several petitions against, so she wasn't just a student on vacation. If I knew her—if she knew *me*—it was from around here. I didn't love that.

But I didn't want to confront her in the middle of a PizzaDome, Kerry and my friends sitting a few dozen feet away. I didn't really want to confront her at all, period. I just wanted to be a little more informed so I could avoid her better.

The best offense is reconnaissance. Yeah, yeah, Granddad. I got it.

I took a picture of her. Or I tried.

And I succeeded, technically. I got a clear picture of her face, if a bit shaky. The problem was the fact that somehow the flash had gotten turned on. So instead of the kid holding his phone at a funny angle, trying to understand how to play air hockey, I was definitely the kid semi-successfully taking a stalker picture of a girl. Great! Knocked it out of the park, Jack.

I looked up quickly, but the girl was already gone. I'd gotten what I wanted, but now she knew that I'd seen her, and I wasn't sure I wanted that yet. I wasn't sure of a lot of things, at the moment.

I frowned. There was something stuck in one of the arcade games that wasn't there before. A piece of paper tucked between two red buttons. I looked around carefully, to be sure the pink-haired girl wasn't still there, and slinked closer.

It wasn't just paper; it was a playing card. I tugged it free. The queen of clubs, staring back at me, unimpressed. I flipped it over. A phone number had been scrawled across the back in Sharpie marker.

Um. Okay. Was that supposed to be flirting? Because I didn't like it.

"Jack."

I jumped out of my skin, hiding the card in my hand like it was contraband. "I thought we could maybe play air hockey later," I blurted, scrambling for my bathroom cover story. The good news was that I wasn't so torn up on the inside anymore, only because the pink-haired girl posed a more pressing problem than what the hell I was going to do if Mom went to jail. She was an unknown variable in an already very precarious operation. I didn't need more of those.

I turned around, expecting to see Remy. Remy always saw through me in the least convenient ways, and the bathroom excuse had been thin to begin with. But instead I found Kerry.

"Oh," I said. I wasn't sure if I was disappointed or relieved. "Are you looking for the bathroom?" I didn't think they were as hard to find as I pretended they were.

Kerry raised her eyebrows, a clear universal signal that she wasn't buying my bullshit. Well. It was worth a try. My phone lit up with a Hullabaloo notification.

[remy]: did you get lost?
[lucky]: did you fall in?
[georgia]: you wanted pineapple on your pizza, right?
[jack]: sorry, I got distracted by the air-hockey table
[gabe]: AIR HOCKEY
[lucky]: oh i'm gonna kick your ASS at air hockey
[gabe]: are you sure there isn't a height requirement?
[gabe]: jaaack she spilled my drink):

Kerry was studying me when I looked up from my phone, her hands buried in the pocket of her hoodie. She leaned against the air-hockey table. "Does Beth know your friends aren't actually from Elkhollow?"

I considered my options. Kerry didn't lie, but she knew what one sounded like. She wasn't likely to believe something just because she wanted it to be true. She got that from Mom. I shrugged and slid my phone back into my pocket, the picture of the pink-haired girl making it heavy. I wanted to get back to the room and show the others. I wasn't hungry anymore.

"What tipped you off?" I asked. "The fact that I've never had school friends before, so why start now?" Kind of bitchy but true.

Kerry definitely wasn't attending my pity party. She narrowed her eyes. "One of them is, like, twelve."

"Fourteen and a half."

"Jack," she said, and it wasn't the same as when Beth tried to admonish me, but that didn't mean I had to like it.

"Are you going to tell Beth?" It was a borderline accusation. Kerry could undo everything in an instant, and there was nothing I could do about it. I could threaten that I was going to live with Dad all I wanted, but Beth wouldn't forgive this. She would see it as a betrayal of her trust, the exact betrayal she was waiting for since the moment she handed me the Onyx card, and she probably wouldn't be wrong. The truth would send her spiraling into mom mode so fast she'd probably launch through the atmosphere and hand Peter Carlevaro the keys to the Golden Age along the way.

Kerry was quiet for too long. My phone buzzed in my pocket, reminding me that my friends were still waiting for us.

"No," she said at last, digging the toe of her shoe into the scratched linoleum. "I'm not a snitch."

I exhaled. All right, maybe I'd been a little worried, but I didn't want Kerry to know that. It wasn't good for older sisters to know they held power over you.

"Where did you meet them anyway?" Kerry sounded more incredulous than suspicious. I couldn't tell if it was because of the fourteen-and-a-half-year-old thing or the Jack-doesn't-play-well-with-others thing.

I froze. Either way, I didn't really have a good answer. I couldn't really mention the ace thing, even if that was what brought us together—it wasn't my place to out them, even if I was reasonably sure Kerry wouldn't care. For that matter, I wasn't really interested in outing myself either. I had enough on my plate without having to break out the *asexuality spectrum and what it means* presentation in the middle of the PizzaDome.

". . . Online," I said, as suspiciously as possible. Why did I have to say it like that? It was *true*. Why couldn't I say a normal thing like a normal person?

"Right." Kerry gave me a sideways look.

"We should get back," I said hastily, ready to move away from the subject as much as possible. I was already wishing we'd just ordered room service instead. "Before they start thinking you kidnapped me."

I stepped around her without waiting for an answer, my nerves prickling with the idea that I was being watched. By the pink-haired girl, by Kerry, even by Carlevaro. There were too many eyes on me and no room to fail.

"You know, just because I'm your sister," Kerry said to my back, "doesn't mean we can't be on the same side."

I faltered. What did that mean? I turned around, but whatever goodwill Kerry was hinting at must have run out, because she only shouldered past me.

I watched her go. Possibilities started to bloom in the back of my head, but I crushed them before they could barely start. It was too late to change course now. Kerry thought I needed her help, but I didn't. I had everything under control.

I pressed my thumb against the corner of the queen of clubs, the thick paper creasing under my fingernail. Well. Almost everything.

CRUSHING

"I DON'T THINK IT'S REALLY THAT BAD," REMY SAID FOR the tenth time since we got back to the room. Gabe had a new stain across his shirt from where Lucky had knocked over his soda, which he'd been bemoaning since. Georgia was struck by some affliction where she couldn't stop talking about Kerry this, Kerry that, Kerry said she'd look at her art portfolio, wasn't that so nice?

And I had a fat lip, from where Remy had hit an air-hockey puck so hard, it flipped over the table and punched me in the teeth.

"It'th fine," I agreed, mumbling past the ice pack pressed against my swollen lip. It really was fine. Except for the fact that I could still taste blood. Just a little bit.

"Kerry might know how to help the swelling," Georgia suggested less than helpfully.

If Kerry had anything to do besides laugh at my mis-fortune, she hadn't volunteered that information before we parted ways. She did find time to give me a sideways look, however. Whatever. I'd learned from my mistake—keep my friends and family separate, at least until we were finished breaking the law. Especially if it meant avoiding any more glowing testimonials from Georgia.

I ignored her, instead pulling out my phone and bringing up the picture of the pink-haired girl. *No more secrets*, I reminded myself. "Have any of you seen her?" I asked, setting it on the coffee table.

I quickly lifted my head up before they all leaned in at once, narrowly avoiding further cranial trauma.

Lucky slid my phone to a better angle. "Cool hair," she said helpfully.

Great. I would let her know that next time I caught her stalking me.

"Wait," Remy said, pulling the phone back from Lucky. They swiped their fingers across the screen and enlarged the picture, focusing on the girl's grainy face. "I've seen her before. Where have I seen her before?"

"She was in the Avalon Club the night we went," I said. The picture caught the pink-haired girl in the same moment she saw the flash, her eyes widening slightly. She was moving, like Bigfoot had infiltrated a PizzaDome arcade. "I thought I saw her watching us leave, but I didn't think much of it. Until now."

"Oh. I guess that could be it." They rubbed their chin thoughtfully. "So what? You think she's following you?"

Well, it sounded paranoid when they said it like that, but it didn't seem that unlikely considering everything else that had happened so far. I pulled out the queen of clubs and showed them the number on the other side. "She left this behind."

They descended on it like a pack of jackals.

"Is that her *number*?" Lucky held it up to the light.

Gabe snatched it from her hand, waving it around like a golden ticket. "Well, *that* explains it," he said. "She has a crush on you, obviously."

"On Jack?" Georgia laughed.

"Shut up." I snatched the card back, my cheeks burning. If I looked at Remy, I'd probably spontaneously combust, but I couldn't help but notice that they hadn't said anything. What did that mean? Did it mean anything at all? "What do any of you know about crushes?"

What did *I* know, frankly? I hadn't had a crush on anything that wasn't a cartoon character before—well, we don't need to get into all that again. You get the point. The whole Remy thing was new, and unexplored, and it would stay that way or I would die. Actually, considering this conversation, dying was an option either way.

"Hey!" Gabe said. "Georgia dated that girl for like a year."

"Four months," Georgia said hastily. "It just felt like a year."

"She was weird," Remy said, speaking up for the first time. They wrinkled their nose, and I looked away again quickly.

They were all starting to make me doubt myself. Maybe I was reading too much into it. Not everything in life was related to drama on a criminal scale. Maybe she *did* just have a crush on me.

No, I didn't like that. It had to be something else.

"She does *not* have a crush on me," I interjected, before they could descend into critiquing the girl Georgia had dated for four months last year. Who *was*, for the record, a bit weird. Or at least could talk for so long about the doomed Franklin Expedition of 1845 for three hours straight, which is at least uncommon. "She was at the Avalon Club. She left me a playing card. It means something. Everything means something." Is that what conspiracy theorists sounded like? Probably. I was two steps away from busting out corkboard and some red string.

"So call her." Lucky shrugged. "She gave you her number."

"*What*? No!" Remy and I squawked at the same time. We locked eyes, startled. My face was steadily going from pink to red.

Lucky squinted, her brow furrowed like she wasn't quite sure what she was seeing. "All right," she said. "Just an idea."

A stupid idea. I didn't call anyone, for anything, if I could help it, especially not a girl whose primary personality trait was *stalking*. I thought we, as a generation, understood that. This wasn't the '80s anymore. I'd watched enough true crime to know that sort of thing was how you got serial-killed.

"Does this change the plan?" Remy asked. I reluctantly dragged my eyes back to them, trying to control my blush even a little bit. Remy's face was carefully neutral.

"No," I said slowly, stealing a glance around the group.

Gabe gave a little shrug. They didn't know where Remy was taking this either. The girl had something to do with the Avalon Club, but frankly, a lot of people did. Whatever she meant to the Avalon Club, or to me, or anything else—the show would go on. It had to.

"Then it doesn't matter," Remy said decisively. They picked up the deck of cards from where Georgia left it before dinner, fussing with the box. "We should keep practicing. Before any pink girls start leaving chocolates at the door." The joke landed a little awkwardly.

Gabe's eyebrows went up, and I saw Georgia exchange a look with him. Lucky had her laptop open again, apparently bored with the conversation. The energy in the room was . . . weird. I shifted my weight. I desperately wished Gabe hadn't joked about the crush thing. Between my reaction and Remy's strangely firm counterreaction, it gave me a little too much to think about.

"Yeah," I said, grateful for the change of subject, even if it felt about as smooth as grinding gears. "Good thinking."

♠

Gabe cornered me that night, after Georgia had passed out on the ottoman and Remy took it upon themself to distract Lucky from overworking herself with their collection of memes.

I was staring inside the mini fridge, trying to decide between chocolate and mint-chocolate-chip ice cream when Gabe sidled up, planting one hand on top of the fridge.

"Can we guy talk?" he asked frankly, leaning in like it was a secret. Or just to meet my eyes. I wasn't *short*, but Gabe was built like an observation tower. Tall, sharp, and not meant to withstand hurricane-force winds.

I blinked at him, holding the mint chocolate chip in my hand like an idiot. The cold was starting to burn, but the idea of guy talk scared me more than frostbite. "Uh," I said. "I thought you said that *male* was too small a word to correctly encompass your identity."

Gabe plucked the ice cream from my hand and shoved it back into the freezer. My spoon drooped sadly in my other hand. So much for midnight ice cream. "Can we talk where you don't try to get out of it by bringing up the complexity of gender?"

Sometimes it was all too obvious that Gabe was going to be a lawyer someday. "I guess," I said warily. I wasn't sure what *guy talk* entailed, or gender-nonconforming talk, but as someone who tried to avoid any kind of talk, I wasn't looking forward to it.

"Where are you guys going?" Remy peeked over their phone. They were stretched across the mustard-yellow couch, a pillow stuffed between their head and Lucky's side. Lucky was using their head as an armrest, still working on her laptop. Remy's attempts at distraction didn't work well enough. Not that I ever expected them too. I wasn't fully convinced that Lucky ever slept.

"The gym!" Gabe chirped, throwing an arm around my shoulder. I looked down. I was wearing sweatpants and an

Elkhollow T-shirt. Gabe was wearing every piece of wearable Golden Age memorabilia he'd been able to find in the lobby gift shop. The basketball shorts with gold stripes down the side were almost too much to look at.

"The gym?" Remy laughed. They paused. "Oh, you're serious? All right, then. Have fun."

"Thanks," I said flatly. Gabe could have put a little more effort in the believability factor. I'd been to a gym once, when Dad decided that sitting in a sauna for two hours was the epitome of father-son bonding. I'd never seen so much chest hair in my life.

"Do we really have to go to the gym?" I asked as we stepped out into the hall. Guy talk was bad. Guy talk on adjacent treadmills was a nightmare.

"Oh, hell no," Gabe said. "Show me someplace cool."

♠

I decided to take Gabe to one of the floating gardens. There were three on different floors, so I took us to lowest one, farthest away from the suite. It jutted out from the third floor, overlooking the largest of the pools. It was going on midnight, but the party was in full swing below. The pool pulsed different colors in time with the music, and someone whooped as they won big at swim-up blackjack. They'd lose it all again just as quickly.

It didn't feel right, watching the Golden Age carry on without Mom as if nothing had changed. Business hadn't flagged since Mom's very public arrest—if anything, it was going stronger than ever, like spectators at a car crash or flies on a corpse.

It felt that way after Granddad died too. Like the world should have stopped moving but hadn't gotten the memo. I needed a minute to stop and breathe.

No time for that. Not when there was guy talk to be had.

"If this is about the pink girl, I really don't care," I said hastily, turning away from the pool below. Gabe was inspecting one of the flowering bushes. "It's nothing. Remy is right, we shouldn't let it distract us."

"Can I pluck one of the flowers?"

Speaking of distractions. "*Gabe.*"

"Sorry! I thought they, like, basically belong to you. I wanted to put one in my hair." He let his hand drop. "Anyway, it's not about the pink girl. It's about Remy."

I blinked. "What about them?"

Oh God, did Gabe—? No, Gabe was aromantic. He'd always been clear that he wasn't interested in anything to do with romantic relationships, and certainly not with Remy. Thankfully. Gabe was funny and charming and, well, *tall*. I couldn't compete with that.

Not that anyone was competing for anything, but I couldn't help the thoughts that flashed through my head. Why would Gabe want to talk about Remy? I thought guy talk meant we were going to talk about me. Or, like . . . football.

Gabe gave me a pitying look, and I was vindictively glad

I didn't give him permission to pluck the flower. He didn't deserve the flower.

He put a hand on my shoulder. "About your big, squishy crush on them, dude," he said with the utmost sincerity, and a little bit of remorse, like he was delivering a terminal diagnosis.

My brain short-circuited. Wires actually snapped, sending sparks in every direction as they careened wildly around my brain. "I don't—" I scoffed, breathless. "I really don't— You're being stupid."

Gabe squeezed my shoulder, his pitying smile intensifying. "Let it all out, bud."

"Shut up," I huffed. "You don't know what you're talking about."

He just nodded knowingly. "Go on."

"I don't have a crush on *anybody*," I insisted. Crushes were stupid. Crushes were infatuation with the idea of someone, not the actual person. "I don't have a crush on *Remy*." A total waste of time. How could I know someone else well enough to love them when I hardly knew myself? And if a crush wasn't love—well, then what was the point at *all*? I never understood how people at school could be so wrapped up in each other one minute and then done the next. I didn't know how they could stand the emotional roller coaster. High risk, low reward. It was a bad bet.

My shoulders drooped. "I don't . . . *want* to have a crush on Remy," I said pathetically. Because I did, and Gabe had seen it, no matter how desperately I tried to bury it. Because

189

I *did* know Remy. I knew them better than I knew myself—or at least if we were books, theirs was the more interesting one. Bent cover, cracked spine. The kind you check out from the library so often, they tell you just to keep it.

"That's what I thought." Gabe gave me a little pat on the shoulder. Were crushes always supposed to be something you comfort people over? I felt like I was at the funeral for my dignity. "So what are you going to do about it?"

I shrugged off his hand. "I'm going to stay focused," I said, steeling my resolve. Now that we were here, I was beginning to see how dangerous this line of questioning really was. It was bad enough that Gabe could tell. I didn't need him playing matchmaker too. "I told you, Remy was right. We don't need any distractions." I turned back toward the pool below us, leaning against the railing surrounding the floating garden. The night was surprisingly cool. I'd forgotten how chilly the desert could get after the sun went down. "Why would I do anything anyway?"

I'd already run the scenarios in my head. Each concluded more or less the same way: Being around Remy was the highest reward I could think of, and there was no way I was risking it. I didn't want Gabe to tell me the odds because I wasn't betting.

Gabe slouched against the railing, resting his chin on his folded arms. He scoffed. "Because they might feel the same?" he suggested like it was the most obvious thing in the world. "Because you saw how defensive they got when we were talking about the pink girl? Come *on*, Jack."

"They want to focus on the objective," I said, carefully neutral, feeling stupid for using the word *objective*. But it was true. Remy knew how important this all was to me. I wanted to stay focused too. "This is a big puzzle for them. They can't help but try to figure it out."

"Do they want to solve the puzzle?" Gabe said. "Or solve it with *you*?"

I shook my head. "We're all going back to where we came from before long," I said, ignoring the fact that I didn't know what that meant for me—if I'd stay right where I was or go back to Elkhollow. "This isn't real. This is like . . . a vacation. Or a weird mass hallucination." Gabe shot me a sideways look. All right, so I wasn't a poet. "We have to go back to real life after this. I'm not going to mess it up for no reason."

Remy wasn't going to chase me down in the airport or show up in my English class one day. Maybe if this were a love story, but we've been over that already. I had to be realistic. I wanted Mom back. That was what was important. It felt like tempting fate in a dangerous way, trying to have my cake and eat it too.

"Hmm," Gabe hummed, unconvinced. He reached out and tickled a palm frond where it stretched out over the railing. I could feel the beat of the bass from the party through the concrete. The DJ must have been right below us. "If you say so," he said. "I won't push, because I'm polite, and it's your business, and my mom raised me right—but don't mistake me, I want to." He pushed up off the railing, stretching his freakishly long arms over his head like a cat lounging in the sun. "But I'm here if you need me, man. Just don't look so hard toward the future that you forget the people you want in it."

I wasn't entirely sure what that was supposed to mean, and I didn't want to examine it. I wasn't going to take advice from a guy wearing a Golden Age limited-edition tank top. "What do you know about crushes anyway?" I complained. "You don't even get crushes." I assumed. Aromanticism was a bit hard to pin down sometimes, but then again, so was asexuality. It was more of a spectrum than a paint-by-number. "Should I really be taking advice from you?"

"Jack," Gabe said, exasperated. He put a hand over his chest like I physically wounded him. "If I've told you once, I've told you a thousand times . . . coaches don't play."

LET'S GET OUR STORY STRAIGHT

WE HAD TO GET MOVING. OUR FAUX YOUTH CON-
ference was only three weeks long. After that, my friends
had to get on planes back to their real lives, Mom would be
in jail, and Peter Carlevaro would be the uncontested king
of the Las Vegas Strip.

Unless we did something about it. Fast.

"All right." Lucky closed her laptop and set it on the coffee
table. It was almost weird to see her without it now. It was
starting to feel like Lucky was part of the decor, lodged
in the corner of the couch, surrounded by crumpled chip
bags and unrecognizable bits of technology that she'd had
overnight-expressed to her. She held up two keycards—both
golden, both with the words *Avalon Club* written in elegant
white script. "Bet you can't even tell which is the fake."

"That one's more scuffed," Remy said, pointing to the
one on the right. "So it must be the older one."

"Shut up," Lucky said cheerfully. She handed me the
original, which I gladly accepted. I'd lent it to her for the sake

of theatrics and to double-check the print shop had gotten the duplicate right, but I didn't like being without it.

Lucky handed the duplicate card to Gabe. "Don't lose it," she warned, her eyes narrowing dangerously. For someone who didn't even weigh a hundred pounds, she managed to be intimidating.

"Me?" Gabe blinked down at the card in his hand.

"Him?" Georgia agreed indignantly. "Where's mine? He can't even play!"

"I'm really good at saying 'hit me,' though," Gabe said, holding his card against his chest with smug satisfaction. "It's harder than you thi— *Augh*! She hit *me*!"

Lucky shot me a look. Evidently taking the heat for this decision was above her pay grade. *Fine.*

"We decided to only make one duplicate," I said, pausing to allow for the requisite chorus of groans. From Remy and Georgia, at least. Gabe gleefully held his card with his fingertips, leaning safely out of Georgia's range. "I know, I know—but one new file in the system is a lot easier to overlook than three."

"So what about us?" Georgia asked. "No offense, but— you kind of need me."

Kind of was an understatement. Remy and Gabe had improved, and I was proud of them, but in the way a parent is proud when their kid starts coloring inside the lines. I made a big deal about it, but that didn't make them da Vinci. Georgia was far and away my best player, even when she wasn't card counting.

"You'll be there—both of you," I said, before Remy could pipe up. They leaned forward, their chin perched on their knuckles, elbows planted on their knees. *Guy talk* with Gabe flashed through my mind, and I looked away quickly, finding a piece of furniture to focus on. A clock shaped like a star stared back at me, orange balls at the end of each of its rays. "They let Remy in with me the first time, so we can only assume that a plus-one is a normal thing. Remy and I have already been seen there together, so it doesn't make sense to make them a false identity. I'll use the original card, and Remy will be my plus-one."

Gabe was boring holes in me with his stare now, I could feel it. If there wasn't a coffee table between us, I would have kicked him in his overgrown shins.

"Gabe, you're still Gabriel Gutiérrez," Lucky said, taking over where her expertise came in. She tossed him a manila envelope. Very FBI, except there were only two pieces of paper stapled together inside. "Except, like, cooler. Now you're the son of a big oil executive."

"Aw." Gabe frowned down at his new identity. "That's problematic."

"You're also a big environmentalist." She leaned forward and tapped the bottom of the page. "Check out your Twitter. It's good."

He perked up again. "Better!" He flipped through the pages. "Cool, I'm rebellious but in a rich way. I probably go to Jack's school."

"Hey," I protested flatly.

"You did, actually." Lucky pointed to a different part of the page.

"That's probably where I learned blackjack," Gabe said proudly, flipping the manila envelope closed and holding it possessively against his chest. We were going to have a hard time getting him to give up Gabe, the oil-heir environmentalist, when we were done.

"Don't tell people that," I said. "It's not exactly a ringing endorsement." Speaking of people who could actually play blackjack, I turned to Georgia. "You'll be his plus-one. Just be yourself, except posing as Gabe's girlfriend."

Georgia was grimacing before I even finished the sentence. "Do I have to? C'mon, you guys know I have better taste than that."

Gabe threw an arm around her shoulders, leaning against her until she had to laugh. "Gabe and Georgia," he cooed. "Aw, our monogrammed towels are gonna be so cute when we get married."

"*Married?*" Georgia laughed and pushed back, rearranging his cheek with her palm. "Nope. Can't do it. Too unrealistic. Why can't *I* be the oil baron? Or Jack's girlfriend, at *least.*"

"You can't be Jack's girlfriend," Gabe said, moving Georgia's hand from where it was smushing his mouth into interesting shapes. "Remy is already his"—Remy looked up— "significant other."

And that's the story about how I strangled Gabriel Gutiérrez to death with my own two hands. Thanks for reading!

I didn't kill Gabe, but I wanted to. Instead I choked and tried to cover it by clearing my throat as my ears went red. I slid my phone off the coffee table. If school taught me one thing, it was how to text without looking.

> **Jack Shannon**
> STOP

> **Gabe**
> I'M HELPING

> **Jack Shannon**
> UR NOT HELPING

"*Significant other* is so awkward," Remy was complaining. "You sound like my grandmother."

Wait, why was Remy's grandmother talking about significant others?

"*Other half*," Georgia said, sickly sweet.

"Partner," Gabriel suggested in a thick Texan drawl.

"Comrade," Lucky said.

"*Anyway*," I said, cutting through the ensuing laughter. "Gabe is the oil baron because he's the most obnoxious."

> **Gabe**
> All right that felt personal

I pushed a hand through my hair and straightened my back, trying to compose myself again. The plan. This was about the plan. I might be people stupid, Remy stupid especially, but I knew the plan. "We work in teams," I said. "Georgia and I will maintain our cover by playing while

Remy and Gabe run reconnaissance. Any dirt on Carlevaro is great, but we really want to dig up this little black book of his. If there's a possibility it's hidden in plain sight at the Avalon Club, we need to find it."

They all nodded, their expressions locked in varying degrees of determination and excitement. Or slight nausea, in my case. It was happening. We were doing this.

"Wait," Georgia said. "Lucky, what about you?"

Lucky and I exchanged a look. That particular problem was one I'd been putting off since the beginning, so I was surprised when she came to me about it herself. Despite being the backbone of the operation, the flaws in her involvement beyond this point were obvious.

Lucky cleared her throat, toying with one of her hair ties—a nervous habit. "All right. Let's be honest, guys," she said. "I'm fourteen."

"And a half," I offered.

Lucky gave me a lopsided smile, but six months didn't change anything. "You guys can all pass for eighteen. This place might be all kinds of illegal, but I think they'd notice if a kid like me waltzed in," she said.

Also true. I'd offered her an even more truncated crash course in playing, but she hadn't been interested. Lucky didn't pull any punches—she knew what was up, and she wasn't going to waste any time pretending she didn't. And if she could avoid unnecessary math doing it, she told me, even better. Evidently tech smart and math smart weren't necessarily the same thing.

"So what are you going to do?" Remy asked, looking concerned.

"We can't go without Lucky," Gabe said, turning to me, as serious as I'd ever seen him. He was still repenting for their fight, I guess. Catholic guilt. I've heard it's a hell of a drug.

"It's fine, guys," Lucky said, waving their concern away. "Really. I'll be busy enough doing the real work while you guys pretend to be hotshots. Carlevaro is bound to have security cameras all over that place. If I can get into them, I'm your eyes in the sky." She paused, shooting me a significant look. "And . . ."

That was where our opinions divided. I rolled my eyes. "Lucky thinks she might be able to hack Carlevaro's system and find something on him that way," I said, doubt coloring my voice.

"It's the twenty-first century," Lucky argued. "Everything is online somewhere. *Everything*." And if it was online, she could get to it.

But I wasn't convinced. "The Carlevaros are old-school," I said, shaking my head. "I doubt he would keep his top-secret, empire-building files on a server that could get hacked from hundreds of miles away."

"I know I make it look easy, but it's not exactly *that* simple," Lucky said blandly.

"But it's worth exploring," I conceded. I didn't like leaving Lucky behind, but she was right. Someday we'd all be over twenty-one and scamming whoever we wanted, whenever we wanted, but for the moment we had limitations. All we could do was make the most out of them.

"You never know what you'll find," Lucky said with a truly sinister smile. For someone so small, she packed a lot of malice into her body. I could only be glad it was being used for me instead of against me. "You just need to know where to look."

A LEOPARD CHANGES
HIS SPOTS

"IT'S NOT THAT BAD," REMY SAID, STIFLING GIGGLES behind one hand. Generous, to pretend they weren't laughing at my misfortune. At least it would have been if I couldn't see their shoulders shaking.

"I really, *really*"—How many times could I say *really* before it lost the emphasis?—"don't think this was necessary." I tugged on the collar of my leopard-print button-down. Well. Not *mine*. Strictly speaking, it was Gabe's, which was why it was stupidly long to accommodate his stretched-out body. I'd just been forced into it for the evening.

We were in the elevator at the Imperium, gliding toward the twenty-ninth floor again. The belly of the beast, swallowed whole by the Imperium's chrome-plated teeth. I felt like Jonah inside the whale, and I didn't know how it was supposed to end. Bible study was never high on the list of Shannon family activities.

"You're the heir to a casino empire," Remy said, composing themself enough to drop their hand. Their mouth kept squirming, like they had to physically hold back a smirk every time they saw my unwilling fashion choices. I thanked God that the walls of the elevator weren't mirrored. "You saw everyone in there last time. You've got to look the part."

"*Heir* is a little dramatic," I muttered. "I'm not inheriting a kingdom." I tugged at my shirt again, self-conscious. Despite having Dad's genetics, I never inherited his love for loud prints. None of us did. There was a reason I'd gone into illegal gambling, and not show choir, when it came time to pick an extracurricular activity.

I forced back a spike of nerves. Actually, I might not be inheriting anything if this didn't go right. Not if Carlevaro was having meetings with Beth and talking about shares and stakeholders. I resisted the urge to kick the Imperium's elevator doors, like Carlevaro's interior-design choices were the problem. It wasn't just Mom on the line. It was everything.

Remy picked up on my growing nerves, and the levity in the elevator died swiftly. They bit their bottom lip, watching the number on the LED screen go up. It was just us first. Gabe and Georgia would be following in thirty-seven minutes. According to Georgia, it was important to keep the time random, so no one would notice. Somehow, I felt like that was the least of our worries.

Remy's eyes flickered toward me, dark even under the elevator's harsh overhead light. "Ready?"

I took a deep breath, steadying myself. I allowed my nerves a chance to say their piece, but their time was over. Now I packed them up and hid them on a shelf somewhere in the back of my mind, with every other inconvenient thing I didn't have time for. "Ready."

The elevator doors slid open.

The receptionist's office was like we'd never left it, with the same woman sitting behind the desk, looking just as bored. I wondered if they ever let her leave or if she was chained to the desk.

She didn't even blink when I handed her the Avalon Club card this time. The real test would be when she scanned Gabe's, but we wouldn't be there for that. Remy and I put our phones in the plastic bin, and it was like cutting off a limb. I had to trust that Lucky's abilities would see us all through, or else this was over before it even began.

"Wait," the receptionist said, and my heart leaped out of my throat and ran back for the elevator. "What's that?" She tapped the side of her head.

I knew she'd ask. I would have been surprised if she didn't. "AirPod," I said, resisting the urge to touch it self-consciously. "Don't worry, it's legal."

I reached into my pocket and brandished an MP3 player with all the teenage impatience I could muster. It was an oblong piece of plastic so old it once belonged to my mom. Modifying it to connect to my AirPod's Bluetooth *and* the WiFi had been surprisingly easy, at least for Lucky. Figuring out how to navigate the screen with the flat wheel on the front had been hard. It didn't even have a touchscreen.

"No way this counts as a phone," I added.

The silence was stretching too long. Shit.

"I really need to get caught up with my podcasts." That was true, actually. I'd been a little distracted lately.

"Hmm," she hummed. "Go on." She waved us through.

"*I don't even want to know what stupid thing you just said,*" Lucky said in my ear, "*but I could feel it. Like someone walking over my grave.*"

I cleared my throat and adjusted the AirPod. Lucky wasn't in the Avalon Club, but that didn't mean she wasn't with us. She was several floors below, in an Imperium suite booked under Dad's name. And I had just one of my AirPods in my ear like a kid playing Secret Service agent.

It worked well enough, but it wasn't perfect. I could hear Lucky, but she couldn't hear me. My AirPod had a functional microphone despite how many times I'd dropped it, but the MP3 player only supported one-way communication. We were already asking a lot from it. Anything more probably would've started melting the plastic casing. It was probably for the best. I didn't need the patrons of the Avalon Club to catch me muttering to myself. Assuming, of course, that Lucky could even get into the camera network. She had a lot of confidence in her hacking ability, but I doubt she'd ever contended with a multimillion-dollar casino—

"*Got it,*" Lucky said. "*We have eyes. Whoa, there you are.*" Her laugh was tinny in my ear. "*I love that shirt; I feel like I'm watching* The Jungle Book."

Bagheera was a black leopard, but *whatever*. I couldn't say that. I pressed my lips together unhappily.

"Nice face, Jack. I guess that means you can hear me loud and clear."

"Are you having a problem?" Remy gave me a strange look. I quickly schooled my expression back into place.

"Lucky," I muttered, grateful that her name was a common adjective to say at a casino. It sure made complaining about her convenient, if nothing else.

We didn't go straight for one of the blackjack tables. I wanted to be slightly less predictable, in case someone had noticed me last time after all. Everyone else seemed to have forgotten the pink-haired girl, but I hadn't. She was connected to the Avalon Club, and now she was connected to me. That made her dangerous. I knew that. I just didn't know how.

Remy and I killed some time at a Texas Hold'em table, which was interesting, considering that Remy didn't know how to play and I was too distracted to bluff. So more accurately, we spent a bit of money losing at Texas Hold'em. I didn't mind. You've got to spend money to make money. Granddad never said that—he preferred "you've got to steal money to make money"—but other people did, and one had to know what they were talking about.

"The eagle has landed," Lucky said. My head twitched, but I couldn't turn to look. As far as anyone was supposed to know, I'd never met Gabe or Georgia before. Success was like a shot of adrenaline straight to the heart. Gabe's card worked. I fought the urge to grin. *"Shut up. Of course it worked."*

And Lucky was getting a little too good at reading my face. Didn't like that.

I tapped the back of Remy's hand under the table, a silent signal that Gabe and Georgia had made it inside, and the corner of their mouth twitched in a secret smile. Something warm sparked in my chest. Didn't like that either.

I was itching to go to the blackjack tables and win something—I kept counting the Hold'em cards by accident before realizing the number didn't mean anything. I could already hear Gabe laughing, twice as loud as usual and weirdly deep. We kept trying to convince him that he didn't need to get in character, but by the end he and Georgia had already constructed an elaborate backstory for their fake relationship. Evidently there was a hilarious anecdote about their first date and bad shellfish that they were just waiting to unleash.

But Gabe and Georgia's arrival was our signal to take our first pass around the rest of the club. We'd put in our time at the table, looking more or less like we belonged. Now we had a little more freedom to move around, especially with Gabe charming the nearest blackjack table, his tall stature and obnoxiously colored shirt drawing in any wandering eyes.

"I'm going to go get a drink," I said to Remy, which really meant the back corner, where the high-rollers' table sat near the bar. I had gotten lucky on my first foray there, but this was a casino, and just about everything here was built on luck—or lack thereof. It was worth the risk if there was the possibility of overhearing something useful again. I couldn't play the waiter as easily in my Rainforest Cafe–esque shirt, but I could probably get close enough to overhear the conversation. Just for a minute. I was already close enough that I could see the glitter of their expensive jewelry, the movement of their mouths as they spoke, the words lost to the ambient noise of the club.

At the last second, I changed course, ducking between two crowded tables. I grabbed an almost-empty drink left unattended, the glass cold against my hand and just about the only thing to keep it from trembling. I told myself I wanted to collect information, but that wasn't true. I wasn't hoping to hear them talk about Carlevaro. I was hoping to hear them talk about Mom.

And that was exactly the kind of selfish sentimentality I couldn't have clouding my judgment. I exhaled gustily. Not that the whole operation wasn't selfish and sentimental, but at least it served a purpose. Being sad about Mom didn't.

I let my momentum take me to the far edge of the club, where tall windows dominated the wall. I needed to clear my head if I was going to accomplish anything useful. I looked out the windows, trying not to meet my reflection's eyes. Most casinos didn't want you to have any idea of what time it was so you'd lose money there as long as possible, but I guessed Carlevaro preferred to have a view of his kingdom. Just the thought made my skin crawl, my hand tightening around my prop drink. The city was beautiful at night, putting off an electric glow that made it look alive. A beast made of neon and poor choices.

"It is kinda pretty, isn't it?"

I startled, making the ice in the drink rattle. I'd forgotten about Lucky in my ear, not to mention above me, watching through Carlevaro's security system. My ears burned, embarrassed. I would have preferred if no one had seen that.

But Lucky's voice was subdued for once, soft around the edges in a way I didn't often hear. Or see, I guess, considering the majority of our friendship had been text based, but the point still stood.

"I used to hate it. Because my mom spent so much time here. With the restaurant and everything." Lucky sighed, the sound tinny through the earpiece. *"But it is kinda pretty. Maybe it was worth it."*

Worth what? Less time with her mom—busy with the restaurant, busy in another city, far away from her? I shook my head before catching myself and covering the movement with a fake sip from my fake drink. I couldn't respond to Lucky even if I wouldn't look like I was talking to myself, but I was surprised by how much I wanted to. I wanted to tell her that Las Vegas was the only place I'd ever really considered home, for better or for worse, that in some way it was what I was fighting for—but it was also what took Mom away from me, even before she was arrested. Corrupt and unsleeping, it really was some kind of beast, even beneath the glowing lights. Like a lot of beasts, you were able to love it and hate it at the same time.

Lucky laughed, and I wondered how much of that she got through the grainy security footage. *"Yeah,"* she said. *"I'm only telling you because I know you get it. And because you can't talk back."* She was quiet for a long moment. *"So yeah, I understand. When it feels like you've never had enough time with her. Just thought I should say that."*

I stared out at the city, focusing so hard on a distant light that it made my eyes hurt. Honestly, I was a bit glad she chose this awkward arrangement to talk about our feelings too. If we were in person, I'd have to figure out what to say. That was the problem with seeing my online friends right in front of me. There was no time to think about my answers anymore. Leave it to Lucky to find the workaround.

I smiled, just a little bit. I wasn't sure if she could see it in the reflection.

Lucky huffed. *"All right, therapy session over. Now get back to work."*

I had to bite back a real smile, turning away from the windows and back toward the club with renewed purpose. It wasn't enough to stand around feeling sorry for myself. I had to act.

Instead, I froze.

There was a bar not far from the high-rollers' table, a circular countertop broken only so the servers could get in and out from the spacious middle, where they moved with practiced efficiency. There was a veritable mountain of liquor bottles in the center, glittering prettily under lights installed specifically for that purpose. The shelving they sat on was gilded, overwrought, and tacky, like everything else Carlevaro decorated, but there was something about it that

I hadn't noticed before. At the center of the structure, the shelves parted around a taller mirror, and in front of it—

A sculpture made from bronze of a sword sticking straight out of a stone.

My heart sped up. I stared, my mouth dry, feeling as though I'd been struck by lightning. A sword in the stone, at the heart of Avalon. I thought that Carlevaro might be dramatic enough to hide his black book in his favorite place, but never before that moment had I been certain of it. It almost disturbed me, how easy it was to see from Carlevaro's perspective, but once the puzzle pieces lined up, it was impossible not to understand. Carlevaro's secrets were what made him king of the Las Vegas Strip, more powerful and more influential every day that I didn't stop him. And what made Arthur king?

Excalibur.

Could it be that easy? Could the key to Carlevaro's downfall be so close, right in front of me? I took a step forward, and then another, my eyes locked on the sword. Was there some fault in it, some hidden compartment in the pommel that might hide what I was looking for? A hard drive, maybe, or a USB stick. I needed to get closer to find out. I needed—

"Jack? What is it? Did you find something?" Lucky said in my ear, but her voice was far away. Suddenly, her tone changed. *"Jack. Go left. Now."*

I obeyed on instinct, nearly twisting my ankle in the process. My hands curled into fists. I had my eyes on the prize, and I wanted it, but as I glanced behind me, I found my eyes on something worse.

Flat Cap. John Fairfield, my fake father, approached the high-rollers' table, silly hat firmly in place. *Shit*. How did he get in? Did he get a new card? Did the receptionist mention his wayward "son"?

Too many questions, too many variables. We had to leave and regroup. Now. My eyes strayed back to the sword in the stone, agonized by my own helplessness. It was *right there*.

"*Jack*," Lucky said in warning, as if reading my mind. "*Live to fight another day.*"

I was pretty sure my grandfather said that once too. "Fine," I muttered under my breath, turning away from the bar and slipping back toward where Remy was watching one of the horse races on the wall-to-wall televisions. We needed time to figure out our next move anyway. It wouldn't exactly be easy getting behind the bar, but far from impossible.

We would be back. I was counting on it.

♠

It was 2:00 a.m. by the time we made it to the circular booth in the back of the McDonald's, a truly horrific amount of fast food spread out in front of us like a greasy medieval feast. Our rendezvous point once we all left the Imperium. Also, functionally our war table as I caught them up with what I'd found.

For everyone else, the mood was buoyant. Georgia had done actually pretty well at the blackjack tables, and Gabe had made several new friends. Remy, for their part, was holding what we'd appropriately dubbed the Money Backpack to their chest, the chips inside clicking together any time they moved. I was mostly trying to swallow my frustration at being stalled. We'd made headway. I should be happy, or at least halfway satisfied. Flat Cap's presence was a concern, but one that Lucky was already looking into, her laptop open amid cheeseburger wrappers and colorful containers of french fries.

Next time, I promised myself. Next time no one would stop me.

"McNuggets really aren't that bad," I said, contemplatively dunking one in honey mustard. I was still wearing the stupid leopard-print shirt, rolled up to my elbows, smelling faintly of cigar smoke the Avalon Club's air purifiers hadn't been able to whisk away. I probably looked more like Dad after a gig at a Miami Beach dive bar, but I'd looked worse before.

"Don't eat that, Jack," Gabe said, watching my McNugget's journey. "Jack. I mean it. I'll kill you if the hyper-processed chicken doesn't first. Jackjackjack—" He cut off with a groan as I shoved the whole nugget into my mouth on principle. He laid his head on the table.

"You can't save us," Remy said, patting his hand.

"Try saving yourself first," I countered. Or I tried to. It was an unusually big chicken nugget. I swallowed painfully. "What is *that* supposed to be?"

Gabe lifted his head with a pout, taking his McDonald's order protectively into his arms. "It's called a cheese fry sandwich," he said, with the same air as someone correcting the waiter's pronunciation of cabernet sauvignon. It was actually a bun, a single slice of cheese, and half a thing of fries dumped in the middle. "And it's the only edible thing in this establishment."

"Except for the ice cream," Lucky added.

"Except for the ice cream," Gabe conceded. "When it deigns to work." He frowned as we exchanged doubtful looks. "Listen, the intersection of vegetarian and fast food, that's also not salad, is not a very big one. I do my best."

"Uh-huh," I said.

"Do you hear something?" Remy asked, cocking their head.

"Is the ice cream machine working again, you think?" Lucky perked up.

"No, no." They flapped their hand at her. "It's like a buzzing. Oh shit, Jack—is that your phone?"

"Oh f—" I jumped, scrambling for my phone. It was half hidden under a discarded paper bag, cushioned on a bed of extra napkins so the vibration was muffled. Getting a call at two in the morning was not good. Getting a call at two in the morning when you were supposed to be having an extended slumber party back at the hotel was *very bad*.

"Watch the shirt!" Gabe squawked, catching my drink as I almost dumped it all over the table. My phone stopped vibrating the split second before I accepted the call.

ONE MISSED CALL: BETH SHANNON

I was so dead. I was seventeen years old, and I was going to die in the next twenty-four hours. At that point, all I could do was hope that I'd at least be remembered on a late-night true-crime show.

"*Shit*. I'll be right back." I pulled my legs up to stand on the hard plastic booth and awkwardly stepped over Georgia, hopping on one foot as I extracted myself from the booth as quickly as possible. No time to lose. The longer Beth had to think about why I didn't answer, the more intricate her suspicions would become. Twenty seconds had passed already. In Beth's world, I was already snorting cocaine off the back of a Cadillac.

"Gabe, I'm about to ruin your life," Georgia's voice floated behind me. "It's about the cheese fry sandwich."

"If you're about to use the words *not* and *vegetarian* in the same sentence, I swear to God—"

I pushed out of the McDonald's, into the neon glow of the golden arches. I ran a hand through my hair, even though Beth couldn't see me. The first step toward being collected was looking collected. I couldn't remember who said that. Fuck.

"Jack?" Beth answered after exactly one ring.

"SorryImissedyourcall," I said in a rush. Wait, why was I apologizing? It was two in the morning. I should be sleeping. No, she must have already known I wasn't, or else she wouldn't be calling. Unless—

My heart stopped. Unless something happened. The last

time I missed a call from Beth, I ended up on a red-eye flight to Las Vegas.

"Where are you?" Beth said in her mom voice. Not her *Mom* voice—Mom dropped news like invading nations dropped bombs. The only time I'd ever seen her hesitate was when she told us that Granddad had died. No, this was a mom voice, or at least a TV-mom voice, which was probably where Beth learned it from. It was tight and controlled, in a way that really said *I already know the answer, but go ahead and lie to me, make my day.*

"Dad took us to a late-night buffet," I said, my heart in my throat. I looked up at the night sky, the stars obliterated by the city's light pollution. I jiggled my foot restlessly. "Some friend of his was playing. You know, the Elton John impersonator guy. Jerry or whoever." As safe a lie as I was going to get. The odds of Dad actually knowing an Elton John impersonator named Jerry were pretty high. I couldn't count on him for a lot, but I could rely on that.

She was quiet for a beat. "Dad's sleeping on the couch in the penthouse."

The blood froze in my veins. My brain short-circuited. A countdown appeared in the corner of my vision. Five seconds before Beth would notice I hesitated. Four. Three. Two—

"Oh my God," I said, exasperated. "Are you serious? He left without us?" I dragged my hand down my face for emphasis, and I hoped she could hear it. I was pacing now, turning in circles in front of the McDonald's. I could feel my friends peering through the windows from the corner booth. I edged around the side of the building, where the windows turned to solid wall. Conveniently pretty close to the dumpster, in case this went badly and I had to throw myself out. "Of course he did. He's Dad."

I pressed my knuckles against my lips, suppressing a string of swear words as I waited for the other shoe to drop. There were some pretty gaping holes in my story—why had we been listening to Elton John covers until 2:00 a.m.?—but leaving a bunch of teenagers to their own devices because he got distracted and then passing out on the couch was pretty in character for Dad.

Finally, Beth sighed. "Of course he did." She sighed again, and I could hear her push up her glasses to rub at her eyes. She sounded exhausted. Was she up at this hour because she hadn't slept at all? "All right, I'm going to pick you up."

My heart jumped right back up to my throat. It was like a yo-yo at this point. That couldn't be healthy. "No!" I blurted, holding my hand out as if to physically stop her. "No, it's fine. We'll take an Uber back. It's not far."

"Jack," she said, a warning in her voice. "It's two in the morning."

"Exactly," I countered, already wondering if I could find a late-night buffet to loiter outside of for when Beth insisted on picking us up. "When's the last time you slept?"

Beth said nothing, but I could practically see her lips purse.

"Go to sleep," I said. "There's five of us, we're not going to get kidnapped." Still nothing. Fine. I didn't want to lay into the guilt trip, but if she wasn't going to give me a choice . . . "I can handle it. I've been handling it. What do you think I do when you're not around? You can't run to Elkhollow every time I need a ride."

A low blow. It also implied I actually went places when at Elkhollow, but it might make Beth feel better to think that I was a normal, well-adjusted teenager. She tried to make it happen when she convinced Mom to send me to Elkhollow, bless her heart, but it wasn't going to be that easy. You could take the Shannon out of Vegas but you couldn't take the years of questionable parenting and ambiguous morality out of the Shannon.

"Ugh," Beth said. Not an answer, but a sign of weakness. We were moving in the right direction. "I'm going to kill Dad."

"Don't mention it to him," I said quickly. "I mean—he's been through a lot lately. We all have. You have." I had. Kerry had. Maybe if I listed our entire family tree, she'd forget what we were talking about in the first place. "You have enough on your plate."

Like secret business meetings with Peter Carlevaro. I chose not to mention that.

"All right," Beth said reluctantly. "Text me as soon as you get back. Do *not* forget."

"Absolutely."

"I mean it, Jack."

"I know you do." All right, a little too sassy. I wasn't entirely out of the woods yet.

I could almost hear her rolling her eyes. "Love you," she said.

"Love you too," I parroted back and ended the call. I leaned back against the wall, my bones like jelly. Another bullet dodged. I wasn't sure how many miracles I'd been allotted, but I was afraid I was going through them too quickly. I exhaled gustily.

"Aw," the pink-haired girl from the Avalon Club said from on top of one of the dumpsters. "That's sweet."

FROZEN

I DID THE ONLY REASONABLE THING THERE WAS to do: I spun around and went, *"You!"* There was finger-pointing and everything. And I accidentally threw my phone in the process. Goddammit.

She was not impressed. The girl frowned, stirring her milkshake with an irritating squeak of plastic on plastic. "Interesting," she said, like she was observing an animal in its natural habitat. And not a particularly cute, charming animal either.

I left my dignity behind and scrambled to pick my phone up off the asphalt. A couple of scratches on the glass screen protector, but it lit up fine. I needed to work on keeping a better grip on my stuff.

There was a text waiting for me.

Remy
u ok?

Not really, but I'd be even less okay with my friends

charging out of the McDonald's like a herd of elephants to see the fabled pink-haired girl. I shot a quick text back.

Jack Shannon
Fine. Be back soon.

I had maybe five minutes before my friends came looking for me. Great.

"Take your time," the girl said, one foot dangling over the side of the dumpster. "Kids and their phones."

I gave her a dirty look. She had to be my age, though today she was wearing oversize glasses that made her look both younger and strangely ageless. The neon lights reflected off the glass and thin gold rims. The effect was somewhere between a moody model and a morally ambiguous anime character.

She sipped her milkshake and tilted her head, her heel drumming against the graffitied and grime-stained dumpster. She clearly had all the time in the world, and she wasn't about to tell me anything I didn't ask for. If she told me anything at all.

I straightened my back and pulled my shoulders into my best pit-boss stance. The one that beat cheaters at their own game and used lacrosse jocks as his own personal Pinkerton. "Who are you?" I demanded, narrowing my eyes. "What do you want?"

She rolled her head, stretching her neck. She was wearing a pastel windbreaker. "I wanted to say hi," she said, "but you never texted me." She jutted out her bottom lip in an exaggerated pout. "Rude."

Time was ticking. You know what? Fine. She wasn't the only one who could play hard to get. "Hi," I said, over-pronouncing the word carefully. "If that's all? Bye." I turned on my heel, my phone tight in my hand.

I made it five steps, almost back in sight of the McDonald's windows.

"Aw, Jack," she called after me. "Come on. You know you're more curious than that."

Was I? I mean, absolutely, but that wasn't how you negotiated. If you threatened to walk away, you had to let them know that you'd actually do it. I kept walking.

"Morgan," she said. "My name is Morgan. Cool?"

I stopped. I could see my friends from there, tucked into the far corner of the restaurant. Georgia and Lucky were dueling with french fries while Gabe refereed, gesticulating wildly. Remy craned their neck, looking for me.

I held my phone up to my ear, like I was still talking to Beth, and waved. Remy waved back.

I turned back, stepping out of sight. I let the phone drop from my ear. "Cool," I said, though my tone disagreed. Morgan. Had I heard that before? I mean, obviously I'd heard the name before, but it didn't set off any memories like other things about the Avalon Club did. I looked closer—she'd shaved off half of her hair and dyed the rest of it pink; she clearly wanted to be noticed—but what I found meant nothing. She was just some girl. "You've been stalking me. Less cool."

"*Stalking* is a harsh word," Morgan argued. She hopped off the dumpster, leaving her milkshake cup behind. Did that count as littering? "I saw you at the Avalon Club, and I was curious, all right? There aren't a lot of people our age there. You know—everyone's too busy with their Xboxes and their vapes." She adopted a stodgy accent, pursing her lips and squaring her shoulders. I didn't laugh, and she dropped her shoulders and straightened up again. "I thought maybe we could form a little club. But it looks like you've already got one."

I froze. Was that a threat? Morgan had seen us all together outside of the Avalon Club. Morgan knew my name—if she knew the *Jack* part, I could only assume she also knew the *Shannon*. She could expose us, if she wanted to. The question was whether she did, and what she stood to gain from it. She couldn't know what we were up to—could she?

"How did you get into the Avalon Club?" I asked, going for casual and missing the mark. My mind was moving too fast, pulling out the puzzle and processing where the new information slotted into place. *Morgan.* I had her name now, at least part of it. She might think it was useless to me, but she didn't know that I had Lucky, or that Lucky had access to the Avalon Club's roster. Lucky would find her. "You're right, there aren't many people our age there."

Morgan actually looked puzzled for a moment, like I'd asked her what gravity was. "Oh, duh," she said, with half a laugh. "My dad was a founding knight or whatever. I'm a legacy kid. Just like you."

"A *what*?" I said, incredulous. A *founding knight*? Really? I knew the Avalon Club came from Arthurian myth—Avalon was the island where Excalibur was forged, among other fun facts—but I didn't know the metaphor went that deep. And here I thought the Golden Age's theme was overkill.

"A founding knight," she repeated slowly. "You know? Like your mom? *Someone* didn't study for his test."

Like my mom, so like Carlevaro too. Of course there was a stupid name for the founders of the Avalon Club. I bet that was his idea. "How many founding knights were there?" I demanded. Had they all sided with Carlevaro in the split? Just how many people were part of this little cabal? How many had secrets held over their heads, tucked away in Carlevaro's little black book? If I could get one of them to help me, if they knew how close I was to finding Carlevaro's weakness—

"Oh, *now* he's got questions," Morgan said wryly, to an invisible audience. "And not even the right ones. C'mon, you're not even going to ask about the secret passages? Because they're pretty cool."

I couldn't tell if she was baiting me or not. I had a feeling that was common when talking to Morgan.

"Anyway," she yawned like a cat. "It's getting late. See ya around, Jack." She turned to leave, her hands buried in her windbreaker.

"Wait." The word tore from my lips. "That's it?"

"It's two thirty in the morning," she said. As if the difference between 2:00 a.m. and 2:30 a.m. was what turned you into a pumpkin.

"I have questions," I said.

"And you have my number. *You're* the one who doesn't want to be my friend," Morgan countered. "But you can always change your mind. Think about it, Jack. But don't take too long. You don't have forever." She winked.

I stared after her, frozen in place. Another threat. Another teasing hint that she knew what I didn't.

It was no use calling after her. I needed to get back to my friends, and Beth was still waiting to hear that I'd gotten back to the hotel. I bit my tongue, swallowing my frustration. My phone buzzed. I looked down as Morgan traipsed off, throwing one last jaunty wave back at me.

Remy
Jack?

I sighed and rubbed my eyes, suddenly exhausted.

Jack Shannon
Coming.

♠

I didn't tell the others about the run-in with Morgan.

A bad idea, I know, but I was getting pretty good at those. We'd promised honesty once we set off on this misadventure, and I fully intended to stand by that.

But—

But I didn't intend to text Morgan, or call her, or do whatever it was she clearly wanted me to do. She'd been following me since that first trip to the Avalon Club, or at least paying more attention than I wanted her to. Maybe my friends were right, maybe she did have a crush, but I doubted it. She'd purposefully shown her hand with the tidbit about the founding knights, like bait on a hook. I might have been curious, but I wasn't stupid. I didn't intend to take it.

Therefore, it really didn't matter that she'd cornered me next to a McDonald's dumpster and said a lot of vague and mysterious things about founding knights and Avalon, because it *didn't matter*. Net-zero outcome. So it wasn't *exactly* lying if I didn't mention it to my friends.

Besides, I had bigger problems. Problems named Beth Shannon.

"It's not a big deal," I said the next day, catching her at a rare moment between meetings with the Dohertys and meetings with the Golden Age shareholders. I didn't want to be having this conversation, but it was better to have it on my terms than to wait for her to show up at the door to our suite. I was trying to avoid having to hastily shove Lucky in a trunk, but I'd do it if necessary.

"He *forgot* you," Beth said, bustling past me. The living room was looking distinctly more lived in since we all arrived—specifically since Dad started accidentally-on-purpose camping out on the couch, even though I'd given him the keycard to a perfectly fine room at the Imperium expressly to avoid conflicting stories like this.

And you're trying to sell us out, what's the difference? I bit my tongue and swallowed the words. The very last thing I needed to be doing was antagonizing Beth about Peter Carlevaro, much less admit that I'd seen him again, even if it was hardly my choice. I knew Beth did what she did because she cared, but I also knew our priorities were vastly, irreparably different. I, for instance, gave half a shit about our family's legacy. Beth couldn't get far enough away from it.

Which would have been fine, if she wasn't trying to put it into Peter Carlevaro's hands. Didn't she think I might have a problem with that?

"Dad's been forgetting me my whole life," I said instead. Probably not my best argument. Beth tossed me an exasperated look. "I mean, I'm used to it. It's no big deal." How could she still worry so much after the Miami incident? That was years ago. I lived, didn't I?

Beth pursed her lips. It would have been more effective if she wasn't dressed for the board meeting, which meant she was dressed in one of Mom's old outfits. A month ago, Beth wouldn't have been caught dead in the Golden Age, much less attending board meetings in Mom's old clothes. I had to bite my tongue again to keep from asking what she'd been telling the other shareholders.

"I don't want you staying out that late again," Beth said firmly. "Even with Dad. You know there's a curfew on the Strip—let's abide by it. I don't need to explain to your friends' parents why they got a ride back in a police cruiser."

I was always quick to sidestep the topic of my friends waiting downstairs, but this time Beth did it for me. She was already halfway out the door, smoothing back her hair with both hands.

"Got it?" she said.

"Got it," I lied.

"Good," Beth said. "Or next time, I'll send Kerry with you."

♠

"Got it?" I asked Dad, my hands on his shoulders.

"Got it," he said agreeably, absolutely slathering a hot dog with spicy mustard. One side effect of a late night was that we didn't move very fast until the afternoon, which conveniently put me on the exact same schedule as Dad. We needed to focus on getting back into the Avalon Club and getting to that statue fast, but I managed to carve out a little father-son time to get our stories straight. Namely—if Beth asked him where I was, I was with him. And for God's sake, stay away from places where she could easily verify the truth.

A big ask for a father, theoretically, but he owed me a couple from all the cases of child endangerment over the years. Still, the least I could do was buy him a hot dog for the trouble.

I dropped my hands from his shoulders, for the sake of avoiding mustard stains on my shirt—another gaudy one of Gabe's, of which he seemed to have an endless supply in his suitcase. I was beginning to grow a bit fond of them. Like Stockholm syndrome.

"But I'm not sure I like lying to Beth, kiddo," Dad said, tearing me out of my thoughts as I tried to decide if I was going to wear the electric-blue squiggly-pattern shirt tonight or the rainbow zebra print. God, I hardly recognized myself. "She does have custody of you while your mom's—uhh, on vacation." His mouth did verbal gymnastics to avoid the word *jail*.

"No one needs to have custody of me," I snapped. If they didn't stop throwing around the word *custody* like I was six years old, I was going to file for legal emancipation myself.

I turned back to the hot-dog stand, exchanging the Onyx card in return for my own hot dog. It shimmered greasily in the hot noon sun. If Gabe was offended by the McNuggets, he'd be horrified by this. "It's just for a little while. My friends came all this way, and you know you can't do anything fun here before curfew . . ." I looked up to find the hot dog guy looking at me expectantly. "Sorry, what?"

"It declined," he said in a flat voice. It was like looking at my future all of a sudden—twenty-one and scraping out a living slinging hot dogs on the Las Vegas Strip. He scratched at his patchy beard. "Do you have another card?"

"Try it again," I said impatiently, my heart thundering in my chest. "It should work. Just try it."

The cashier didn't break eye contact with me the whole time he stuck it in the pin pad and waited for the angry beep. Declined.

"Sorry," he said, without sounding very sorry at all. Bored, maybe. Or stoned. "Can I have the dogs back?"

That was it then. The Onyx was gone, basically a useless piece of plastic to look back on with fond memories. The realization was like losing a limb. The Onyx card was the only reason I'd gotten this far in the first place. I'd already stretched my Blackjack Club winnings thin, buying the chips to playact at the Avalon Club, and my regular account had been frozen from the beginning. Now whatever winnings we had from Avalon were all we had left.

I fumbled for my wallet, pulling out a crumpled twenty-dollar bill. "Keep it," I said, leaving it on the counter. My hands were trembling as I shoved the Onyx card back into my wallet. The grease on my hot dog looked disgusting now, my entire stomach twisting itself into knots.

"Embarrassing!" Dad laughed, one hand on his belly like this was all one big joke. Like our lives weren't falling apart around our ears like the sky was cracking open, just a little bit at a time. "Oh, I hate when that happens."

Except that didn't happen to me, not except for the lobby in the Imperium, when I first discovered that Mom's accounts were frozen. But the Onyx card was supposed to be separate. Safe. Hidden.

What had Beth said? *The Dohertys think we have a little while before anyone finds this one.* A little while. Not long enough.

"It's fine," I said, as much to myself as to Dad. "It's all right." This would all be over soon anyway. We had our lead, now we just had to act on it. And we could. Act on it, I mean. We still had our winnings from the Avalon Club. We still had the Golden Age. I still had my team. My friends.

For now.

Q&A

FOR NOW. THE WORDS WEIGHED HEAVILY ON ME, making every step forward feel more important. Nothing had changed, despite the pressure mounting on all sides— we were going back into the Avalon Club, we were going to get Carlevaro's black book, and we didn't really *need* the Onyx card to do those things. But losing it had rattled me and—surprise, surprise—I didn't tell my friends about that either. I couldn't afford to rattle them too.

Lucky took care of the keycard. She couldn't tell from the system, but Flat Cap must have gotten a new one if he was at the Avalon Club the other night. Still, we couldn't risk making a new profile when the receptionist already knew me as his son. Lucky ended up cloning his profile instead so that the system wouldn't ping it if Flat Cap was already in the club when I arrived. A Band-Aid more than a solution, but we were operating on the desperate assumption that we wouldn't need to go back after this.

The plan wasn't much different from the last one, except

that this time we had a focused objective—the sword-in-the-stone statue behind the bar. Difficult to get to, considering it was right out in the open, but I supposed that was the point. Hiding in plain sight. In the direct line of sight of anyone visiting the bar, to be more specific.

Despite Remy's minor stint at theater camp, we chose Gabe as the one to get behind the bar under the guise of a bartender. He was the oldest, and his sheer height meant that he looked it too. Never mind the fact that he was the best liar and also begged to do it. If I could impersonate a server for even a couple of minutes, then I had every confidence Gabe could get close enough to that statue to find what we were looking for. The rest of us would run cover, ready to cause a distraction if things got hairy.

We were calm, clear, and focused. It would be fine. It would all be fine.

If Morgan was there—

Well. I hoped Morgan wouldn't be there.

"What's with the face?" Remy asked.

"What face?" I tried to school my features into something neutral.

We made it past the receptionist again, which was its own relief, but even stepping into the Avalon Club for the third time, I couldn't help the unsettled feeling making my skin crawl. My instincts were nagging at me, but I couldn't tell what they were trying to say.

Remy snorted. "Uh, that one's worse." They looked at me closely, their thumbs hooked through the straps of the

Money Backpack. I think they liked to carry it to feel the weight of the chips, though we all knew that Georgia would have the most to contribute by the time we consolidated them at the end of the night. I'd yet to break it to them that, if all went according to plan, we wouldn't exactly be able to cash them out. "Are you sure you're up for this tonight?" It was all they could say here, where anyone might be listening.

No more secrets. I knew I should tell them. That was what was bothering me, I realized uncomfortably. There was a lot riding on getting this right tonight, but only I knew the full extent of it. I hadn't told them so they wouldn't suffer from the same nerves I was battling now, but the guilt only made them harder to bear. Talk about a no-win situation. Emotions were so stupid.

"I'm fine," I said, and the Avalon Club swallowed us up before Remy could question the obvious lie further. Gabe and Georgia would be following us in soon, but before we could get to business, we had to blend in for a bit.

Blackjack, at least, would help settle my nerves.

"The only Morgan I'm finding is an investment banker from Phoenix," Lucky said in my ear as the dealer put down a king of diamonds and my hand busted spectacularly. I was playing like shit tonight; I could barely keep track of the count. No wonder Remy thought I was sick and/or on the verge of a breakdown. *"I take it that's not the one?"*

I shook my head, covering it by scratching at my ear. Addendum: I told Lucky part of the truth, which actually might have made it more of a lie, in the grand scheme of things. She knew Morgan was a person of interest regarding the club, but she didn't know she was the pink-haired girl. If she suspected, she didn't let on.

Lucky grunted, unhappy. She didn't like to fail, but I wasn't surprised. Morgan wouldn't make things that easy.

"*I'll keep looking,*" Lucky said, and for the moment my AirPod-turned-communicator went quiet except for the steady clicking of her keyboard.

"He's been lusting over that gaudy thing for years," a man in a rumpled purple suit said as he joined our table. "I'm only surprised he didn't make a move sooner."

His companion snorted. "Lusting over the hotel or the woman?" he said in a clipped English accent.

"Both." The purple-suit man laughed, tossing his chips in without even looking at them.

"What do you think he'll do with it?"

"Who knows. Sell it. Rebrand it. Burn the place down."

The Englishman rolled his eyes. "If he calls it Camelot, I'll scream."

They were talking about Carlevaro. The realization hit like a ball-peen hammer right between the eyes. Carlevaro and the Golden Age. I didn't even look at my hand, my eyes burning a hole in the green-velvet table to keep from glaring at our tablemates. Just knowing that people were talking about him made me furious, but beneath it was a quiet spike of terror. Other people knew about Carlevaro's plan to take the Golden Age. Suddenly the possibility that it might actually happen was far, far more real.

The man in purple snorted. "You'll be lucky if that's the least of what he does. If his company keeps eating up property, we're going to be calling him King Carlevaro before long."

Something brushed my wrist, and I startled, but it was only Remy, wrapping their hand around mine. They kept their eyes forward, inspecting their cards as the dealer worked around the opposite end of the table. But their hand was warm around mine, small but solid. They squeezed, and my heart squeezed back.

Thank you, I wanted to say, but I couldn't, and not just because of the lump in my throat. Remy's dark hair was edged with gold under the hanging light illuminating the table, their other hand tapping thoughtfully against the green felt. They looked sideways, out of the corner of their eye, and smiled a small, secret smile. Just for me. Remy winked.

"*Oh my God*," Lucky said, so loud that the little speaker crackled. "*Are you guys holding hands?*"

I jumped, dropping Remy's hand so fast, I cracked my knuckles against the edge of the table.

"*You were!*" Lucky crowed. "*You totally were!*"

"*Shut up*," I hissed, going red in the face. I was going to dismantle every camera in this place with my bare hands—

"Just a bug!" Remy said, their voice going up an octave. They hopped off their seat and stomped theatrically around our chairs. They raised their hands—either placatingly or in victory, I couldn't tell. "Just a bug! Don't worry, I got it."

The rest of the table was looking at us like we'd lost our minds. English Guy was staring at me like I was something he found on the bottom of his shoe, but Purple Suit looked considering. I accidentally locked eyes with him. Was he someone I knew from the past, like Flat Cap? One of Mom's old friends?

I turned away quickly. Better not to find out.

Lucky was still laughing so hard she might cry. "*Sorry,*" she wheezed. "*Sorry, but oh my God. I'm so glad I've been recording.*"

Great. Fantastic. Stupendous.

My face resembled a cherry tomato again. "Let's go," I muttered, tugging on Remy's sleeve. Whatever moment we'd had was thoroughly crushed under Lucky's heel like an imaginary bug, and I was back to being . . . whatever I was now. I felt like everything was moved slightly to the left, just enough to throw me off-center. It had been that way ever since arriving back in the city, though I could feel it getting worse as time ran out. I couldn't let myself stop to think about Mom, but it was affecting me worse than I thought. "There's got to be a table with fewer bugs." Maybe one not in Lucky's virtual direct line of sight.

Georgia caught my eye from one of the other blackjack tables and raised her eyebrows, questioning, but I only shook my head infinitesimally. She wasn't the only one giving us weird looks as we escaped the table, but they were quickly losing interest. In a place like the Avalon Club, we weren't really the weirdest thing around. Tonight there was someone in an entire fur suit playing craps near the exit. If there was anything worse than losing, it'd be losing to a neon-green wolf.

I tripped over my own feet. The new shoes Gabe had picked out for me didn't fit quite right, and I'd been afraid of experiencing death by metallic gold loafer all night, but that wasn't what threw me off.

It was Morgan. She stood across the room, leaning against the doorway to one of the lounges. There were a handful of them off the main floor, some for smoking, some for betting on races or fights, and some for things better left unsaid. Morgan was playing on her phone, her pink hair falling in her eyes. I shouldn't have been surprised she was bold enough to sneak it past the receptionist.

Had she seen me? Probably. The whole place had seen me, quite unfortunately.

Morgan looked up and winked, before she turned and disappeared into the lounge. She wanted me to follow after her. That was her bet, the way we were all betting on something here—that my curiosity would be stronger than my good sense.

"*Oh shit,*" Lucky said, the laughter gone. "*That was her, wasn't it? Pink hair? This footage is all in black-and-white, I can't tell.*"

And now Lucky had noticed. She was already connecting the dots. Sometimes, Lucky was too smart for anyone's good, most especially mine.

I hesitated. I had maybe ten minutes before Gabe would be exiting the bathroom, having thrown a close approximation of the bartender's red vest over his uncharacteristically conservative outfit. I was supposed to be watching from the corner by the high-rollers' table, where I'd have a clear view of the statue—and anyone else watching it too. If things got tense, I'd give Remy the signal to cause a distraction and give Gabe time to bug out of there, hopefully with the metaphorical black book in hand.

Ten minutes. Less, the longer I waited.

I had time. Barely.

Sorry, I thought, before I turned to Remy. I put my hand on their elbow. Their eyes flickered from my face to my hand and back again. Or maybe I just imagined that. "Why don't you go check out the other table? I think I need to sit down for a minute."

That was what I was supposed to say, but sooner than I was supposed to say it. Remy gave me a curious look, their eyebrows pulled together, but they couldn't really argue with me in the middle of the club.

"Okay," they said, almost warily, and it took everything I had not to wince. I hated lying to them like this—just not enough to stop, I guess. Something changed in their expression, like they were coming to a realization, and my stomach dropped as Remy's concern transformed into quiet understanding. They thought I was still upset about the conversation about Mom. They thought I needed to be alone, and they were willing to give that space to me.

As if I didn't feel like enough of a piece of shit already.

"Got it," Remy said with a soft smile, and they reached out and squeezed my fingers again, quickly, where Lucky couldn't see.

"*I saw that,*" Lucky said flatly. "*We can talk about that later. Where the hell are you going, Jack? This is not part of the plan.*"

I waited until Remy had joined Georgia's table, sliding into an empty seat on the opposite end. Georgia threw me another questioning look, but I twitched my hand, silently warding her off. The plan was still on. I just needed to make a detour.

Morgan was a rogue element. She knew things I didn't, and I had no idea if I'd ever be able to find her again if I passed up this opportunity. If all went according to plan, I would have Mom back, but I was realizing that I had opened something bigger than I'd bargained for. I couldn't just go back to Elkhollow after all this and pretend it had never happened. There were things I wanted to know, things Mom never really told me. Answers to questions I hadn't even thought to ask.

Answers that Morgan might have.

Only one person left to shake, but that was easy.

"*Jack,*" Lucky said, her voice steadily growing louder. "*She's Morgan, isn't she? The pink girl? Jack, listen to me. I think I've found something. Jack, you big idiot, I'm going to eat your kneecaps—*"

I pulled the AirPod out of my ear and stashed it in my pocket, Lucky's tinny little voice still yelling expletives at me. My heart thundered in my chest. Whatever Lucky thought she found, it would have to wait.

I did a lap of the club, skirting around the bar before ducking through the patchwork crowd watching a soccer game. The Avalon Club wasn't very large, all things considered—nothing compared to the casino floors downstairs on the lower levels of the Imperium, or the Golden Age's own, but it used its space well. Each table felt like its own little universe, lit up bright among the gloom of the club. There was a reason it was so easy to lose time there, as well as your money.

Which made it easier to shake any lingering eyes that might have been watching me. Half of the crowd erupted into victorious whooping as someone on the TVs scored a run, or whatever they did in soccer. I darted between them, dodging careless elbows.

The row of lounges stared me down, each door leading to the belly of the beast. Some had open doorways, some had muffled voices inside. One notably had a man wearing a dark suit and a serious expression standing outside of it, his feet planted wide. I scurried past him without making eye contact and ducked into the lounge I had seen Morgan disappear into.

I didn't realize how warm it was in the club until I was greeted with a blast of cold air. I slowly closed the door behind me, the hair on my arms rising. The lounge was . . .

Surprisingly boring, which I should have expected after the receptionist's lobby. It was softly lit, but in less of a Hollywood way than the rest of the club. The furniture was tasteful but conservative, long leather couches and dark wooden desks with ergonomic swivel chairs waiting behind them. It looked like the kind of place businessmen paid extra to wait in when they had a long layover at the airport. Thinking back, I could remember playing in rooms just like this, tucked into a wide leather chair with an iPad while Mom argued with investors on the phone.

"You didn't want to bring your friends?" Morgan said from beside me, making me jump. The lounge was empty, except for us, but the walls seemed to swallow the sound, like they were made to avoid disturbance at all costs. "Aw. Do I embarrass you?"

I glared at her. I wasn't there to play around. I didn't have time to. There were no clocks here, typical of a casino, but I could feel time ticking down.

Morgan rolled her eyes at my silence, tucking her hair behind her ear. She was dressed like it was Halloween and she was going as the '90s given human form. If I thought the pastel windbreaker from outside the McDonald's was daring, she'd stepped it up with the metallic vinyl skirt and velvet choker necklace. Suddenly I wasn't feeling so bad about my Gabe-inspired wardrobe.

"I preferred meeting next to a dumpster," I said.

"Of course you did," she said with a scoff, "but this is more fun. You know games *are* supposed to be fun, right?"

"This isn't a game for me." I bit out the words.

"And that's why you're starting to get gray hair."

I frowned, touching my temple reflexively. No, I wasn't. Was I?

Morgan pushed off the wall she'd been leaning against, lazily dancing as she scuffed her feet against the floor. She was wearing black combat boots. "Let's cut to the chase—you've got questions. Obviously," she said. "What do you want to know? Or should we start with what you *do* know?" She gave me a coy look that made my pride bristle. I was usually the dealer—I wasn't used to playing a game where I didn't know the rules. "You're a legacy kid, but you're not here with your mom. Why?"

"My mom's in jail." The words came out like pulling teeth.

"And the first thing you do is start gambling?" She dropped onto one of the long couches. "That's a hell of a coping mechanism."

"Thanks," I said blandly. I made a note to ask Beth if our health insurance would cover therapy. Morgan might have a bit of a point.

But I'd worry about that later. A little time never hurt anyone's festering neuroses. She didn't know why we were really there, which is what mattered. I stepped forward, lingering next to one of the leather chairs. I leaned against it but didn't quite sit down. "How did the Avalon Club start? Who started it? How many founding knights are there?"

Who was her dad? Did I know him? Did I know *her*? Maybe I'd been away from the city for longer than I thought.

Morgan's smirk wilted, her whole obnoxious persona faltering. "Oh," she said, her eyebrows coming together. They were pink too. "You really don't know anything, do you? I thought—"

She cut herself off, shaking her head, and pushed herself off the couch. Her hair obscured her face on the way up, and when she tossed it back again, the Morgan I'd encountered before was back. Cocksure and overly familiar, mysterious in a way that meant she was trying to be. She smiled, the corners of her eyes crinkling.

"Guess we should start at the beginning then," she said. "C'mon."

FIRST-NAME BASIS

"DAD LIKES TO USE THIS ROOM A LOT," MORGAN SAID, gesturing expansively to the lounge. "Because it's the most boring, I guess. No one ever comes here. It's supposed to be for if you need to, like, take calls or do business or whatever, but people don't really come here to do business. At least not that kind of business, if you know what I mean." She winked.

It was hard to imagine worrying about stocks and board members in a place like the Avalon Club. Maybe that was why people like Mom and Carlevaro liked it so much. For everyone else, the Las Vegas Strip was escapism in neon. For people like us, it was business.

Like this is business, I reminded myself.

"Is something in your eye?" I asked with a frown. Morgan was still winking, or experiencing some kind of facial tic.

"I'm winking," she said, indignant. "*You know what I—* Never mind. Anyway. The first thing to know about Avalon Club—"

"Don't talk about Avalon Club," I suggested wryly.

"Don't make jokes," Morgan said. "You're not good at them."

She crossed the lounge. "The first thing to know about Avalon Club," she repeated, daring me, with a single raised eyebrow, to interrupt again, "is that all roads lead to Rome." She reached up and pulled a book off one of the bookshelves lining the back wall. I had assumed they were props to look esteemed and pretentious. It turned out it was actually a hidden lever.

My eyes widened, and I was too impressed to scoff. A bookshelf turned secret door was even more pretentious than fake books, but somehow I was completely okay with that, as it swung open on well-oiled hinges. I wasn't proud. Or, well, I was proud—but some things were more important than pride. Namely, every childhood dream of having a secret doorway hidden behind a bookcase, and maybe a slide between floors.

Morgan grinned like a shark. "Cool, right? Get used to that. It's all kinds of dramatic."

"I got the feeling," I said faintly. I closed my hanging mouth before I could start catching flies. "I mean, they called themselves the *founding knights*."

She laughed. "You don't even know the half of it. C'mon."

I hesitated. Again. I'd lost track of how much time I had left, but I knew there wasn't enough of it. Soon my friends would be moving into position. For me.

Morgan raised her eyebrows. "Now or never, Jack. I don't have all day."

Now or never.

The new doorway led to a hall remarkably identical to the beige-painted cinder block network in the security offices downstairs. I hesitated at the line where carpet gave way to mottled linoleum, but the bookcase was slowly starting to close, the lock on the other side blinking in warning. Morgan didn't even spare a glance back to make sure I followed her.

I'd made my decision. Too late to regret it now. My heart thundered in my chest, my head spinning with new information. There was more to the Avalon Club than I'd guessed. The statue had felt so obvious when I first saw it, but now doubt was starting to creep into my heart, sickly and cold. Maybe I needed Morgan's answers even more than I'd thought.

I jogged to catch up, my footsteps loud in the chilly hallway. It snaked and branched. Every so often a door interrupted the mass of beige, but the deeper we went, the more the walls started to change. Framed Vegas memorabilia lined either side of the hallway, a different vintage poster or yellowed newspaper clipping every few feet. It was like a weird back-alley museum, a covert love letter to the city of sin.

"There are hidden doors all over the place," Morgan said offhandedly. There were little plaques on each of the doors, but she was walking too fast for me to read them. "Avalon isn't the only thing on this floor, let's put it that way."

Clearly. I wished I had Lucky looking over my shoulder. My hand brushed my pocket where the AirPod hid. I swore I could still feel it vibrating with her voice. I could only imagine the increasingly colorful expletives.

"Where are we going?" I finally asked, more curious than wary now. It wasn't that I didn't believe Morgan before, about being a legacy kid, but this made doubt impossible. There was more to Avalon than I had ever imagined.

"The place is called Avalon, Jack," Morgan said, twisting around so she was walking backward. "What did King Arthur have?"

I squinted. "A round table?"

"N—well, yes," she said. She bounced off the wall without breaking stride and twirled around, tripping forward as we turned the corner. The hall ended with an oak door, incongruous with the bland wall around it. "But more importantly"—she pushed the door open—"a throne room."

I didn't know if the founding knights actually called it the throne room—I wouldn't put it past them—but it certainly looked the part. It was everything I had expected from the first lounge. Dark wood and thick carpet, warm lighting and dusky shadows. You could practically smell cigar smoke and bourbon built into the foundation, but in a men's soap kind of way, where it had a name like Midnight Thunder and didn't give you lung disease. Morgan watched smugly as I drifted into the room, and I was reminded of showing my friends our suite at the Golden Age. There were few things more satisfying than watching someone's jaw drop and knowing what they're looking at is yours.

And this was mine, at least as far as it was Morgan's, if all of this was true. It had to be. It struck me all over again that Mom had had all of this all along—on top of the Golden

Age, on top of three kids, on top of Granddad's failing health in the end—and I hadn't realized what it really meant. It had looked different then, before her falling out with Carlevaro and before the Imperium was built, but I had no doubt that it was just as grand. I hadn't even thought about it enough as a kid, taking it for granted as one more oddity in an already fairly odd life on the Las Vegas Strip. I tried to remember the last time I spent at her elbow, looking over the edge of the blackjack table, but the memories were more of a feeling than color. My heart ached. Since I'd left for Elkhollow, I could count on one hand the number of times I saw Mom in a year. I hadn't even realized how much had changed.

"Nice, right?" Morgan said. She wandered through the lounge, her hands in her jacket pockets. It was cold there too. Despite being in the middle of Las Vegas, it felt more like we'd stepped into a European study. I almost expected to look around and find a roaring fireplace, and maybe a few swords on the wall. Avalon, indeed.

"C'mon, this is the interesting part," she said, and I followed her like I was being tugged along on a string. The walls were painted a dark red, like a fine vintage of wine, and artfully cluttered with more memorabilia. I had to tilt my head back to look at the highest pieces.

Most were pictures, interspersed with framed letters with elegant letterhead or novelty poker chips set between glass and dark velvet. The pictures were what interested me the most. They didn't have plaques beneath them, like a museum, but I felt like they were telling a story. It was like reading a picture book without any words—or maybe just words that I didn't know how to read.

I touched my fingers to the glass of the photograph closest to me. "This is the Golden Age," I said, quickly retracting my hand before it smudged. The lighting was poor, and it was old enough that the quality was grainy, but I knew that room. In the photograph, it had a few poker tables and a pool table stretching out in front of the camera, lit by a stained-glass lamp hanging over it. It had changed quite a bit since it became the speakeasy in the Golden Age's basement, but I'd know it anywhere.

"That's where the first Avalon Club was," Morgan said, her head tilted as she surveyed the photograph with me. "It moved around a couple of times before the Imperium was built. I think they rotated it. Made it harder to find. More *exclusive*." She shimmied her shoulders.

I snorted softly, my eyes roaming the photos adjacent to it. More rooms, ones I didn't know. But there were plenty of things I did recognize. Like Mom.

Mom smiling from the dealer's position at a blackjack table, coyly hiding her face behind a fan of playing cards. Mom, centered in a group of five, one arm around Peter Carlevaro's shoulders, the other around the waist of a woman who used to give me chocolate coins like she was paying me to keep a secret. Only they were all younger, the years washed away like dirt. Mom looked so much like Kerry that I actually did a double take. Young Mom had Kerry's coloring and Beth's way of holding herself. Proud.

The difference was that Mom took pride in things like illegal high-stakes gambling rings, and Beth took pride in staying far away from them.

"Recognize him?" Morgan pointed to one of the higher-up pictures. It was Mom again, with a little boy perched on her knee.

I was maybe three years old, my hair like dandelion fluff. Granddad always said I was so much like her, it was hardly as if my dad participated at all. I retroactively wrinkled my nose at that. Gross, Granddad. Not exactly what I wanted to think about.

"Where are you?" I asked, scanning the pictures. I didn't imagine she had the pink hair then, but kids stuck out among pictures of smiling people in front of poker tables or bars. But there were only a couple of me, sitting on Mom's lap or poking my nose over a blackjack table.

Morgan went uncharacteristically quiet. "Dad never really brought me around Avalon," she said belatedly, like she had to remember the question first. She laughed shortly. "I wasn't around the city much at all, really. I mean, would you bring a kid to a place like this? Your mom was kind of a renegade, I guess."

"I don't know," I said, still staring at the photographs. "I think I turned out all right." Except for the slightly illegal gambling ring and the *very* illegal gambling ring and all the extensive lying that had gone into both. We all had our faults. Some, clearly, were genetic.

But she seemed disappointed, like the question pressed

on a bruise she was trying to hide. It scratched at the back of my mind, stirring up the questions still unanswered. I scanned the photographs. There was no frame helpfully labeled "The founding knights and their names, just for you, Jack, you're welcome." Familiar faces cropped up in some and were absent in others, friends and patrons and business partners, but not with any frequency that set them apart as particularly important. There was just Mom, and—

My stomach dropped like a lead weight. Mom and Peter Carlevaro.

"Morgan," I said carefully. "Who's your dad?"

Morgan blinked, overly innocent, like I'd just caught her with her hand in the cookie jar. "Well . . ." she started, tugging on her sleeves. "Well, about that . . ." She looked up suddenly, cocking her head. "Do you hear that?"

"I'm not falling for that." How many of the oldest tricks in the book was she going to pull out? Throw a rock down the hall to distract the guards? She was playing dumb, which meant she knew I would be mad. She knew what Carlevaro did to my Mom, and she still didn't tell me that she was his daughter—

"No, for real," she whispered furiously, slapping a hand across my mouth.

"*Mph!*" I protested, affronted. I fought the childish urge to lick her palm, only because I didn't know where her hands had been. Knowing the Carlevaros, probably running greedily over dirty money and dragonesque hoards of gold.

Actually. I glanced toward the door. Now that I was listening, it did sound like there were voices. Muffled by the thick oak door but getting louder.

My eyes cut back toward Morgan's. They were wide and brown. *Brown like Peter Carlevaro's eyes.*

Well. A lot of people have brown eyes, but I was still kicking myself for not realizing who she was. I really just found it hard to believe that someone chose to procreate with Peter Carlevaro in the first place. It wasn't an idea I wanted to linger on.

"What day is it?" Morgan demanded.

"*Mph*," I responded, her hand still over my mouth. I meant, *Oh, let me check my calendar,* but she got the idea. She let her hand drop.

"Shit. It's Friday, isn't it? I forgot. *Shit.*" She grabbed my arm but instead of pulling me, she started pushing me downward.

"What?" I said, baffled. "What are you doing?" She pushed down on my head, and I swatted at her. "Stop that!"

"*You* stop that." Morgan swatted me back. "Dad is always here on Fridays."

My eyes widened. "Shit."

"*Yeah*," she agreed, renewing her efforts to shove me downward, behind the couch. "Just—hide here for a minute. I'll distract him."

"How?"

She hesitated.

"Shit," I groaned again.

"I'll figure it out. Now *shut up.*" She gave me a final shove as the door opened.

I hunched behind the couch like an Olympic runner, or maybe a lemur, my hands planted in the carpet and balanced on the balls of my feet. I didn't like trusting Morgan, *especially* not now, but I didn't have much of a choice. Some things I could charm my way out of, but this sure as hell wasn't one of them.

"... Legality is really not one of my concerns." Carlevaro's voice filled the room. God, he sounded like a cartoon villain. Maybe if he didn't look like a brown-bag lunch left on the school bus all day, it'd be intimidating. Instead he had to resort to blackmail. "I—Morgan?"

"Hi, Dad!" Morgan chirped. She was almost an entirely different person than any version of her I'd encountered. She sounded younger—more real than the mysterious persona she was unfortunately fond of, but still a little hollow to the trained ear. I was a little too well-versed with lying to be fooled that easily.

But Carlevaro wasn't. Or maybe he just wasn't well-versed enough in his daughter to know the difference.

"I— Hold on. I'll have to call you back," Carlevaro said. My shoulders relaxed by a degree. He was on the phone. That meant I only had one person to sneak past. "What are you doing here, sweetie?"

I inched forward, holding my breath. I could see a sliver of the door if I peeked around the edge of the couch; Carlevaro's feet, and Morgan's, one of her boots awkwardly scratching at the back of her calf. I ducked back again. They were still in front of the door. There was another on the opposite side of the room, but that was in Carlevaro's direct line of sight, and I didn't know where it led anyway. An escape was no good if it just trapped me in a beige hall of locked doors anyway.

"I—" Morgan faltered, and I winced. *Come on.* Surely, she could lie to her father. I'd been lying to Dad ever since he gave me a sip of his rum and Coke and asked if I liked it. "I missed you?"

There was a pregnant pause. Then Carlevaro sighed. "Do we have to do this right now, Morgan?" No more *sweetie.* "I was in the middle of a very important phone call. You're not even supposed to be in here. You know that."

"They're all very important," Morgan countered, an edge to her voice. "I can only ever find you here. Friday nights. Like clockwork."

"To think," Carlevaro said. *"Alone."* He made the word weigh a thousand pounds. My stomach dipped. I hadn't—it wasn't like I'd heard that line before, not exactly, but I knew what it looked like; the *I'm really busy right now* and the *Can't we do this later, Jack?* Interrupting always felt like it was a little bit my fault for needing things in the first place.

Morgan huffed, and I heard her cross the room. I shoved my thoughts aside. I could muse about how we weren't so different after all—two sides of the same coin, etc.—later. Morgan was drawing him away from the door. Good. Maybe I could count on her after all.

"To drink bourbon and stare at old pictures." Morgan's

voice was rising. I had the feeling it was a familiar argument. "It's sad, Dad. Move on."

Carlevaro snorted, and his expensive Italian loafers scuffed against the carpet. I peeked around the couch again. The door wasn't quite closed. Carlevaro had pushed it, but the latch didn't take. There was a still a bright strip of beige from the hallway.

"Don't start this again, Morgan," he said, a warning in his voice. I shifted my weight onto the balls of my feet.

"What?" Morgan said, the bubbly daughter act completely discarded. Or at least twisted into something darker. "So it's just a coincidence that you haven't been to Avalon since Aileen Shannon was arrested?"

I crept forward, using the sound of Morgan's rising voice to cover the scuff of my feet. Carlevaro's back was to me, one of his hands resting on the back of an overstuffed couch. There was a chair between me and the door, just big enough for me to hunch behind. I pressed a hand over my mouth to silence my ragged breathing.

"Or that half of this room is still pictures of her?" Morgan went on. I could see her gesture wildly from around the side of the chair. "And you just happen to spend *every* Friday night right here."

"If you don't think I'll revoke your club privileges—"

"You won't," she said. "You promised. And you *always* keep your promises, don't you, Dad?" There was something in her voice I couldn't pin down, an unusual way she put the words together. A threat?

There was a sickly beat of silence. "Is this about Jack Shannon again?" Carlevaro said, and I froze like a rabbit, biting the inside of my cheek. No *Arthur Shannon* here. I *knew* he was just pulling that to mess with me. "Did something happen?"

"I don't want to talk about Jack Shannon right now," Morgan said quickly. Yeah, I *bet* she didn't. What exactly were they saying about me around the Carlevaro-family dinner table? And what did it have to do with promises? "You just don't get it."

"Morgan—"

"Maybe if you'd paid half as much attention to Mom as you did this stupid club—"

"Do not bring your mother into this—"

"She's not Beetlejuice, Dad, she's not going to teleport from Dubai—"

All right, time to go. I sneaked one last peek around the chair to be sure the coast was clear. They were standing toe to toe now, Carlevaro stiff backed like a cadaver while Morgan was practically stepping on his toes, her pink hair falling in her face. I stole across the room, crouched low and scuttling like a demented crab until I got to the door. I eased it open, slid out, and eased it back, almost closed again as Carlevaro and daughter tried to outshout each other.

I leaned against the cold cinder block wall, my hands on my knees, my legs turned to jelly. Holy shit. Holy *shit*.

"Whatever, enjoy your sad old-man time," Morgan scoffed with enough teenage cruelty to take down a horse. "*Don't* follow me."

I pushed myself off the wall, wincing at the sound my shoes made against the linoleum. I was halfway down the hall by the time Morgan ducked out of the lounge and slammed the heavy oak door behind her. It cracked like a gunshot, leaving the hallway horrifically silent. I stopped, and our eyes met.

Then I was moving again. Bye. I'd pull on doors until I found the right one, if I had to.

"Jack," Morgan called after me in an undertone. "Jack, come on." She jogged after me, snagging her fingers in the crook of my elbow. I yanked my arm back. She didn't get to touch me.

"Leave me alone." I didn't look back. I'd figure my own way out. It couldn't be that hard. I pulled open the door nearest to me. A storage closet. What kind of janitor did you hire to clean a clandestine hallway? Fucking ridiculous.

"Jack." She was starting to sound like Beth. "At least let me help you find the way out."

"I don't need your help," I said obstinately, hurrying to the next door down the hall. "I can do just fine on my own."

I threw the door open and was rewarded by a faceful of cigar smoke. I coughed, and my eyes watered. A table of heavily tattooed men stared back at me, their cigars drooping from their lips. One ground his in an ashtray and made to stand.

"Excuse me." I wheezed and slammed the door shut again.

"Clearly," Morgan deadpanned. "Will you slow down for, like, one second?"

I responded with a glare and reached for the third door.

Morgan lunged forward and grabbed my wrist. "Not that one," she said quickly. "Just—trust me, okay?"

I didn't want to trust a Carlevaro about anything, but I took her word on that one.

"Let me explain," Morgan said, pushing her hand back through her hair, leaving it in disarray. It was the closest to real Morgan that I'd seen so far. Or at least as far as I could tell, considering I'd already been duped once. But it was enough to make me pause.

She exhaled gustily, her hands dropping to her sides. "I knew you wouldn't trust me if you knew who my dad was—"

"Correct."

"So I—"

"Decided to stalk me?"

"Will you shut up?" Morgan snapped. She shoved her hands in her pockets, her shoulders curving sulkily. "So I wanted you to get to know me first. So you'd trust me when I finally told you the truth."

"And what is the truth, Morgan?" I asked, ignoring the hypocrisy nagging at me. I was probably the last person to be talking about truth. My friends were still waiting in the club, wondering where I'd gone. With the exception of Lucky, who was probably researching ways to curse me and my name for the next thousand years. "The whole truth."

She bit her bottom lip and looked back over her shoulder, where a long beige hallway separated her from her father. Me from Peter Carlevaro. "I know that my dad is the reason your mom is in jail," she said. She looked back at me, her expression determined. "And I want to help you."

"Why should I believe you?" I asked. I legitimately wanted to know. Morgan seemed so sure of herself, even after getting caught in the lie.

"Because you don't have a choice," she said. "Your stupid plan isn't going to work."

"What would you know about my stupid plan?" I countered.

"Enough to know that you can't do it without me," she said. "I've seen you snooping around. What you're looking for, you're not going to find in the club. That's all just dramatics he puts on to distract everyone from all this." She nodded at the hall around us, beige and bland and not totally unlike Carlevaro himself. "Anything important—really important—he keeps in his office." She paused, clearly for dramatic effect. "I got you back here. I can get you back there too."

I stared at her, my mind moving a thousand miles an hour. We were wrong, fallen in the trap that Carlevaro set for just that purpose. The Avalon Club was a decoy, a peacock flashing its feathers so we didn't notice the much more mundane answer beside it. Or Morgan could be lying.

And yet here we were, standing outside the Avalon Club in a whole world I hadn't even known existed. If there was this much hiding beyond Avalon's walls, what else had I missed? What else had I miscalculated?

"Why?" I asked again. "Why help me?"

She smirked. "C'mon, Jack," Morgan said. "If Peter Carlevaro was your dad, wouldn't you want a little teenage rebellion too?"

IN REAL LIFE

"ABSOLUTELY NOT," REMY SAID.

"Are you on drugs?" Gabe added.

"I really don't think this is a good idea." Georgia frowned.

Lucky was still not talking to me.

"Okay, just listen," I said, flapping my hands to ward off the fresh wave of dissent on the horizon. A Dad move, usually when he knew he was losing. Bad sign. "She said she wants to help us, and I think she means it."

It was still fairly early in the evening, at least for a Friday, meaning it was before midnight, and the Strip was bustling with tourists and partygoers. We were crammed around a café table outside of a smoothie place, bathed in streetlights and neon marquee. I was pointedly not looking at the man across the street in some sort of leather harness taking selfies with tourists, for which I unfortunately had the best view in the house. I was still thinking too fast to eat anything, but Lucky had two smoothies in front of her, presumably saving one to chuck at me if she got angry enough. The look on her face said she was considering it.

"We had a plan," Remy said. Their face wasn't much better.

I winced. "I know."

"And you ditched us."

"I know."

"You could have ruined everything."

Okay, now that wasn't entirely fair. I could have, but I didn't. And if I took a risk, I wasn't the only one. By the time I made it back into the Avalon Club, Gabe had already figured out that there was nothing to be found in the sword-in-the-stone statue and had progressed to mixing drinks as if he were a real bartender.

"There was nothing to risk," I said, an impatient edge to my voice. I didn't know why they all seemed to think I *wanted* this setback—the statue was a bust, and Morgan was our only choice left. How was that *my* fault? "We were wrong. *I* was wrong, okay? But we have new information now. We can keep moving forward." I had to keep moving forward, even if there was the very real possibility that it would be forward right off a cliff.

"I don't know, dude," Gabe said. He was wearing the silver suit jacket that Georgia had been carrying for him, like he couldn't stand not to be gaudy for a moment longer than necessary. He wrapped his arms around the Money Backpack, which was slung over his chest BabyBjörn style. To foil pickpockets, he said. Despite my misadventures and the overall failure of the evening, Georgia had still made out pretty well at the blackjack table. If Mom went to jail, and Beth sold the Golden Age, and I became a homeless grifter, the two of us could probably make decent money counting cards in Atlantic City. Something to consider. "Isn't Carlevaro's whole thing, like, *being a criminal*? You don't think his daughter maybe, like, inherited *the lying gene*? How are we supposed to trust her?"

"Yeah, but . . ." I faltered, my argument weak even in my own ears.

"We *said*," Lucky spoke at long last, "no more lies."

She turned each word into a bullet. She should have looked ridiculous, a fourteen-(and-a-half)-year-old beanpole-shaped girl sitting with her arms folded across her chest, her two puffy pigtails lit up green and pink respectively by the city lights, but I certainly wasn't laughing. Lucky had come to the Morgan Carlevaro conclusion before I did, and she would have warned me if I hadn't taken out the AirPod.

In conclusion: I fucked up. I knew I fucked up. But I didn't see why we couldn't move past that in light of recent events.

"I'm sorry," I said. I turned to Lucky. "I'm sorry I didn't listen to you." To Remy. "I'm sorry I lied." To Gabe and Georgia. "I'm sorry I wasn't there when you needed me."

"Jack," Georgia warned, "don't say 'but.'"

"*But.*" Too late. "This could be our chance. It wasn't in the statue, okay? So what now, if not Morgan? What other leads do we have?" I was letting frustration leak into my voice. The truth was worse than they even knew, but I couldn't admit that now, not with Lucky still shooting me a death glare. We were out of time. *I* was out of time. I couldn't afford to retreat and regroup. Literally. Without the Onyx card, the chips in the Money Backpack were all we had left.

Georgia was watching me with a careful expression that made me want to bristle, like I was a wounded animal she was trying to coax out of the corner. "What about the money?" she suggested gently, gesturing toward the backpack hanging off Gabe's front. "Is there something we could do with that to help your mom?" Gabe and Remy nodded sort of half-heartedly.

It was like a slap to the face. Or maybe a bucket of cold water over my head. They didn't get it. This wasn't about *money*. If there was one thing that the Shannon family had—above honor or goodwill or even love—it was money. "If a bank account could save my mom, it would have already," I said, unable to keep the venom from my voice. It was better than the hurt, at least. "It was kind of the first thing we tried, actually."

It wasn't enough. The helplessness came over me like a wave. For the first time in my life, money meant nothing, and I didn't have much else. I had everything Mom ever taught me—how to play cards, how to make a risky bet, how to lie my ass off—and I had my friends.

And even they didn't believe in me anymore.

"I'm not saying we should start making friendship bracelets with Morgan," I said tersely, sticking to my guns, because I couldn't say any of the things I was actually feeling.

I couldn't show that kind of weakness—not now. If I started, I might never stop. "But we should at least listen to what she has to say."

"Listen to *her*?" Remy repeated. They were sitting opposite me, I realized suddenly. Not next to me. It was enough to make my thoughts stumble. Remy usually sat next to me, but even at the little café table, they'd managed to avoid it. "You won't even listen to *us*."

I would later have a couple of regrets about what I was about to say.

I was stung about my realization about Remy, and confused about Morgan, and frankly still worked up over seeing the pictures of Mom lining Carlevaro's inner sanctum. But, as my therapist would say, those are excuses. And I'm trying not to make those as much anymore.

I reacted badly.

"Oh, so it's all good when you guys are having fun playing spies," I said, "but when it comes too close to actually getting somewhere, suddenly it's too dangerous."

Gabe pulled a face. "There's a little bit of a difference, Jack."

"You know it's not like that," Georgia added.

No, they didn't know what it was *like*. They didn't know the Onyx card was useless now, and even if they did, they'd never understand the stakes. We only had one shot at exposing Carlevaro, and I couldn't waste it. I didn't get to go home after this. Not if we failed.

I would lose everything.

AMANDA DEWITT

"Fine. I'll do it myself," I snapped, my hands planted on the sticky café table. The delicate feeling that had been trembling in my chest since boarding the plane back in Boston was cracking now, and a roaring wind hid on the other side of it. There was a hurricane inside my chest, almost too loud to hear over. "Like I should have from the beginning."

I thought the moment the words left my mouth would be like a gunshot. Like an earthquake. But it wasn't. There was no recoil, no aftershocks, no chorus of descent. It was silent, except for the babble of the street crowd and the distant honking of traffic. People talking and laughing and living their lives, as if mine wasn't ending.

I had to go.

I banged my ankles against the metal bench as I pushed myself to my feet. I tried not to think of it as running away, but it was hard to call it anything else. I couldn't look in their eyes, so I looked at the neon lights instead. "I'll see you back at the hotel."

When Mom left the Golden Age in handcuffs, she'd done it with her chin held high, her eyes icy, wearing a cream-colored pantsuit and not a single hair out of place. I left my friends with my hands shaking and my eyes burning, shouldering my way through foot traffic and trying not to break into a run. I didn't know what I was supposed to do. I couldn't talk to my friends, couldn't talk to Beth. I definitely didn't want to talk to Morgan.

I wanted to talk to Mom. I wanted to hear her voice. The thought struck me like a punch to the chest, driving the

264

breath from my lungs. I gripped my phone so hard it hurt, but I had a feeling it was after hours at the county jail.

I let my feet drag, losing momentum the farther away I got. I made it to the Fountains of Bellagio, which meant it was crowded, but toward the end of the show, which meant the crowd was starting to break up and move on. I drifted forward, toward the stone barrier as the fountains sprayed in elegant choreographed arches. The Bellagio Resort and Casino rose like two great wings behind them, a crowned dome at its center. The stone barrier was cool against my palms. There'd be another show in fifteen minutes. I decided to wait. I wouldn't be able to face the suite again for a while anyway.

"Jack."

Shit. I hadn't even realized how scratchy my eyes were until I wasn't alone anymore, and there was nothing to do about it now. The only thing worse than crying was trying not to cry. It was like holding your thumb over a hose. The longer you pressed down, the worse the pressure got.

But it was better than the alternative. Shannons didn't cry. Anywhere. I leaned forward and rested my forehead against my folded arms as the fountains died down. It was easier than looking back at Remy. "You didn't have to follow me," I mumbled.

"You wanted me to follow you." I felt Remy come up beside me, stirring the night air.

Yeah, I did. I couldn't admit it, but Remy didn't need me to. They knew I didn't really want to be alone. Even mad at me, they were good enough not to let me.

"I think we should probably talk," Remy said. I peeked sideways, lifting my head just enough to see that Remy had mirrored me, their chin resting on their arms. Of course, they didn't have to hunch so much to reach the stone railing. One very specific benefit to being short.

"I'm not sure I want that," I said weakly. My heart beat painfully in my chest, like it'd been dislodged during my escape and was stuck someplace that wasn't entirely healthy. I suddenly wished I'd listened to Gabe's guy talk after all. I felt like something was about to happen, but I didn't know what.

"Too bad."

They gently prodded my elbow with theirs, and I finally lifted my head. I scrubbed under my eye with the back of my hand. "I shouldn't have said that to you guys." Somehow it was the first real apology I'd come up with. It was easy to say the word *sorry*. It was harder, almost impossible, to admit that you were wrong. At least for a Shannon. "Especially to you."

Remy watched me, blue light from the fountain's spotlights playing across the curve of their cheek. "But?" they prompted.

"There's not always a *but*."

"With you there is."

I winced. There was always an asterisk, always a way out of it. I wanted to think it was a Shannon thing, but maybe my family was just another excuse. Maybe, for once, it was just Jack. For better or for worse.

"It's not always a bad thing." Remy leaned forward until I couldn't help but look at them. Their lips quirked victoriously as I met their eyes. "I mean, sometimes it's annoying as hell, don't get me wrong, but it means you're always thinking. You never stop moving, Jack. It's why you can do things like organize secret blackjack clubs and convince all of us to fly across the country to participate in your stupid schemes."

"The convincing really wasn't all that hard," I muttered. Not really among my top-ten biggest grifts.

"*But*," Remy said heavily, "you seem to keep forgetting that you're in the middle of the worst thing that's ever happened to you. You need to slow down."

"Well—"

"Including the time you were forgotten at the airport in Boca Raton, yes."

Of course Remy remembered that story. It was a good story, but I still felt my throat close up as I battled a wave of emotion. I closed my eyes, steeling my nerves. "I'm sorry," I said. "I know you guys were having fun, and suddenly it's not fun anymore, but"—fuck, there was that word again—"*but* I don't get to go back to real life after this. I don't get to get on a plane and go back to school and Hullabaloo and pretend like this never happened. If I don't save my mom, *soon*, I won't have a real life to go back to."

I wasn't sure I ever did at all. Was real life Christmases in Aspen and the cold penthouse living room and summers training blackjack dealers in the library basement? This was the closest thing to real life I could think of—the soft night breeze ruffling my hair and the spray of the fountains as they kicked up the next show, the way they came together to dust Remy's curls with little droplets of water that glittered like diamonds.

The thought was so heartbreakingly hokey that it snapped me right out of it. I didn't get to think things like that. It was exactly what I told Gabe: This wasn't real life, however much it might feel like it. I already stood to lose my mom, and the Golden Age, and I didn't even know what else yet. I couldn't lose my friendship with Remy too just because I was stupid enough to be in love with them.

Remy stared at me for a long moment, their eyebrows furrowed just enough to form a little crease between them. "Ugh," they said, dragging their hand down their face. They pushed off the stone railing, away from the fountains. "Gabe was right. You're such an idiot."

I—what? I turned to follow them, my hands held out helplessly in front of me. That wasn't exactly the reaction I was expecting. "You talked to Gabe?" My heart skipped a beat, and my eyes widened. "You talked to Gabe about *me*?"

Remy scoffed. "As if *you* didn't talk with Gabe about *me*."

"How do you know?" Wasn't guy talk supposed to be sacred or something stupid like that? If Gabe thought just because I quibbled about the name *guy talk* there weren't any rules, he had another thing coming—

"Jack," Remy said, exasperated. "I knew you weren't going to the *gym*."

I pressed my fingertips against my temples, trying to make some sort of sense out of my chaotic thoughts. I'd gone from frustrated to depressed to confused in short order, and it was all starting to blend into a headache. This was exactly why I usually did my best to repress the messier emotions and call it a day. "Wait, wait, wait," I said. "Okay, I get why you were mad at me before, but why are you mad at me now?"

"Because it's not a game for us, Jack!" Remy threw their hands in the air. People gave us a careful berth, but didn't really spare us a second glance. People yelled at each other about games a lot around there. "None of us are here to have fun, we're here for *you!*" They poked me in the chest, right at the center of one of the big blue polka dots covering my latest horrible fashion choice. "This *is* real life, Jack. I'm here with you *in real life* and . . ."

They faltered, their lips parted, like they didn't know how they got this far, and it was too late to go back. I knew the feeling.

"That's all I wanted," Remy said, and they poked me again in the chest for good measure, but there was no fire to it this time. "To be here with you in real life."

"Oh," I said, and it was like the space between us was every moment since I read their first post, back when I was lonely and confused, and all I knew was that the words *Is something wrong with me?* felt like they were ripped straight from my most secret thoughts. There was Hullaballoo, and conversations at three in the morning, and pictures of their dog when I couldn't admit that I was unhappy, but Remy somehow always knew anyway.

There was this moment—fountains and city lights and *real life*.

"Oh," Remy agreed softly. "I—" They hesitated, and their eyes slid past me. "Is that Gabe?"

I blinked, dazed. "What?"

"Gabe." Remy pointed, and I turned, combing the crowd. "Coming toward us. Look. Why's he running?"

There. It was hard to miss Gabe's metallic silver suit jacket. It made him look like a B-movie astronaut sprinting down the sidewalk running after a kid wearing a dark hoodie and carrying a—

"Oh my God," Remy said. "*Oh my God*. It's the Money Backpack."

GLADIATORS

REMY AND I TOOK OFF RUNNING. THE KID WAS PAST us before we could even move, Gabe hot on his heels, but somehow giving chase felt like the only sensible thing to do.

We always had the Money Backpack, ever since I handed it to Dad and he came back with the first chips, though I hadn't had an obvious nickname for it then. We needed somewhere to carry our chips, and whatever we cashed in, and I'd rather die than carry it in a briefcase. If I got to that point, I might as well buy a plaid flat cap and age forty years. It was a prop, the chips all a part of our cover at the Avalon Club, but that didn't mean they weren't worth real money.

Our *only* money, now that the Onyx card was frozen. Without that money, there were no more second chances. No plan B. The chips were useless outside of the Avalon club, but we wouldn't be able to even go back in without enough chips to make it look like we belonged.

Shit.

"Sorry!" Remy shouted as we shoved, slipped, and negotiated our way through the crowd. "Sorry, sorry! Excuse me!" The Bellagio's fountain show was ending again, which actually made it worse, as the crowd started to disperse. Moving targets filtered back toward the sidewalk, a swaying forest of colorful shirts and baseball hats through which I could just barely keep track of Gabe's silver jacket. I couldn't see the thief, but if Gabe was still moving, I trusted that he could.

I wasn't sure what we were supposed to do once we caught the thief. Citizen's arrest? The thousands of dollars in illegal gambling winnings might be hard to explain.

"Watch out!" Remy yanked me backward by the collar as a man in a fantastically pink Hawaiian shirt stepped out in front of me. I glanced off of him instead of straight-up colliding, but the encounter wasn't without casualties. He spooked, and his drink went flying—thirty-two fluid ounces of red Slushie collided with my chest and dripped down my shirt like a boozy bloodstain.

Oh God, it was *cold*. I made a strangled sound and touched my sticky chest, but Remy pulled me forward again, their hand around my wrist. I staggered after them, leaving the tourist to mourn his lost twenty-dollar drink on his own.

"Gabe," I squeaked as I saw the intersection of Las Vegas Boulevard and East Flamingo rapidly approaching. Ten lanes of traffic plus two turn lanes that merged onto the Strip to form a total of twelve chances to become a piece of roadkill. "Gabriel, *donotcrossthatroad*!"

The thief sprinted out onto the asphalt just as the cross-street traffic started to go. The cars on Flamingo sat like racehorses at the gate, their headlights cutting stripes against their legs as Gabe and the thief took off, blatantly ignoring the bridge specifically meant for foot traffic and avoiding vehicular manslaughter.

We were at the intersection sooner than I expected, and I came to the realization that my advice was harder to follow than I wanted it to be. The stairs to the foot bridge were around the corner, which would cost us precious time. Not to mention the stairs themselves. Let's just say there was a reason Remy found our gym excuse so unbelievable. My lungs already burned, and my legs were rapidly turning to lead. The moment I stopped moving, I fully intended to collapse to the ground.

My eyes flickered to the streetlight; still red, but it wouldn't be for long. I felt my shoe connect with the sidewalk and knew I had to make a decision before it left the ground again. No time to hesitate.

I glanced at Remy—just for a second, just long enough to meet their eyes—and we ran out into the road after them.

And then we got hit by a— Okay, no, just kidding. But we did get lucky.

Just as we started across the road, one of the cars turning right off of Las Vegas Boulevard almost hit the thief. The red Mazda slammed on the breaks, with an unhealthy-sounding screech, at the last moment. The thief only flinched and scurried forward, the Money Backpack thumping against his back. Gabe executed this weird slide across the hood of the sedan, like he was starring in a buddy-cop movie from the '70s and the only thing keeping him moving was a heady cocktail of cigarettes and police brutality. It was actually impressive until he tripped on the landing. The thief looked back.

They were too far away for me to see a face, the hood casting shadow across their eyes, but I saw enough. A flash of pink.

I stopped in my tracks, which was not the right reaction when one was standing in the middle of traffic. *Morgan*. It was all I could think. My friends were right. Morgan was playing us, and I was the fool who wanted to trust her.

Remy shoved me forward, forcing me back into the reality where I was standing in the road.

We bolted to the soundtrack of discordant honking as cars stacked up behind the increasingly pissed-off Mazda. I threw up the little *thanks for not running me over* wave as we streaked past them. As we hit the pavement on the opposite side, the light for Flamingo Road turned green.

Which was enough pulse-pounding adventure for me, thank you very much, but our quarry didn't agree. Morgan veered left and hotfooted it across the parking lot, straight into Caesars Palace.

"Shit," I wheezed. That was the kind of heat we definitely didn't need. Hotel and casinos didn't take well to people running through the premises at breakneck speed. And that was assuming no one had already called the police. Suddenly the stakes changed, and collecting Gabe and getting the hell out of here became more important than getting our money back. The only scenario worse than losing the Money Backpack was getting caught with a backpack full of poker chips from a casino no one had ever heard of. All while being distinctly under the legal gambling age, as a cherry on top.

Not that I expected an explanation would be strictly necessary. The dots would connect themselves pretty well on their own.

Remy and I reached the lobby doors just in time to meet a group coming out of them. A college girls volleyball team, by the looks of it, but I was more focused on their mascot. Ironically, a Roman soldier. Less ironically, a Roman soldier I collided with at top speed, my face cushioned by his soft-foam pecs. Not as fun as it might sound. I wasn't interested in getting to second base before, and I definitely wasn't then.

I tangoed with the sweaty college kid inside of the mascot as I tried to extract myself from his foam embrace. I might have thrown a few more elbows than strictly necessary, but I finally emerged, bouncing like a pinball through the throng of girls in matching varsity jackets. I could see Remy doing the same, sans mascot groping. It didn't seem fair that all the particularly bad things kept happening to me.

Finally, we burst into the lobby, slipping on the extrav-agantly patterned marble floor. I grabbed Remy by the arm before they could tip over, and we leaned against each other, breathing hard. The air-conditioning blew in my face, drying the sweat in my hair and testing the limits of my already burning lungs. The lobby was all white marble and gold, and people stared at us like we were from another planet. I felt the vicious urge to tell them who I was, so they knew I wasn't a weird teenager who looked like he was about to throw up all over the marble, but a weird *Shannon*. If they were going to look, they should at least know they were looking at rock bottom. Maybe it'd make them appreciate their vacations a little more.

Gabe had semi-trapped the thief. There was no doubt it was Morgan now. No one else would wear bug-eyed sunglasses to a heist, her hair half obscuring one of the lenses in a damning wave of pink. There was a circular fountain at the center of the lobby, a trio of Grecian women casting judgment from the center. Gabe had managed to get her on one side of the fountain and him on the other, so they both kept spinning back and forth, feinting one way and then the other like they were cursed to live their lives in a cartoon.

"Gabe," I gasped, still holding on to Remy like they were a lifeline. My legs were trembling, berating me for going back on my promise to collapse at the first opportunity. "GabeGabeGabe," I added, like a particularly stupid Pokémon. I meant, *We need to grab Gabe and go before we get arrested*, but that was too many syllables for my lungs to support.

"Gabe," Remy agreed. They nodded furiously, their curls flopping in every direction. Less crystalline-droplets-and-poetry than in front of the Bellagio, but I was grateful to have them there with me.

We moved forward as one.

Or at least I thought we did. It turned out that what I thought was a coordinated plan to get Gabe, Remy interpreted as a plan to *help* Gabe. When I went forward to grab him, Remy went in the other direction as if to trap Morgan in a pincer movement between the two of them. Which might have worked (sort of), if I didn't take the opportunity to wrap my arms around Gabe's middle and haul him backward.

Remy darted forward the same moment that Morgan made a break for it. They managed to get their hands on the backpack, but rather than pulling it out of Morgan's grip, the zipper split open like a mouth, spewing poker chips across the marble floor. Remy stared down at it, dumbfounded. Meanwhile, Morgan dropped the backpack and flat-out ran, taking the opportunity to zag sideways and disappear onto Caesars' casino floor.

All of this happened in the span of about three seconds while Gabe thrashed against my grip.

"What are you doing?" he grunted. "He's getting away!" Well, at least he couldn't tell that it was Morgan who threw our entire winnings all over the floor of Caesars Palace.

"And you're on camera," I muttered in his ear. Or I tried to. Maybe two words got out before Gabe accidentally bashed me in the nose with the back of his head. At least I hoped it was accidentally. Stars bloomed across my vision, accompanied by a hot gush of blood. I choked and tripped backward, still holding Gabe around the middle, and we tipped into the circular fountain sitting proudly at the center of the lobby. After our brisk jog, the cool, stale water closing over my head was almost soothing. Except for the part where I sputtered, gagged, and shoved Gabe off of me before his freakishly tall body could drown me.

I dragged myself to my hands and knees, dripping water and gaping like a fish as blood and chlorinated fountain water dripped down my face. Any lingering hope for a clean getaway was lost among the slimy pennies slipping under my palms. Maybe, I considered, just maybe, drowning was the better option here.

A hand grabbed me by the collar and help pulled me up. "Remy," I croaked. Except my nose was still bleeding freely, so it sounded more like *Rdhemny*.

Not Remy, unless Remy had turned into a man wearing a Caesars Palace security polo and grown a truly impressive mustache. The security guard looked down at me over it, one hand holding me up like a misbehaving puppy while the other held a walkie-talkie up to his mouth. I could hear Gabe splashing as he got a similar treatment.

"Yeah," the security guard drawled into his walkie-talkie, so close he could probably taste the plastic. "We got 'em, Mr. Carlevaro."

♠

What I know now that I didn't know then: On April 8, 2016, a company known as Galahad Properties purchased Caesars

Palace. Galahad Properties, as anyone with a passing knowledge of Arthurian legend, and how dedicated one man can be to a theme, might guess, could be traced back to Peter Carlevaro.

Which is how I ended up getting caught by Peter Carlevaro for the second time that summer, only in considerably worse shape than the first time.

Let's take stock of the situation. I had:

— No money. Morgan got away, and our winnings were all over the floor of the Caesars Palace lobby. Asking security if we could collect them before they took us in was a little too bold, even for me.

— No results. Morgan had been our last lead on getting our hands on Carlevaro's book of dirty little secrets, and I sure as hell wasn't about to give her a call now.

— A bloody, but not broken, nose. A member of the casino's security team patched it up, but I was already developing two black eyes where Gabe's thick head endeavored to drive my nose back into my skull. Not my best look, but it did make me look cool in a *Fight Club* kind of way.

— A lot—*a lot*—of explaining to do.

They put me in an empty room in the Caesars Palace security office—I was getting pretty familiar with the behind-the-scenes security offices of famous hotel-casinos in Las Vegas. I was considering writing a guidebook. In the meantime, I was planted on a swivel chair, pressing an ice pack to my nose. I looked like a prisoner of war. My clothes were beyond saving; there was a giant red stain from the Slushie incident right over my chest, which paired nicely with the blood on my collar. I was slowly starting to dry out, but no matter how many times I ran my hand through my hair, it still stuck up in ridiculous spikes. I groaned and closed my eyes, leaning into the ice pack.

Gabe and Remy had been stored in another room. Or maybe separate rooms, to keep them from getting their stories straight. I didn't know where Georgia and Lucky were. All I really knew was that my head felt like it was going to explode, starting with my aching nose.

That, and I knew Beth had arrived.

I could hear her voice, muffled on the other side of the door. I could hear Carlevaro too.

"I hope you plan on doing something about this, Bethany." Carlevaro's voice dripped with icy condescension. Just the sound of it made me want to grit my teeth, but my jaw ached too much to go through with it.

"I do." Beth sounded tense.

"I've decided not to press charges. The Shannons have had enough trouble with the authorities, I think," Carlevaro continued haughtily. "You're all lucky that I have properties all over the Strip. And that I informed my security teams to keep an eye out for our friend Arthur there." He paused. "Somehow, I suspected we might have this problem."

He'd been watching me the whole time then. I'd put too much faith in the idea that Carlevaro underestimated me, that he didn't expect me to come back. Did he know just how much time I'd spent inside the Imperium? Did I only make it into the Avalon Club because he allowed me to? My stomach roiled, but all I could do was adjust the ice pack.

"This is . . ." My sister paused, taking a deep breath. "Thank you, Peter. I'll take care of it." Something in her voice promised a reckoning. Even safely on the other side of the door, I flinched.

"See that you do." Another pause. "I'd like to talk to him, with your permission."

I opened my eyes. The wood grain of the door stared back at me.

"I don't—"

"It's fine." The words left my mouth before I could stop them, my voice pitched loud enough to carry to the other side of the door. I heard them stop at the sound of my voice. Did they know I could hear them the whole time, or was making me listen to my own humiliation an unexpected side effect? "I want to talk to him."

The door opened a moment later. Carlevaro stood in the doorway, the office's harsh light reflecting blindingly off his shaved head and casting gaunt shadows under his eyes. He looked like the Grinch on Christmas morning, his mouth curled in smug satisfaction. Beth stood behind him. She exhaled gustily when she caught sight of me.

"Jesus, Jack," she murmured.

"It's not as bad as it looks," I said, even as my bruised nose and fat lip slurred the consonants a little. I looked away from her guiltily, turning to Carlevaro instead. "Come to gloat?"

His eyes flickered up and down pointedly, like my entire state of being was satisfaction enough. He turned and muttered one last thing to Beth before closing the door behind him. We were alone in the dusty little office, the linoleum and white cement block making the room seem colder than it was.

"Always the path of most resistance, I see," he said, his voice like an oil slick. "I can't say I'm impressed, Arthur."

I lowered the ice pack. "Jack," I said, my tongue thick and nearly useless. My mouth tasted like blood and chlorine.

"What was that, Arthur?"

"My name is Jack," I spat. "Jack Shannon. Didn't Morgan tell you?"

His expression didn't change but mine did. That told me everything I needed to know. It wasn't an accident that Morgan had stolen the Money Backpack and led us into a hotel conveniently owned by her father. It had been a trap.

I'd been so ready to believe her—because I hated her father too, I guess, or maybe just because I knew how hard it was, growing up when one of your parents had more important things to do than actually parent. Clearly, I was the fool.

Carlevaro hummed to himself and pulled something out of his pocket. My heart lurched. A poker chip, white and gold. The Avalon Club logo flashed in the light as he rolled it over his fingers. He'd gotten all his money back in the end too. I wondered when the indignities would stop piling up.

"What do you want?" I pressed the ice pack against my nose again. It was starting to melt, but at the moment the cold against my skin was the singular good thing in my life.

"Just say it and go. I'm in enough pain without having to listen to your voice."

Carlevaro only smirked. There was a flash of movement, and I dropped the ice pack, my hand going up on instinct to pluck the poker chip out of the air. It was warm in my palm. A gold 500 was scrawled on one side.

"Keep it," Carlevaro said, staring down his nose at me. He considered me like I was a tool he didn't know how to use yet. He must have come from dinner because he wasn't in his usual Lex Luthor–ass suit and tie. His shirt collar was open, one button away from being Dad levels of too much cleavage. If I could see the cross necklace nestled in his chest hair, it was too many buttons. "In case you want to try again." His smile twitched.

I bristled. He was mocking me. There was no way I'd be able to try again. Not now. Beth was probably interrogating my friends as we spoke, and Carlevaro's network went even further than I'd thought. That was it. Game over.

Unless, my mind chorused. *Unless, unless, unless*—I stopped every possibility before I could consider it. I wouldn't give him the satisfaction of seeing me hope.

"And if not," he said, as if reading my mind. He chuckled. "Consider it something to remember me by."

♠

Dad picked me up in the red Honda Civic.

I knew things were bad then—like really bad, probably end-of-the-world bad. Beth didn't rely on Dad for anything, much less to be my parole officer. If she was trusting him to take me home, it meant that she was busy with much worse things.

The penthouse was cold and dark by the time I dragged myself through the door. The lights from the city cast a dusky glow through the bay windows, throwing shadows over the white carpet and the white furniture and the white walls. I sighed, and the silence swallowed it up.

Dad put a hand on my shoulder, his palm warm and calloused. I blinked at it. We weren't really a very tactile family—sometimes we were hardly a family at all. A warm glow burst in my chest, so unfamiliar it actually made me a little nauseous.

"You'll be all right," he said, with the kind of misplaced confidence that only Dad could muster. Usually I didn't like empty platitudes, especially the ones that were absolutely not true, but I was feeling pretty low. At that point, I might have even taken an "everything happens for a reason."

I swallowed, my throat tight with a swell of emotion. I almost even believed him. "Thanks, Dad."

He smiled, and we savored the rare father-son moment.

"Are you gonna . . . ?" He gave a little jerk of his head. Right. I was standing in the middle of the doorway. Well, two and a half minutes of emotional vulnerability wasn't too bad. It might have even been a record.

"Sure, Dad." I dragged my unwilling carcass into motion. I didn't want to have this conversation in front of Dad anyway. If Beth thought she was mad now, she'd be really mad if she knew how much I'd semi-tricked Dad into being a part of my schemes. Take nuclear and make it apocalyptic.

Beth found me in my bedroom not long after. I'd changed into sweatpants and a hoodie, both to complete the depressed-chic look and because my semi-damp clothes were starting to itch. The door opened, and I looked up.

She didn't close the door behind her, which made my anxiety spike. Beth loved to fight with Mom, but she didn't like airing our dirty laundry. She always closed the door, even when it barely muffled their voices. Either she wasn't planning on yelling at me, or we were past the point where she cared what anyone else heard.

I wasn't sure which was worse. I'd expected yelling. I actually might have enjoyed some yelling, if it meant I got to yell back.

"I spoke to your friends' parents," Beth said, her voice rough with . . . exhaustion? Emotion? I couldn't tell the difference anymore, even in myself. At some point they just became one in the same.

My stomach dropped. There was a middle ground between *Beth thinks I've been running through the city playing extreme tag at all hours of the night* and *Beth knows the truth.*

She knew my friends were not who I said they were. Worse than that, she knew we'd lied to their parents to get them here in the first place.

"You told me I could invite friends over," I said, but the argument was pathetic even to my own ears. Beth told me I could invite people from *Elkhollow,* not people off the

Internet whom I'd never technically met before, and I conveniently never mentioned that I'd branched out from the idea a bit. It wasn't technically a lie, but that was the kind of Mom logic that would only make her more upset.

Beth clearly wasn't impressed. "I want the card back, Jack," she said softly.

I hesitated, just for an instant, before I pulled my wallet off my desk. The Avalon Club card winked at me from where it was tucked behind my new PizzaDome rewards card. I brushed over it and pulled free the Onyx card.

I couldn't help but sound sulky as I handed it over. "It stopped working anyway."

"I just—" Beth bit off the words with a frustrated sound and pressed her fingers to her forehead, her head bowed. My stomach dropped a little further. I imagined there were probably sightings of it around the fourth-floor gym by this point.

"Beth—"

"I trusted you, Jack," she snapped, dropping her hand. Her voice was raw, like the past few weeks had scraped away any patience she had left. "Do you have any idea how hard all this has been? Do you have *any* idea?"

I almost could have laughed, I was so taken aback. Is that what she wanted to talk about? Trust? "What? Because it's been *easy* for me?" I countered.

"I *know* it's been hard for you," she said. "Which is why I tried to help you. I gave you the Onyx, Jack. That's why I gave you space. And all you did was turn around and throw it right back in my face."

I had been slumped in my swivel chair, one leg tucked underneath me, somewhere between sad puppy and teenage rebellion. I was standing now, my hands clenched into fists at my sides. I was yelling too. "All *I* did," I said, poking viciously at my own chest, "was try to save this fucking family. From Peter Carlevaro *and* from *you*!" She stared at me, stunned. I swallowed thickly. "He told me you wanted to sell him the Golden Age. Did you think I would never find out?"

Silence reigned as we stood opposite one another, frozen like two gunslingers waiting to pull the trigger.

It took me a moment to realize that Beth was crying. No—Beth was trying not to cry. After all, Shannons didn't cry.

And while Beth was a Shannon through and through, she wasn't Mom; not my mom nor anyone else's. Beth had been nearly the only responsible figure in my life for so long that sometimes I forgot that she was only a twenty-three-year-old dental assistant.

Beth shook off the moment of weakness like an old coat. She pushed back her hair from her face. "I can't do this, Jack," she said, without looking at me. The anger was gone, or at least put somewhere else. Now all that was left was resignation. "I can't take care of Mom and you. I tried, but I can't."

I didn't need taking care of, but the words died in my mouth. "What does that mean?"

"Tomorrow, your friends are going home," Beth said. She straightened her back, like a general about to go to war. "And you're going back to Elkhollow."

She might as well have slapped me. "You can't do that," I said. My heart was pounding in my ears, and suddenly I felt more helpless than when I was sitting in front of Peter Carlevaro. I knew Beth would probably try to send my friends home—I already had arguments queued up for that—but I already *was* home. Or I was supposed to be. She couldn't send me away too.

Things were bad now. Pretty *very* bad, actually, but I could work with it. Granddad had less when he came to Las Vegas, and he managed to found the Golden Age. Sure, it took a little bit of organized crime to get it done, but everything did back then. Everything did *now*. The Avalon Club chip was still in my pocket, Carlevaro's last challenge taunting me.

I'd never get the opportunity if I was in Massachusetts, relegated back to the library basement like an exiled prince, waiting until the day I turned eighteen and could do what I wanted. But that wasn't until December, and it'd be too late by then.

"Beth," I started, trying to put on my best reasonable-young-adult voice, but inside, the scared kid was clawing at the inside of my chest. "Please. Mom—"

"Let Mom worry about Mom," Beth snapped, and it was our conversation in the Imperium parking garage all over again, only this time she didn't sound quite so understanding. I had the feeling that it wasn't going to end with an unsolicited credit card again. "Let me worry about Mom. You've done enough."

I shrank back, falling back into my chair as effectively as if she'd pushed me. "Can I say goodbye to my friends?" I asked, my voice tight.

If I could see them one last time, I might be able to come up with something—anything—to salvage the entire mess. That was what I told myself, but really, truthfully, I just wanted to see them. The last time I'd seen most of them, it had been as I walked away, back when I thought arguing with my friends was the biggest obstacle I had. Gabe's head connecting with my face wasn't going to be in the top ten of our most cherished memories either.

And then there was Remy. My heart twisted painfully. *That's all I wanted. To be here with you in real life.* I wanted to grab on to that moment at the fountains—real and terrifying and exhilarating—and hold on to it forever. I wanted to believe Remy when they said that was real life. But my friends were leaving, and so was the fantasy. Maybe real life would always be a poorly lit basement in Massachusetts, my friends hundreds of miles away and my family even farther.

I knew Beth's answer before she even said it. It hung in the air like a rainy day, dreary and sad. "I don't think that's a good idea," she said stiffly. "Get some rest, Jack. You can pack in the morning."

She turned away and shut the door behind her with a soft click.

ROCK BOTTOM

IT WAS THE WORST I'D EVER SLEPT.

I slept on top of the comforter, but I still managed to get it tangled around my legs as I tossed and turned. I'd barely been in my bedroom since coming back home, and it felt wrong now. I should be in our suite with my friends, listening to Gabe snore from the other bed and Georgia shuffle around making coffee, always the first person awake. I had weird, fractured dreams where I was there with them, except sometimes Mom was too, or Peter Carlevaro. Every time, I tried to leave, and every time, Morgan was waiting outside the door, shaking her head and telling me to try again. I woke up to the sun splintering through the blinds and, somehow, I was more exhausted than I had been before.

I moved mechanically, refusing to look at where my suitcase still lay, where I dropped it upon arrival. I showered. I brushed my teeth. I considered my shirt from the night before, stained red and smelling of cherry vodka, before

I tossed it into the trash. I didn't need any keepsakes. The sooner we all forgot about all this, the better.

I grabbed my phone on instinct, my thumb already going through the familiar motion of unlocking the screen and opening the Hullabaloo app, before I realized that it didn't survive my dip in the fountain at Caesars Palace. Water actually dribbled out of the case, and the screen remained black. I stared at my reflection in the dark screen, my hair still wet and my eyes bloodshot. Phones could be replaced, but at that moment, standing in the middle of my room, as alone as I'd ever been, it felt like the end of the world. I dropped my phone back onto my bed.

It was over. It was all over, and I had even less than I did to begin with.

"It's past noon, you know."

I looked up. I'd kicked the door shut when I got back from the shower, but it didn't latch. I hadn't heard Kerry push it open again. Now she leaned against the doorframe.

I was so not in the mood for cryptic Kerry bullshit. "So?" I said, not bothering to hide my impatience. If she wanted to lecture me too, she could get in fucking line. Maybe it was a good thing I was flying across the country soon after all.

"So you're still sitting around feeling sorry for yourself?" Kerry said. "That's kind of sad."

I glared. I had a perfectly good reason to feel sorry for myself, thank you very much—

"Don't you remember what Granddad always said?"

Kerry said, cutting off my internal rant as if she could actually hear it.

"Racehorses aren't shooting stars, you can't just wish on them?" I didn't know what that was supposed to mean, but I suspected it had something to do with fixing horse races.

"That too," she said, "but I meant 'Rome wasn't built by sitting on your ass.'"

Ah, that one. Granddad was a colorful man.

But I was tired of Shannon wisdom. It hadn't gotten me anywhere good so far. I sighed and scrubbed at my face with one hand. "What do you want, Kerry?" I asked. "I have to pack." I deeply didn't want to pack, but it was better than continuing that conversation. My patience for just about anything had run out.

Kerry took a step inside my room. "You really think you can save Mom?" she said, and something in her voice was enough to get me to really pay attention. The purple ends of her hair hung in her eyes, partially obscuring her face. "If you're right, I mean. About Peter Carlevaro."

Was this a trick? Did Beth send her to dig up any lingering plans I might have in motion? I didn't want to believe that. Kerry might be *my* older sister, but she was Beth's younger sibling too. We had a common ground there that made us stronger together, when we chose to utilize it.

Maybe this wasn't a trick, but what was it? A scheme? Kerry didn't scheme. She was the only Shannon smart enough not to partake.

Carlevaro's poker chip was heavy in my pocket. I was

sure that I was right. I was less certain that I could pull it off. Morgan was working for her dad, but I didn't think it was that simple. Not after overhearing the way they talked to each other in his inner sanctum, when Carlevaro didn't know I was there. There was a bitterness in her tone that I didn't think could be faked. Morgan couldn't be trusted, but something told me that her information could be.

Then again, Carlevaro wanted me to try again. More likely than not, I was playing right into his hands.

But what did I have to lose?

"Yeah," I said. "I do."

"Do you think you can do it in twenty-four hours?"

Okay, she didn't need to make it *more* complicated. "Maybe," I said, hesitating. "But not alone."

Kerry looked at me sideways, a funny little smile pulling at her lips and one eyebrow quirked. It was a look I recognized— I'd seen it on myself often enough. For a moment, I saw my sister in a new light. Maybe she had a few schemes up her hoodie sleeves after all.

"Who said anything about doing it alone?" Kerry said.

♠

"Beth is with the Dohertys, so she put me in charge of you and your accomplices," Kerry told me in the elevator. I'd hastily combed my hair and changed out of my depression sweatpants, but otherwise we weren't wasting any time. I could hear that twenty-four-hour clock ticking down.

"You?" I didn't mean to sound so incredulous. Some things just slip out.

"It was either me or Dad." Kerry gave me a sideways look.

"Point taken."

The elevator was too big and too quiet, filled with a thousand things we weren't saying. I couldn't tell Kerry how grateful I was, or how scared. Every time I tried, the words froze on my lips. Kerry and I didn't talk about things like that. Sometimes I thought it was because we were afraid that if we talked, if things got too real, then we'd find some break between us that couldn't be resolved, the way Mom and Beth did. We'd spent too many nights listening to them fight, nights where we only had each other and our own careful silence.

"Beth wants to sell her shares to the Golden Age," she said suddenly, like she couldn't bite back the words anymore. Her eyes flickered toward me. "She wants to be done with it."

My stomach tied itself in knots. "I know," I said. "But not because she told me." It was impossible not to sound bitter.

Kerry snorted softly. "Of course she didn't," she said, and the elevator door slid open. She jostled me with her elbow. "She was afraid you might do something stupid."

"Thanks," I said dryly. I preferred the word *ill-advised*. I was less surprised that Beth had told her than the fact that Kerry cared so much. I didn't know that anyone cared about the Golden Age as much as I did. I guess there was more to my middle sister than she let on. Or more than I'd ever looked for.

"Don't take it personally." Kerry looked up and winked. "If I didn't want you to do something stupid, I wouldn't be here."

♠

Kerry produced a keycard from her hoodie pocket that opened a suite on the tenth floor. It was one of the suites styled after the future, which explains how she got it so easily. During the 2008 recession, Granddad needed something different to convince people to come spend money they didn't have. Thus, the future rooms were born. They were a hokey, *The Jetsons*–esque kind of idealization of the future, which I guess might have been appealing at the time, but they hadn't aged very well. Now they just felt patronizing.

I would take patronizing. I would take silver-foil couches and weird teardrop-shaped lamps. I would even take the fake windows filled with screens of nebulae and shooting stars, though that was really pushing it. I would take anything if it held my friends.

But I still dragged my feet as I followed Kerry inside the suite. What if they didn't want to see me? Beth had said she talked to their parents, which meant I wasn't the only one in trouble. I didn't know what the normal-person punishment for faking an educational conference and running away to Las Vegas was, but I had a feeling it wasn't getting banished to Massachusetts to attend boarding school.

I peeked over Kerry's shoulder. The mood in the room was subdued. Remy and Georgia sat on the floor, playing cards. Go Fish, by the looks of it, but it still made me smile. Gabe was stretched out on the metallic silver couch, his long legs hanging over the end, one arm thrown over his eyes. I hesitated. Something wasn't right.

"Where's Lucky?" I said.

For a moment, you could hear a pin drop. Gabe lifted his arm, Georgia's cards drifted downward, Remy twisted where they sat. My heart lodged itself in my throat. Why weren't they talking? Was I supposed to talk? If the moment went on any longer I was going to—

The room exploded into chaos, and everyone was talking at once. I was vaguely aware of Kerry flattening herself against the wall before Gabe was holding me by the face.

"I'm *so* sorry," Gabe gushed, leaning against me like an oversize puppy. "Oh my God, look at your beautiful face. It's a curse, you know. My brother lost his first tooth because I head-butted him in the chin. That time it was on purpose, but still—"

"*Mph*," I said eloquently. He was squeezing my cheeks together. My abused nose throbbed painfully.

"Get off of him before you break his nose for real this time," Georgia said, exasperated, as she hauled Gabe off. Again, a bit like grabbing a puppy by the scruff. Gabe wore an appropriately hangdog expression and a bandage on his forehead where he scraped it against the fountain. "We're glad you're okay, Jack."

Remy stood in what was left of the game of Go Fish, still holding their cards. I met their eyes, and they smiled nervously. "Hey," they said.

The butterflies that lived in my stomach fluttered in response. "Hey," I said. Were they thinking about the moment beside the fountains? Or were they thinking about my raccoon eyes? Should I say something so they knew I was thinking about the fountain too, like a little wink? Should I—no, no I should definitely not literally wink.

Gabe untangled himself from Georgia, looking disturbed. "Okay." He held up a finger toward each of us. "Something happened here. What happened here?"

Oh no, we were not having that conversation right now. Or ever, preferably. "Anyway," I said quickly. "Forget about me. Where's Lucky?"

The mood in the room took a significant dip, and they all exchanged looks.

"Lucky's mom picked her up this morning," Kerry said, inserting herself back into the conversation. I'd kind of forgotten she was there. She leaned against the wall, rubbing one elbow. "Since she was already in the city."

I winced. Right. I imagined Chef Favreau wasn't entirely happy about that. "And the rest of you?" Did Kerry already talk to them? She'd seemed so confident we wouldn't have to do this alone, but now I wasn't so sure. I was already surprised Beth hadn't personally put us all on planes that morning and washed her hands of it. Thank God for the Dohertys, or she might have.

"Well, I'm over eighteen," Gabe said, a hand to his chest. "So I can do whatever I want."

"But," I supplied for him.

"*But*," he continued, "I was guilted into it, and I will be murdered promptly on arrival back home, so please enjoy this precious time we have left together." He pulled a face. "Your sister is hard-core, man. She had me confessing more than my priest. The other sister, I mean," he quickly clarified to Kerry, "but you're cool too."

"My parents are flying in tomorrow," Remy said.

"And I'm leaving tonight," Georgia added.

"No, you're not." Kerry was dangerously close to wearing a hole in her hoodie sleeve now, digging at it nervously with her thumb. We all turned to her with varying degrees of surprise. So she hadn't told them about her scheming, but I wasn't as worried as I had been before. My friends, despite being a haphazard collection of asexual teenagers with only a handful of useful skills among us, had a way of making me feel like I could do just about anything. "Beth put me in charge of booking your flights." She shrugged, looking uncomfortable with every eye on her. "I couldn't get anything until tomorrow. It's hard to book a flight last minute, you know."

Another beat of silence. Another explosion of noise. "Ker-*ry*," Gabe enthused, throwing his arms around her. Georgia reeled him back again by the shirt collar.

"Sorry about him," she said, but she was looking a little starstruck as well.

"No hugs necessary," Kerry said hastily, her hands up. "I'm only here for selfish reasons. Remember that any time you get the urge to hug."

I laughed, and the knot of tension that lived in my chest felt a little bit looser. It would never be gone entirely, but it was easier to breathe. We hadn't accomplished anything yet, but we had a chance now. A chance was a lot more than I'd had an hour ago.

"Are we doing this?" Somehow Remy had materialized beside me, their eyes bright. "Are we really doing this? *Can* we do this?" They frowned like they were calculating the odds but couldn't quite figure out the math. They nodded, apparently reaching a good conclusion. "We have to do this."

I couldn't help but remember that Remy was not very good at math.

I opened my mouth, a familiar wave of guilt washing over me. They'd already done so much, and they already had hell to pay when they got home. Lucky was probably already paying it. Mom and Carlevaro and everything in between were my responsibility—and Kerry's now. I never should have dragged them into this.

Georgia cut me off before I could say as much. "Jack, if you're going to say something all sad and noble, can we save it for after we kick ass?" She caught my eye and winked. "Carlevaro took my winnings, so you could say it's kind of personal now."

She was trying to make me feel better about the mess I'd gotten us all into, and it halfway worked. *I never should have dragged them into this,* I thought again, but I was so glad that I had.

"Besides," Georgia added, "what's the worst that can happen?"

"We get arrested," Gabe answered cheerfully.

"We die," Remy speculated.

"We fail," I said simultaneously. Well. Maybe my priorities were a little off.

Georgia rolled her eyes. "I guess technically," she conceded. "But we're not going to. Because we're . . ." She trailed off expectantly. We stared. "Our team name, guys. Our name?"

Gabe squinted. "We had a name?"

"Oh, the name!" Remy said, smacking me on the shoulder with the back of their hand. "Right, it was a whole thing. Aces—"

I snapped my fingers. "Aces Wild."

"There we go," Georgia said. "Great job, guys. Off to a good start."

"Aces Wild?" Kerry frowned. "What does that mean?"

"Don't worry about it," I said, waving her off and moving on to a much more unpleasant topic. "We don't have a lot of time. Carlevaro knows we might be trying something, and I . . ." I faltered. "You guys were right about Morgan. I should have listened to you."

"Well, *yeah*, but—*hnng*!" Gabe wheezed as Remy elbowed him in the ribs. "I was kidding!"

"It's going to be a challenge. What else is new?" Georgia shrugged. "So what do we do?"

That was the problem. I didn't know. I hated those words—they felt wrong, so unlike me that I hardly recognized myself. I was supposed to be the one with the plan. Even when I didn't know what came next, I could usually fake it. But I'd never been this low before. I was still struggling to pick myself back up.

My eyes scanned the room. We were down Lucky. We couldn't count on Morgan. We had fewer assets than we had before, and somehow I was supposed to put together a plan to pull off more than we'd been able to accomplish already. We needed to get into Carlevaro's inner sanctum. *Challenge* was an understatement.

"I don't know who Morgan is," Kerry interjected, quietly raising her hand. "But you do have me."

ONE LAST TIME

THE IMPERIUM LOOKED JUST THE SAME AS IT DID before, all dark marble, gold, and tacky artistry, but somehow it felt colder. Like it could sense my intentions, and it wanted me out.

That was fair. I didn't much want to be there either.

But there was no choice anymore. One night left to find a way to hit Carlevaro where it hurt. One night to save my mom, my family, and the Golden Age. One more night with my friends.

And I wouldn't even be there for most of it.

I wanted to be at the Avalon Club so badly I could feel it like an ache in my chest, like my heart was twenty-nine floors above me. But Carlevaro expected that—he wanted that. He'd made that clear enough with the five-hundred-dollar chip he'd flipped to me like it was a piece of candy.

I felt like an idiot now, and for a lot of reasons. Morgan had lied to me, and Carlevaro had known that we were playing at the Avalon Club all along. We'd been puppets in a show, only we just hadn't known it yet. That almost bothered me more than the idea of failure. The whole time I thought I'd been outsmarting him, I was only playing right into Carlevaro's game.

Which was exactly why I couldn't be there now. If we were going to succeed, if we were going to find what he didn't want found, then we had to do something a little different. He was expecting me, which meant that we had to do the unexpected.

Which was where Kerry came in.

People underestimated Kerry—because she kept to herself and wore oversize hoodies and used to hide her hearing aids behind her hair. *I* underestimated Kerry. But there was one universal truth about her that was best not to forget: Kerry was still a Shannon.

She didn't just play poker. She won.

If I closed my eyes, I could almost see it. Right about now, Kerry would be walking through the doors of the Avalon Club, probably trailing Gabe like a publicist does a celebrity. She would be Gabe's plus-one tonight. It meant Georgia had to stay behind, but she was downstairs, in the Imperium room that used to be Lucky's station, monitoring Kerry's phone and throwing Beth off the scent if she got too suspicious.

Once inside, she would pick a table. For Kerry, it was Texas Hold'em. Card counting at the blackjack table was a bit of a team effort, especially once you got into the serious operations, but Texas Hold'em was a little different. It wasn't a numbers game like blackjack; it was a human one. It wasn't the cards you were trying to game but the other players.

That was the thing about Kerry Shannon. Kerry didn't lie, but that didn't mean she couldn't.

She would take that five-hundred-dollar chip that Carlevaro had so graciously provided me, and she would grow it until stacks of chips sat in front of her like a miniature city. People would notice. They'd start to pay attention, start watching. The pit boss would be circling like a vulture.

And Kerry would turn and say, "Excuse me. You can tell Mr. Carlevaro that I'm ready to play him whenever he has the balls."

I mouthed the words silently, as if I were there saying them with her. Carlevaro wouldn't be able to stop himself. He might have guessed my every move so far, but there was no way he would have expected Kerry to get involved. *I* never thought that would happen. He'd know we were up to something, but he'd be misdirected. While Carlevaro was busy with Kerry, his inner sanctum would be left unguarded.

And I would be where it all started. With Remy, of course.

"Got it," I said, meeting Remy around the side of the Imperium, where the tall metal doors for the delivery bay were closed up for the night. I flashed a black staff keycard I'd lifted after a run-in with a bellhop in the parking lot. He wouldn't notice until he went outside to have a smoke break. In the meantime, it would get us behind the scenes.

"Ready?" I said. The outside of the delivery bay was dark, the night throwing a cold wind across the expanse of oil-stained concrete.

"For a real heist?" Remy grinned. "I thought you'd never ask."

It was a weird parody of my first foray into the Imperium, but that was the point. I'd been so focused on the mystique of the Avalon Club—exactly like Carlevaro wanted me to be—that I'd forgotten there was another way into the heart of his operation, one that I'd already seen at the very beginning. The keycard let us into one of the side doors, into the cavernous delivery bay. It was darker than the outside, all the lights turned off for the day except for two emergency lights, one above the door back into the hotel and one above the elevator, which was exactly where we were headed. The service elevator was nothing like the gilded cages out on the hotel floor. Scuffed metal walls and thin industrial carpeting greeted us when I pushed the button to go up, the lights inside the elevator so bright in the gloom that we had to squint.

I knew the service elevator had to go up to the twenty-ninth floor, the same way I knew that Carlevaro's office had to be there. That was where Flat Cap had been going the day I stole his keycard, and Carlevaro would never put his office anywhere but. The Avalon Club was the beating heart of his enterprises, and he would be holding his cards close to his chest.

I tapped the Avalon Club keycard against the pad and hit the button for the twenty-ninth floor without hesitation.

Kerry couldn't distract Carlevaro forever, no matter how good she was at bluffing. It was now or never.

"Nervous?" Remy asked as the elevator lurched upward. It was the first time we were really alone since the Fountains of Bellagio. Not that the fountains really counted, considering it had been in the middle of a crowd of tourists, but at the time it had certainly felt like we were the only two people in the world.

"A little." For a lot of reasons. I couldn't shake the idea that this might be the last moment alone I'd have with Remy—ever? Maybe not ever, but certainly for a while. The world already felt a little dimmer.

I turned back toward Remy, my mouth open to say something—I don't remember what, I didn't even really know what I was going to say at the time, I don't think—but I never got the chance. Because when I turned, Remy was right there, and I was right there, and suddenly the space between us didn't feel very big at all.

I didn't really intend to kiss Remy before it happened. Or maybe I did, and I just didn't realize it. Frankly, I'd spent most of my life up until that point not really intending to kiss anyone at all. If it had been anyone else, anywhere else, that probably wouldn't have changed.

But Remy always knew what was on my mind, even if I didn't.

Actually, *kiss* is probably an overstatement. Somewhere between Remy being short and me being closer to tall and neither of us quite knowing what we were doing, the trajectory got a little jumbled. Our lips brushed together for a singular moment, and a tingly burst of warmth lodged firmly in my gut.

And then our noses bumped together, and we sprang apart again as if we'd been burned. I was very aware of the hot blush crawling up my neck and the ache in my nose. I may have forgotten it was bruised, but my face sure didn't.

"Sorry," I squeaked, my voice probably higher than it had been since puberty.

"Sorry, sorry, sorry," Remy said at the same time, their hands over their nose. "Maybe not a good time."

"Maybe not ideal," I agreed hastily. Did Remy regret it? Was it that bad? Suddenly I'd rather let Carlevaro push me off the top of the Imperium than be in that elevator.

Remy peeked between their fingers. "That was some dramatic 'We might not make it out alive' shit, wasn't it?"

A startled laugh escaped me. "A little," I admitted. "Sorry," I said again, looking back at the elevator screen, avoiding my warped reflection in the metal walls. We were almost to the twenty-ninth floor, and I was pretty sure I looked like a cherry tomato. "I don't—I mean—I've never had a crush before." And I felt extremely stupid just saying the word out loud. Shannons didn't like things they weren't good at, and they liked admitting it even less. It just wasn't natural.

"You have a crush on me?" Remy asked, and I nearly popped a vertebra, my head whipped around so fast. They regarded me with wide eyes. What did—but at the fountains—what was "All I wanted was to be here with you in real life" *supposed* to mean?

Remy's composure cracked into a shit-eating grin. "I'm fucking with you," they said, dissolving into giggles.

"Shut up," I muttered, jostling them with my elbow, but my mouth twitched in a matching grin that refused to be ignored. Their hand slipped into mine, but Remy didn't say anything. They only laced our fingers together, and my heart beat its stupid, lovesick pattern against my chest. Remy's hand was as about as sweaty as mine. They were nervous too.

But we were together. But our friends were somewhere nearby, even if we couldn't see them. But whatever happened tonight, at least I'd always have them, all of them, even if we were hundreds of miles apart.

I gave them a sideways look. "Still ace though, right?" This wasn't some sort of awakening for them, was it? I so did not need that on my plate on top of everything else. Navigating a relationship (was that what this was?) was hard enough when we were both on the same page about the sexuality-and-lack-thereof thing.

"Are you kidding me? Uh, yeah." Remy gave me a sideways look right back. "You?"

"Oh, absolutely." Frankly, I didn't know where people found the time to have sexual attraction.

"Oh, thank God." Remy laughed.

The screen lit up with the number twenty-nine, and the elevator rumbled to a halt. The laughter died.

"It's go time," Remy said with a determined look on their face. They squeezed my hand and I squeezed back.

I snorted. "That's not going to be our catchphrase."

"We'll workshop it."

"We'll see about that."

♠

The elevator opened to a very cold, very empty hallway.

It stretched endlessly in either direction, where it finally connected with other legs of the maze we were stepping into. I recognized the back network of hallways that Morgan had led me through immediately, and not just because the walls were the same shade of beige. They were also lined with framed newspaper clippings and old photographs and blueprints set against burgundy backing. Immediately across the elevator hung an illustration of the Imperium, only it wasn't the one we'd stepped into. It was six feet across and depicted a sprawling black stone monstrosity that arched toward Las Vegas Boulevard like wings, a grand garden at its center. The original Imperium sat at the center of the structure, reaching to touch the sky. At its very top was an angel wielding a sword.

The same angel that stood on top of the Golden Age. I stared at it for a moment, resolve hardening in my heart. Carlevaro had big plans for the future.

I looked both ways, trying to gauge which direction was the better bet just based on the gaudy decor. Had I seen before that newspaper clipping from the year the Sands was demolished, or was I just imagining it? God, what I wouldn't do to still have Lucky watching over us. I touched the AirPod-turned-communicator in my pocket like a talisman. It didn't feel right to leave without it, as if it were a little piece of Lucky still with us, though that had been another awkward explanation when Kerry realized I'd rooted around her room to find it. Oops.

"This way," I said, making a decision. I turned right. The Imperium was big, but not nearly as big as Carlevaro wanted it to be. There were only so many places his office could be. If we could find the lounge Morgan took me to before, it would be a start, and luckily the dramatic oak door would more than stand out.

We stole through the hall, sticking close to the wall, even though there was no hiding if someone spotted us. We had to move quickly and hope that Kerry was keeping the Avalon Club, and Carlevaro, thoroughly distracted.

"There," I said, hooking a sharp right turn, Remy trailing behind me. I could see the heavy oak door like a light at the end of the tunnel. It was so close—and then we heard a door open around the corner behind us, followed by a deep voice. Someone was coming.

Remy and I exchanged a look, and in a heartbeat we both knew our options were limited. The oak door was too far away and the voice too close. Even if we ran, whoever was coming would see the door close. Assuming that wasn't where they were headed in the first place.

"Go," Remy whispered, jerking their head toward the oak door. "I'll distract them."

"Remy—"

"Go, idiot." They gave me a little push and I stumbled, still looking back, where the voice was only getting louder. "I'll be fine. Just focus."

I didn't like leaving them, but they were right. We came here for a reason.

I spun on my heel and all but ran for the oak door—I would have, if the sound of my footsteps wouldn't have given the game away anyway.

I stumbled into Carlevaro's lounge. Or—the founding knights' lounge. I didn't like to think of it as his, but I didn't like to think about how *the founding knights* meant Carlevaro and Mom either. The thought made me pause, even as my heart beat in my throat.

I exhaled as I closed the door behind me, and my breath scraped against the silence and sank into the thick carpet. My hands hung uselessly at my sides, afraid to touch anything, as if I were standing in a tomb that should be preserved, or maybe one that was cursed. My eyes swept the room. Could Carlevaro's little black book be here? Maybe, but I didn't think so. This was the place he came to relax. The secrets of the Las Vegas Strip were his greatest prize, but they were also work. There was no desk in the lounge either. It couldn't be what Morgan meant by his office. It had to be somewhere else.

I didn't like this place, and not just because I'd had to

lose Remy to get here. There was even a strange energy in the air, buzzing in my fingertips like—

Oh no. That wasn't energy. Or if it was, it was concentrated on my left hip.

I stuck my hand in my pocket, one ear toward the door. I pulled out the AirPod-turned-communicator, and a tinny buzz filled the room. It vibrated gently, pulsing unevenly with the sound. I stared at it like I'd never seen it before. Was it picking up interference? Some weird CIA shit Carlevaro had going on to keep people from spying on him? The buzzing stopped, then started again, fluctuating like a faraway song.

It almost sounded like—

Words.

I slowly lifted the AirPod up to my ear, holding it with my fingertips like it was a snake about to bite, until the electronic fuzz turned into words.

"JACK, YOU SON OF A— Oh, hey."

I never thought I'd be so happy to hear Lucky's voice screaming in my ear. I almost dropped it. I fumbled with it, before hooking it around my ear. It fit awkwardly, meant for my sister who was much younger at the time, but at the moment it was worth its weight in gold. Or poker chips.

"Lucky, I—" I cut myself off awkwardly. Right. The MP3 player didn't allow me to talk back to her.

"Yeah, I still can't hear you," Lucky deadpanned. *"But I can see you."*

"You can?" This time I slipped up out of surprise. How could she see me? It didn't surprise me that Carlevaro had surveillance in the Avalon Club—all casino floors had eyes in the sky, even the ones that didn't explicitly invite people there to commit crimes. But here? In his inner sanctum?

Lucky took a deep breath. Her voice sounded scratchy; I wondered how long she'd been yelling into the microphone, trying to get my attention. Oops. In my defense, I'd already counted Lucky out for this leg of the misadventure. I should have known better than to count Lucky out of anything.

"*Mom put me on tech lockdown after she picked me up from your sister,*" Lucky said, talking fast. "*Dad's flying in, I'm in big trouble, blah, blah, whatever. Once Dad gets here, I'm toast, but my mom doesn't know all the tricks I have up my sleeve. I could probably hack with a smart fridge, if you gave me enough time.*"

Did we have time for bragging? I didn't think we had time for bragging.

"*Anyway,*" Lucky said, clearly having the same idea. I doubted she ran out of things to say about her own prowess. "*I couldn't get ahold of any of you assholes through Hullabaloo*"—Not my fault. My phone was still deader than a doornail—"*but I knew you wouldn't give up that easily. So I did some more looking, and I discovered a network I missed before. Real hush-hush, with security tighter than a—never mind. It was tight. Keyword: was. It took me like an hour to get into.*" She sounded disgusted that she couldn't do it faster.

"Can we cut to the chase?" I muttered, whether Lucky could hear me or not. My eyes flickered to the door. I didn't know how much time Remy had bought me.

"Look to your right," Lucky said. *"The big ugly clock. See it?"*

I considered a grand, sturdy-looking bookcase against the wall to my right, filled with books and paraphernalia that looked like they came out of an evil professor–themed escape room. I ignored the black-and-gold miniature globe—though it sure looked like it still featured the USSR—and focused on the clock instead. It was a squat oak clock that—well, it looked more like Cogsworth from *Beauty and the Beast* than anything else. Whatever. I'm not a clockmaker. I squinted at its face.

There. A little fish-eye lens winked back at me, hidden at the center of the clock face, where the arms met. My heart pounded in my ears, sticking me with a shot of adrenaline. I leaned in and waved hello.

"Hey, there," she said. *"Okay, back up. I don't need to see your nose hairs."*

I leaned back again. "Office," I said, enunciating the word the best I could. How did you mime *office*? I pretended to type and hoped she got the idea.

"What are you doing? Jack, listen to me," Lucky said, uncharacteristically subdued. *"There's one more thing I found on Carlevaro's secret network. But I don't know if you're going to want to hear it."*

I dropped my hands. That was never a good sign, but I didn't have time to be fainthearted. Not tonight. Lucky knew that Morgan was a Carlevaro before I did, and I'd learned my lesson about not stopping to listen to what she had to say. I looked the camera dead in the eye, and nodded.

Maybe I didn't want to hear it, but I needed to.

Lucky took a deep breath. "*Okay*," she said, and it sounded like she was steeling herself as much as I was.

Okay, this is the part in the movie where someone leans over to whisper in the hero's ear and explains the plan, even though they'd been talking at a perfectly normal volume before. There's a reason they do that, because no one wants to sit in the theater and listen to the idea of a plan for twenty minutes before seeing it executed. This is the part where I should tell you what Lucky told me, the way I've told you every personal, mortifying detail up until now—the truth, the whole truth, and nothing but the truth (as far as you know)—but I won't. I'll tell you that you'll find out soon enough. I'll tell you that it changed everything, and nothing at all.

Just trust me.

I stared into the camera, strangely numb, wondering if anyone else could see me through its eye besides Lucky. Her words still echoed in my ears, making them ring. Nothing to do but move. Nowhere to go but forward.

"Can you direct me to Carlevaro's office?" I asked out loud.

"*I can't read lips*," Lucky said, "*but I can direct you to Carlevaro's office.*"

THE SWORD IN THE STONE

THERE WAS A DOOR ON THE WEST WALL OF CAR-
levaro's private lounge, opposite from the one I entered. I
probably I should have known that would be the way forward, but it was easier with Lucky in my ear, guiding my
footsteps.

This hall was different. It was a straight shot, maybe fifty
feet or so. The walls were the same beige cinder block I was
growing used to, but the plush carpet extended from the
lounge and down the hall until it reached the foot of a door.
Oak, like the one that led into the lounge, but with one big
difference: A keypad sat next to the door.

I had expected this. Though maybe *suspected* was a better word. Carlevaro couldn't let it be that easy. Even now,
when I was so close to the end.

But I was ready for it. Or Kerry was. My sister had one
other trick up her sleeve.

I pulled a golden keycard out of my pocket. It was different from the one I'd grown familiar with. It was gold on both

sides, and there was no script on it either. The only thing denoting it related to the Avalon Club was the sword-and-crown symbol on one side, the same symbol printed on the club's poker chips. This one was special.

Because it was Mom's.

The edges were crisp and sharp, like it had never been used before. It probably hadn't. The Imperium opened its doors after Mom's falling out with Carlevaro, but that hadn't stopped him from sending her a card anyway. Kerry had found it in Mom's jewelry box, hidden under a row of rings. I wanted to laugh at Carlevaro for sending it, but I couldn't. After all, Mom had kept it.

I couldn't think about what that meant now; I could only hope that it was what I needed. I held it up and tapped the edge against my lips thoughtfully, like a gambler blowing on dice. I needed this to work. If it didn't, the door was just another dead end.

I tapped Mom's keycard against the pad, and it lit up green. The door unlocked with a heavy *snick*.

I pushed it open carefully, every nerve prickling. The room beyond was . . .

Deceptively normal. Well, rich normal. The same kind of normal the Golden Age penthouse was: leather furniture, Italian marble, and a kind of chilly, distant vibe that told you the last person to care about it significantly was the interior decorator. It almost felt like home, except it was done in neutral browns and beiges instead of stain-me-I-dare-you white. A bit of a Tuscan flavor.

I gave myself a little shake. I wasn't there to critique the decorating. I gingerly closed the door behind me.

"I've lost you," Lucky said. *"You're on your own from here."*

Of course, the one place Carlevaro didn't have watched. Luckily, Carlevaro's suite was much more straightforward than the path I took to get there. Looking at it, you might almost think it was a normal apartment and not the end of a convoluted network of secret rooms and illicit activity.

I moved through the suite, my footsteps impossibly loud over the soft hum of the refrigerator. I ignored the kitchen and the living room and made a beeline for a row of closed doors. The first one was a bathroom. The second was a bedroom, and I paused. A teenage girl's bedroom, clearly, from the mess of clothes on the bed and the computer on the desk, covered with a snarl of charger cords. Morgan's room, it had to be, but it was strangely impersonal. The walls were beige, decorated with an oil painting of a winter landscape. I changed my mind. Less like a teenage girl's bedroom and more like a guest room a teenage girl happened to live in.

I closed the door again. The next one gave me what I needed.

Carlevaro's office wasn't exactly the den of villainy I imagined it to be. Again, it was disarmingly average, though the crystal decanter of whiskey was pretty fucking pretentious. The view was everything I expected it to be, though. The far wall was all glass, looking out over the nighttime Strip. I could see the Golden Age in the distance, the angel at the top glowing like a star. No way that was a coincidence.

I went to Carlevaro's desk, running my hands along the lacquered wood. Where would he keep his secrets? I'd been so sure about the sword in the stone back at the Avalon Club. It was just the sort of overdramatic move that would appeal to him, and I couldn't help but look for something similar here.

It would make him think of Mom. As much as I hated the thought, it was true. They'd built everything around the theme of King Arthur, like a sly inside joke between the two of them. Even my name—the first one, that teachers always flubbed on the first day of school. *Arthur*.

And Morgan.

The door flew open, rattling in its frame, and Morgan stood there, breathing heavily, her hair hanging in her face. She flipped it back dramatically, and her face was flushed, like she'd just sprinted the entire way. My back went stiff.

And then she grinned. She didn't look like she was about to call security. She looked . . . relieved.

"You did it," she said. "You made it all the way here. I didn't think you would."

Anger welled up like blood in a wound, surprising me. I should have been panicked. I should have grabbed the nearest sword-shaped object and made a run for it the moment the door opened, but instead I was rooted in place, my hands curled into fists at my sides. I hadn't expected to see her again, but a part of me hoped I would. I wanted revenge against Carlevaro more than anything.

But I also wanted the truth.

"What do you want, Morgan?" I said, a razor's edge to my voice. "What do you *actually* want? Besides selling me out to your dad."

Morgan flinched. "You weren't supposed to know that was me."

"Wear a wig next time," I snapped. I turned away, trying to rein in the furious thing in my chest. I needed to focus. Anger wasn't useful. Anger wouldn't get me out of there or find what I needed before it was too late.

"Oh," Morgan said, and I could feel her noticing the single AirPod in my ear. I resisted the urge to take it off. Lucky was blind here, but she still had eyes everywhere else. I didn't know when I might need her again. "That's why you're so mad at me. Your hacker friend. She told you."

Yeah, she told me. "What do you want from me?" I said again, my nerves fraying, threatening to snap.

"I want to get to know you," Morgan snapped back. "Is that such a crime?"

"Yeah, actually, in this specific instance, it's involved a lot of crimes!"

"I deserve to know my brother!" Her jaw closed with a click, looking abashed. The word *brother* hung in the air between us.

And there it was. Ta-da.

"*There's an email to your mom, Jack,*" Lucky had said carefully, back in the lounge. "*It says that Carlevaro is your—*"

"You don't get it," Morgan went on, her eyes burning. She looked desperate, her hair falling over her eyes. "I'm *helping*

320

you. I've been on your side this whole time." She took a step forward, one hand reaching. I jerked backward. I didn't want her touching me. I didn't want anyone touching me. "Dad wanted— He wanted to know that you could handle this. You had to prove yourself. But you *weren't*. You were just wasting time with your friends like this was summer vacation. You just needed . . . a push." She shrugged. "It worked, didn't it? You're here. You did it. And now . . ."

"And now what, Morgan?" I said flatly. My fingernails were digging into the palms of my hands. "We can be one big happy family?"

"Well . . . yeah." Her eyes were big and shockingly innocent, for all that she'd done. And in that moment, I saw her for what she was.

She was lonely. It wasn't just about me. Maybe she wanted a brother, but I suspected she wanted a father more. There was a reason that I'd forgotten about Morgan's existence, despite the role the Carlevaros had played in the Shannon family all my life. She wasn't important to Carlevaro, easily shuffled off to her mother, who apparently didn't want her either. I wasn't just a (half) brother to her. I was her key to a family.

"*Jack,*" Lucky said in my ear. She sounded far away, secondary to my heart pounding in my ears like a jackhammer. "*Jack, can you still hear me?*"

"You know it won't work that way," I said, my anger dampening into something more like pity. Or understanding. She wasn't the only one who had been betrayed. Mom hadn't told me the truth. Who else knew? Beth? Dad? Everything I thought I knew was coming unraveled in my hands, and I was caught in the knots, paralyzed. My life was falling apart (again), and I felt bad for *her*. "He's not going to change just because of me."

"You don't know that," Morgan countered.

"Then why didn't he tell me?" I said. "Why all these stupid games?"

"Jack. I don't have eyes on Carlevaro. He—he's not in the club anymore."

"Because I made a promise."

Morgan and I jumped. I took a step back, until I bumped against the desk.

Peter Carlevaro stood in the doorway, the same way his daughter had, but much more collected. He looked like the grim reaper, between his shaved head and deep-set eyes and the fact that seeing him made me want to die. My heart lodged in my throat, threatening to choke me. I wanted answers, but I didn't want to have this conversation. I didn't want to look at his face and try to find myself in it—was that my nose? My chin? Did I look that much like a ferret?

"Morgan," Carlevaro said. "Go to your room."

Her cheeks went red. She threw a desperate look at me, as if I wasn't the one caught breaking and entering. Well, entering. It was his own fault that the keycard still had access. "But—"

"Go."

Morgan slunk to the door, her face hidden by her hair, and I saw an opportunity where there sure as hell weren't many left.

"Morgan," I said. I would have liked to say, *See, your dad is an asshole, isn't he?* or *Wow, I was right, who would have guessed?* But I didn't really have the time to get into specifics. I had to settle for *Morgan* and hope she heard *He's not on your side, but I could be.*

She hesitated in the doorway, meeting my eyes. Maybe she did.

But then she turned and left, leaving me alone with Carlevaro. I tried not to let my disappointment show.

"I want to call my sister," I demanded the moment Morgan was gone. The stakes had changed irreversibly. Beth finding out that we were here wasn't the worst possibility anymore.

"Do you?" Carlevaro said, and I couldn't tell if he was mocking me or if I just expected him to. "Because I get the feeling that Bethany won't be pleased to find out you're here tonight."

"I don't care." My heart was beating so fast, it felt like it would give out. I didn't want to be here. I didn't want to look at him, and I definitely didn't want him to look at me, his eyes bright and hungry like a predatory bird. "I want to see my friends." What happened to Remy? Did he have Kerry and Gabe cornered somewhere too?

Carlevaro took a step away from the door, his hands spread wide. As if I could just stroll out the door. I doubted that. "You're the one who came to me, Arthur," he said. "And

323

I have to say, I'm impressed." He smirked, and his refrain ran on loop through my head. *Come back when you can impress me.* He'd meant it, and as more than just a taunt. All along, this was a test.

And I'd passed it.

"I'd say you've earned the truth," he said.

I hesitated, the desk corner digging into the small of my back. The truth. The kind of truth I might not get anywhere else, even from Mom. The kind of truth I'd be wondering about for the rest of my life.

Carlevaro smelled weakness like blood in the water.

"I loved your mother. I still do," he said softly. "This— Avalon. Our secret city of sin. Our greatest creation . . . before you."

I flinched. "You sent her to jail," I spat. "You can't have loved her too much."

"And what's the appropriate response to seventeen years of lies?" Carlevaro retorted, a snarl on the edge of his voice. "She kept you from me. She lied to me. To you too." He shook his head. "I know you think I'm the villain here. The fact that you made it this far is quite charming, but the game is over now, Jack. You're here, and you know the truth."

Something inside me trembled. "What did you mean?" I asked. "About making a promise?"

Carlevaro titled his head back, considering me with snakelike eyes. "Your mother didn't know from the beginning. I believe her on that count," he said, "because I remember the day she pulled away from me. I knew she'd never let me have her completely, she was too proud for that, too independent. But I had her, in part, for so long. I thought that was enough. But suddenly things changed, and I didn't know why." He actually looked troubled, like he was still running the conversations over in his head, trying to find a way he could have won. "My father told me the day he died. Of course he knew—he knew everything that happened in this city. I was furious. Think about everything she's stolen from us, Arthur. Every year."

There was the *Arthur* again. My skin crawled. But Carlevaro wasn't done.

"She had to be punished. I had more than enough to bury her." He said it so offhandedly, like sending the woman he supposedly loved to prison was an unfortunate but unavoidable turn of events. "But she made me make a promise first, and I supposed I owed her that much. She would go easily— not kick up a fuss, not try to take a plea to implicate me as well—and I wouldn't approach you about your parentage. Not unless you approached me first."

I could feel my mouth hanging open, but I couldn't seem to close it. My brain had short-circuited. Mom could have easily flipped on Carlevaro. It might even have saved her. The Golden Age was everything to Mom—to the Shannon family. It was Granddad's legacy, Mom's inheritance, our home. Mom wouldn't give up the Golden Age for anything. Except to protect me. To protect me from *him*.

"And now you're here," Carlevaro said softly, "and there's so much to show you."

I unstuck the words from my throat. "You may be my father," I said, the words still weird and hollow to my ears, "but you're not my dad."

My dad was irresponsible and inconsiderate and spent his nights impersonating Freddie Mercury under neon lights, but he wasn't Carlevaro. He might forget me in Miami nightclubs, and put me on a plane without unaccompanied-minor paperwork, and—

Okay, that wasn't the point. The point was that, at the end of the day, he cared about me. Peter Carlevaro couldn't say the same. I wasn't going to fall for the same dream that Morgan had. I couldn't.

Carlevaro's mouth twisted ugly. "Pay attention, Jack." Oh, suddenly I was Jack again, now that he was trying to win me over. Real convenient. "You can be everything you should have been from the start. The Golden Age is for *you*, Jack. Once you're ready for it. You didn't take all that personally, did you? I only knew that you needed a challenge to . . . inspire you. You are still a Shannon, after all." His smile twitched.

"You can merge our legacies, the way your grandfathers always wanted. The Carlevaros and the Shannons were meant to work together, not against one another. You're proof of that." He took a step forward, holding out his hand like I was supposed to . . . take it? Whatever movie scene was playing in his head, it was a different one than I was seeing.

"What happens to my mom?" I said.

His smile grew indulgent. He was laughing at me, the way you laughed at a toddler who had misjudged their own strength. "Jack . . . you can't have everything," he said. "Be reasonable. I only want to give you your inheritance."

I hesitated. The Golden Age was everything my family had worked to build—my grandfather, my mom. Me, some-day. Or I would have. If I walked out of this room without shaking Peter Carlevaro's hand, I could kiss the Golden Age goodbye. I could only imagine what a man like Carlevaro would do to it after he'd been spurned for the second time.

I felt something shift inside of me, an echo of something that wasn't there anymore. It was like seeing another version of myself considering it—a lonelier Jack, more desperate and more afraid. The same Jack who taught rich kids blackjack and collected their money as some sort of simulation of power he didn't have anywhere else. A Jack who didn't have anything without the Golden Age waiting for him someday. Who would have done anything to protect the Shannon family legacy.

But that wasn't true anymore, was it? Maybe it never was.

"Your mother and I always dreamed of owning this city together," he said. "It's something I've worked very hard toward, even after her unfortunate betrayal." He paused. "It's something I would like to have a worthy successor for. I think you've proven yourself to be one, Jack."

He leaned forward, and I saw it. A flash of gold around his neck, fallen out of his shirt collar. I'd seen it at Caesars Palace, but I'd assumed it was a cross like any other middle-aged Italian American man might wear. I was wrong.

It was a sword.

"What about Morgan?" I asked.

Carlevaro's evil ambition flickered. "What about her?" He sounded genuinely confused.

And then the fire alarm went off.

I had a heartbeat to make a decision. So I did.

I bolted, shoving past Carlevaro and skidding into the suite's living room with something close to cartoon physics. The door to the hallway and back to the lounge banged open and Morgan appeared, her eyes wide.

"Come on!" she called over the blare of the alarm. The flashing light turned the suite into a very beige rave.

"Jack!" Carlevaro shouted behind me.

Morgan had made her decision too. Hello, new sister.

"Come on, come on, come on!" Morgan snapped her fingers as I threw myself after her, slamming the door behind me.

We didn't look back.

♠

They ended up evacuating the entire hotel and the casino, all fifty-three floors of guests enjoying the tables, the pools, and their beds all herded outside the hotel in an amorphous blob of humanity. It was easy to blend in with the crowd of tourists ranging from confused to furious, bathed in the stuttering red-and-white lights of the fire engines and police cruisers.

"Good thinking, pulling the fire alarm," I gasped, still out of breath.

Morgan shot me a confused look. "Oh," she said. "Oh. I guess I could have just pulled it, yeah." She cleared her throat and looked away. "Good idea."

I blanched. "Did you—"

"It's fine, it's fine." She flapped one hand at me. "The firefighters are here. It was only a small fire. Look—is that your tall friend?"

The top of Gabe's head stuck up over the crowd, in all his treelike glory. I caught glimpses of the others through the bodies between us. I nearly went boneless with relief. They'd made it out, even Remy. Not that I thought the Imperium was about to burn down—we couldn't even see any smoke— but there was still the very real possibility Carlevaro would have had us arrested for trespassing. I suspected he wouldn't take my rejection very well, the same way he never took Mom's. Though clearly "rejection" was a more fluid concept than I previously thought. I actually gagged a little.

Morgan and I shoved through the crowd until my friends and sister appeared. They stood clustered under a grimy streetlight, but they might as well have been an angelic chorus surrounded by divine light. I moved as if by momentum alone, tripping forward. Kerry looked up and met my eyes the instant before I wrapped my arms around her.

Kerry and I didn't hug. Except under special circumstances.

"Oof," she said, but she hugged me back, her lion's mane of hair bunching against her hoodie collar and tickling my nose. I didn't mind.

"Group hug?!" Gabe enthused, and I still didn't mind when he collided with us. I heard Remy and Georgia laugh and felt them join the human knot, warm against my back.

"*What's happening?*" Lucky crowed in my ear. "*Did you light the place on fire? They're not saying much on the police scanners. Someone had better call me! Jack! Come on!*"

It was all devastatingly wholesome, minus all the crime and drama and the fact that I now had Carlevaro genes lurking inside me like a live grenade. Except—

Except that I could see Morgan standing awkwardly to the side, pretending she wasn't watching us. She ran her hand through her hair like a nervous habit. I felt an unexpected stab of guilt. Morgan had made the right choice in the end, and, well—

I guessed we really weren't that different. Without my friends, or maybe with friends that weren't so great, I would have been alone too.

"Gabe," I whispered. "Someone's missing."

"Lucky?" He raised his head and must have reached the right conclusion on his own when he spotted Morgan. "Her? Are you sure?"

"Yeah," I said. "I'm sure."

He accepted it with a shrug and called over my head. "Hey! No one gets out of a group hug! C'mere!"

He practically dragged Morgan inward as soon as she got within arm's reach. I caught a glimpse of her trying not to smile. That was the beautiful thing about Gabe. He never did anything halfway.

"All right," I said after we'd all had our Hallmark moment. I untangled myself. "Someone had better call Lucky and tell her what happened before she blows out my eardrum."

"What *did* happen?" Remy said. "Did you get what you were looking for?" They gave Morgan a sidelong look, their eyes flickering pointedly to her pink hair. I decided to save the introductions for later. Long story.

"No," Morgan said before I could even open my mouth. She rubbed the back of her neck, looking almost cartoon-ishly guilty. "It was my fault. I—" She looked at me, our secrets stuck on her tongue. I gave my head a little shake. I'd have to tell them—especially Kerry; maybe Beth knew, but I was sure that Kerry didn't—eventually, but not here. "I messed it up," she said simply. "I'm sorry."

The group deflated a little, and they exchanged looks, none quite looking at me or Kerry.

"Well," I said. "I did find this."

Sorry, remember that movie-whispering moment? The artificial dramatic tension and big reveal? I'm afraid I didn't warn you about this one, but you shouldn't be too surprised. You were perfectly fine reading about me lying to just about everyone else.

I held up Excalibur—in miniature, yanked from around Peter Carlevaro's neck when I shoved past him on the way out. A little trickier than pickpocketing a hotel keycard, but not too much. It gleamed in the flashing lights, two inches long and perfectly balanced, like the artist expected a rat to pick it up some day and go to battle. It also had a seam.

I tugged, and after a moment's resistance, the sword split in two where the hilt met the blade. At the end of the hilt was the end of a mini USB stick. I held it up to the light.

Of course Carlevaro kept his secrets the only place he could really trust them to be safe. Right over his shriveled little heart.

On a fairly weak-looking gold chain too. Rookie mistake.

"Is that—?" Remy started.

"*What?*" Lucky's voice crackled from Georgia's phone, the screen filled with her face from an unflattering angle. "*What is it? I can't see. Hold me up straighter!*"

"What's on it?" Gabe said.

"I'm not sure," I said. I felt a smirk start to crawl over my face, pulling at the corners of my mouth. "But it's probably something pretty interesting."

DENOUEMENT

PETER CARLEVARO WAS ARRESTED ON MULTIPLE counts of illegal gambling, organized crime, narcotics trafficking, and felony conspiracy. The story broke shortly after 345 pages of incriminating files, photographs, and video were delivered simultaneously to the offices of the *New York Times*, CNN, and the *Las Vegas Review-Journal*, quickly followed by charges being filed by the FBI and the LVPD. He had a couple of friends too. I couldn't really talk about the rich and corrupt of the Las Vegas Strip, but it only felt right to use the information we had on them for good instead of evil. Carlevaro wasn't any worse than the rest of them, after all, just because he chose to spite me specifically, and I probably had some familial bad karma to make up for. Still, it was Carlevaro I watched being led out of the Imperium in handcuffs, the morning sun glinting off his shaved head like a billiard ball. He struggled against the FBI agent holding his elbow, spitting curses that CNN was smart enough to cut the audio for.

I watched it from the waiting room at the Clark County Detention Center.

"Jack," Beth said, touching my shoulder. I startled, my eyes jumping away from the silent TV screen in the corner of the waiting room. "Are you ready?"

"Yeah," I said. The plastic chair creaked as I got to my feet. My new phone was cold against my palm, the screen crowded with Hullabaloo notifications. All of my friends were safely back home, and in trouble so deep it would take the better part of the year to climb out of it. But we still managed to keep in touch. Maybe this was real life again, and maybe that meant they'd be far away, but only physically, and not forever. They were always only a tentative 4G connection away.

And they knew what today was for me.

"Yeah," I repeated, my mouth dry. "I'm ready."

I moved through security numbly, leaving my phone and my friends behind. Even Beth kept her distance as I sat down on the opposite side of the cold metal table in the middle of the visitation room.

Mom sat on the other side of it. I couldn't decide if this was a nightmare or a dream—I never wanted to see her like this, dressed in a baggy beige uniform, under the careful eye of the jail's security cameras watching our every move. She looked nothing like how Aileen Shannon was supposed to. There were no gems on her fingers, no makeup, no sharp pantsuit and sharper heels that made the Strip bow at her feet.

But she still looked like my mom.

"Hey, Jay," she said softly, and she smiled. "I hear you've been busy."

Something cracked in my chest, and I laughed, the sound edged with tears I could only just barely stave off. I was sure Beth had told her all about it. Only Mom would hear that I'd spent the summer playing illegal high-stakes blackjack and be impressed.

"Yeah," I agreed. "A bit." I wet my lips, resisting the urge to bite my tongue. This wasn't a conversation I wanted to have here, but phone calls to the jail were recorded, and I wanted to have it that way even less. "Mom," I said, and I faltered. "I know. About Uncle Peter."

Mom closed her eyes and exhaled slowly. Her hand half reached out toward me, curled against the table. They kept it so cold in there, trying to combat the simmering desert afternoon outside. "Jack . . ."

I reached out and grabbed her hand, the edge of the table pressed against my chest. "So it's okay," I said quickly. "You can take a plea deal. Turn state's evidence. Whatever." I was throwing out whatever *Law & Order* buzzwords I could remember. "They arrested him this morning. Everyone's talking about it."

"Jack," she said again. "I lied to you."

"So what?" I said, panic rising in my throat. One of the guards glanced toward me, and I forced myself to lower my voice. I let go of her hand and gripped the side of the table until my palms ached. "I forgive you. It's over. Carlevaro is going to jail. We can—"

I cut myself off abruptly. *We can go back to normal.* Is that what I wanted? Is that what any of us wanted? Boarding school on the other side of the country and holidays in Aspen, perfunctory gifts and listening to her and Beth fight behind closed doors. Was that what real life was? Did it have to be?

"We can do better," I said weakly. We could try again. Not everyone got a second chance. Carlevaro certainly wouldn't—the information we'd found on the sword USB had been enough to ensure that. Morgan was in Dubai with her mom currently, but last I'd heard, she was floating the idea about doing her senior year at a little place called Elkhollow Prep.

Mom reached across the table this time and took my hand again, prying it away from the cool stability of the table. She wrapped my hand in hers. No nail polish, I noticed. She liked to keep them painted gold.

"I lied to you, Jack," she said again, her voice soft but firm, insisting that I stop and listen. I couldn't remember the last time she'd looked at me like that, like I was the only thing on her mind. "Do you remember your appendix? The hospital stay?"

My stomach dropped, probably into the space my appendix had left behind. "Yeah."

"They asked for your dad—for Robbie's blood type. And I realized—I realized that it didn't make sense. It *couldn't* make sense." Her lips thinned. "I knew it was possible, when I was pregnant with you, but I didn't want to think it might be true. And I knew what he would do, if he knew we had a son. He was already so ambitious, we both were, but I'd realized that some things were more important. I loved him, but—"

"You told me you hated him," I said.

"I hated him a little too," Mom said. "Our relationship was . . . complicated. Things with Robbie were easier. I thought it would be better for you to grow up without Peter hounding you about, oh, all his stupid dreams about the Strip and his empire. I didn't want that, not anymore. But I did want you." She squeezed my hand, and the lump in my throat grew painful. "I thought that made it okay, that I was doing it for you. But it wasn't." She hesitated. "I've done a lot of things that weren't okay, Jack."

My lips trembled, but the one time it might have been okay to cry, I couldn't. My eyes burned, but the tears wouldn't spill. "What are you saying?"

"I'm saying that maybe your sister was right. Maybe it's time for the Shannon family to go straight." Mom smiled sadly, and without makeup I could see the worn lines around her mouth, the wrinkles at the corners of her eyes. "Maybe it should start with me."

I stared down at the table, at our joined hands, and I tried to remind myself that I was really there. This wasn't a nightmare. As much as it felt like my heart was sinking, falling, disappearing into a deep, dark pit, I was still there, sitting on a hard metal bench, watching my life fall apart again. But—

But it was different this time. I wasn't in the library basement, watching people I barely knew and scarcely liked losing money to my blackjack dealers. I wasn't alone. I had my sisters—three now, however weird that still felt. I had friends who would lie, scheme, and run through the streets of Las Vegas for me, and I knew somewhere deep down that they'd do it again. Not that I was planning on it. But you have to keep your options open. Maybe this time it was different.

Maybe, in time, it would be okay.

"What am I supposed to do?" I asked, like I wanted to ask her all along. I looked up and met her eyes.

"I don't know," Mom answered truthfully, and something about the way she said it struck me in the chest. The truth. We told the truth now. The truth, the full truth, and nothing but the—you get the idea. "But I think maybe you're right. We can do better."

She squeezed my hand one last time, and my heart squeezed back. The room wasn't as cold as it was before.

"Do better, Jack," she said, "and everything else will figure itself out."

♠

That fall, I started my senior year at Elkhollow Preparatory Academy. I spent the rest of the summer in Las Vegas, visiting Mom and helping Beth with the Golden Age's affairs. Actually helping, not spending a bunch of money, winning more money, and then losing it all again anyway. Sort of. We actually had quite a few Avalon Club chips after Kerry killed Carlevaro at Texas Hold'em, before he made his retreat to go confront me. Too bad they were useless now that the Avalon Club itself had gone defunct along with Peter Carlevaro. But just knowing that Kerry had beat his ass was almost as good.

The Golden Age would survive—for the moment, at least. Nothing was certain on the Strip, but you took each hand as it was dealt. It turned out that Beth was actually kind of good at running things, when she could do it her own way and not Mom's. Without Peter Carlevaro whispering in her ear, trying to convince her that it would be best for us to sell the place, she was willing to give it a try. The night before I left for Massachusetts again, I'd caught her researching Las Vegas apartments. I smiled just thinking about it. A lot of things could change, but the Golden Age penthouse would still remain empty most of the year. I think I preferred it that way.

It was the week before classes started when I stood in the library basement, surveying my kingdom again. It looked smaller than it did at the beginning of the summer, the carpet thinner and the air mustier, but there was something a little comforting about it too. It was no Avalon Club—but then again, I wasn't in jail, so I still had one up on Peter Carlevaro.

I watched Morgan bounce around like an overexcited puppy, even though it just looked like a normal basement now. It hadn't seen a hand of blackjack all summer, though I heard that a couple of the sophomores had tried to run it without me. Keyword: *tried*.

"Are you sure?" Morgan said, poking her head over a stack of boxes filled with textbooks twenty years out of date. She was more excited to attend Elkhollow Prep than anyone had the right to be, but it was nice to see. I still didn't quite know how to act around her, and the feeling was clearly mutual, but we were trying. My family was ten different kinds of messed up, but at least I had one, and at least I knew they loved me. Morgan deserved one too. If I could give it to her, I had to try. "We could make pretty good money. Especially the two of us. Oh! I could do some sleight of hand and skew the count, to keep people from counting—"

"I'm sure," I said quickly, before she could change my mind. *Do better.* Not really the family words Granddad would have gone for, but they were worth a try. "Maybe we could try running a real club."

Morgan shot me an incredulous look. "Like what?"

"I don't know." I really didn't have a huge non-poker skill set. I shrugged. "Math? Math club?"

"Math club?" a muffled, half-static voice said. "Did he really just say math club?"

I frowned. Okay, we'd had a pretty unusual summer, but I didn't expect to start hallucinating Gabe's voice. If I was, he could at least be nicer.

I gave Morgan a sideways look. "You heard that too, right?"

She met me with wide-eyed innocence. "Heard what?" she lied. Badly. Her mouth wiggled with a barely contained smile.

I narrowed my eyes. "What's going on?"

Morgan broke immediately, rolling her eyes. She jerked her head toward a door at the back of the basement, raising her eyebrows significantly. I frowned, more confused than ever. The door led to a musty old closet, filled with technology thirty years out of date. Even if somehow my friends were all hiding in there in some sort of surprise-party situation, they'd end up with a floppy disk to the eyeball for their trouble.

Well, only one way to find out.

With one suspicious look over my shoulder, I pulled open the closet door to find—

A laptop open on a card table.

"Am I going to have to solve a puzzle to get out of here?" I asked.

And then my friends suddenly populated the screen, all uncovering their webcams at once with assorted attempts at saying "*Surprise!*" Over the laptop's tinny speakers, it mostly ended up as a lot of enthusiastic yelling.

I grinned anyway, stepping closer and leaning down so the camera could see me better. It felt weird to see them all in their rooms, hundreds of miles apart, each background a perfect little capsule of who my friends were. Lucky sat on what appeared to be a throne of stuffed animals; Georgia's backdrop was a wall of crystals in different colors and shapes, organized in a way that I was sure made perfect sense to her. Remy had a golden retriever trying to muscle his way into the frame, and Gabe was in his backyard, the late-summer sun reflecting off his mirrored sunglasses. He grinned.

"Are you surprised?!" he said.

Remy rolled their eyes. "He might have been before you had to open your big mouth!" Their dog stuck his nose in their ear, not totally un-Gabe-like.

I laughed. "I'm suitably surprised," I said, knowing Gabe would accept nothing less. I looked over my shoulder to where Morgan lurked in the doorway, leaning against the doorframe with a smug look on her face. Or maybe not *smug*. Self-satisfied. "What is all this?"

Morgan shrugged, still smirking. "Ask them," she said. "My job was just to get you here."

"Well, we heard that you have a lot more free time now that you're not doing Blackjack Club," Georgia said when I looked back. "So we thought we might make a new club."

"Since none of us are really allowed to leave the house for the next calendar year anyway," Lucky said, with a devilish little smile that said not even being grounded could stop her from wreaking havoc if she really wanted to. Lucky didn't have to leave the house to work her mayhem.

Not that we were going to wreak any more havoc anyway. Doing better. Right.

"Oh yeah?" I said, surprised by the bloom of warmth in my chest. My friends were still far away, and yet just as close as they'd ever been. Nothing had changed just because I couldn't reach out and touch them. "What kind of club?"

"Ever heard of Dungeons & Dragons?" Remy said.

"It's got all your favorite things." Gabe's square shook as he adjusted his grip on his phone, holding up his other hand

and ticking off his fingers. "Hijinks. Tomfoolery. Math. It's like the Jack Shannon playbook."

"And Gabe is DMing, so you don't even really have to know the rules," Georgia added.

Morgan nudged me with her elbow. "How does that sound?"

I realized I was staring, lost in the fact that I was actually looking forward to the year ahead at Elkhollow for the first time. Mom was still in jail, and I still had Carlevaro genetics, which was a tough pill to swallow, but we were here. Together. And even through the computer screen, it felt an awful lot like real life.

"Great," I said, grinning so hard it hurt. "It sounds great."

A NOTE ON MOVING FORWARD

THIS WAS NOT A LOVE STORY; THAT WASN'T A LIE. I told you, I'm done lying. I wouldn't be here telling you the truth if I wasn't.

But there might have been a little love along the way. I used to think that love was something simple, in an unattainable kind of way. Love was the Hollywood ending—the sunset kiss and the fade to black. I didn't think it was something I was allowed to have. I didn't think it was something I wanted.

But my mom lied to me because, whatever else may have happened, she loved me, and I forgave her, however slowly, in fits and starts, because I loved her too. I now have more sisters than can be healthy, and I have friends who would drop everything to follow me to Las Vegas, even if there are a few more miles between us again.

So yeah, all right, maybe it's a little bit of a love story after all. But you probably guessed this would get sappy when we started.

This is my confession, all down in black and white. Take it or leave it, because I'm done with it.

I'm going to do better.

THE END

ACKNOWLEDGMENTS
\ik-ˈnä-lij-mənts\

I COULD WRITE A WHOLE OTHER NOVEL ABOUT all the people I have to thank for this one, but in the interest of time we'll try to keep it short and sweet.

A huge thanks to my agent, Cate Hart, and everyone at the Harvey Klinger Literary Agency who believed in this book even when my faith got a little wobbly and worked hard to find it a home. To my editor, Ashley Hearn, who fell in love with Jack and his messy little life as much as I did, and more importantly, helped me take a hammer to it and straighten out all those crooked plot edges. Not to mention my copy editor, Rebecca Behrens, whose heroic efforts overcame my loose understanding of proper grammar. Thank you to everyone who made this book into a beautiful book-shape, including art director Adela Pons, designer Lily Steele, cover artist Victor Bregante, and Terry and Michelle and the entire marketing team at Peachtree.

I never could have done any of it without the people who made the person who went on to write the book. My parents, my grandparents, all my cousins, aunts, uncles, and family friends who have always loved and supported me. My mom and my brother especially, who didn't get to see this book, but are people I carry with me always. Kelly and Staci, who first taught me how to navigate publishing. Lindsay Bandy, Christine Cohen, and Tom Hoover, who talked me off the edge so many times, because publishing will do that to you.

Thank you to all the friends who have always been there for me and helped shape my stories just by being the colorful, funny, lovely people that you are. August, who reads everything, even when we both know it's not very good. Dino, Annamarie, and Soraya. Susannah, Charlie, Lena, and Tiff (and Sage, even if she can't read yet). All the online communities that have supported and enjoyed my writing, especially my friends from CTABB, who are too many to name but know who they are. Anyone I might have forgotten, and anyone who just decided to pick up and read the book! That's pretty important too! This book was born during a very difficult time in my life, and it will always be a bright spot that I'll cherish. Thanks isn't enough for everything I've been given, but it's all I've got—thank you.

ABOUT
THE AUTHOR

AMANDA DEWITT is an author and librarian, ensuring that she spends as much time around books as possible. She also enjoys *Star Wars*, Dungeons & Dragons-ing, and even more writing—just not whatever it is she really should be writing. She graduated from the University of South Florida with a master's in information and library science. She lives in Clearwater, Florida, with her dogs, cats, and assortment of chickens. *Aces Wild: A Heist* is her debut novel.

amandadewitt.com

Find Amanda on Instagram @am.dewitt
or Twitter @AmandaMDeWitt.